Born in Salford, DAVID Cc [barcode: CW00545020] volumes of poetry, as well as short fiction: including the (Comma, 2005), *Tea at the* won the Frank O'Connor International Short Story Award in 2013, and *The Dressing-Up Box* (Comma, 2019). David's story 'Tea at the Midland' won the 2010 National Short Story Award, and his story 'In Another Country' was adapted into the Oscar-nominated film *45 Years*. He is a translator of Hölderlin, Brecht, Goethe, Kleist, Michaux and Jaccottet. With his wife Helen, he edited *Modern Poetry in Translation* 2004–2012. He is the winner of the Queen's Medal for Poetry 2020.

Praise for David Constantine

'David Constantine is the consummate writer of short fiction, and in *Rivers of the Unspoilt World* he once again shows us his great sympathy, understanding and interrogation of the human condition.' – Stuart Evers, author of *Ten Stories About Smoking*.

'Reading the intriguing histories and curious lives that fill this new collection, I felt I was being held by an author with abundant love and integrity and, most of all, impeccable patience. What more can I say about this master of literature other than to implore you to read him?' – Lara Pawson, author of *This Is The Place To Be*.

'Perhaps the finest of contemporary writers in this form.' – *The Reader*.

'One of the short story-writers who matter, poetic, passionate and humane.' – Maggie Gee, author of *The White Family*
'*The Dressing-Up Box* does the deepest work of fiction – it tells

us strange, hard, beautiful truths for our time.' – A. L. Kennedy, author of *The Little Snake*

'David Constantine's fifth collection of stories is a fierce and tender meditation on our struggle to live – a lyrical and plainspoken portrait of humanity at its pernicious worst and its suffering, creative, resilient best.' – Carys Davies, author of *West*

'Precise in their intensity, unsettling, suddenly and unexpectedly luminous, these stories will stay with you and unfurl within you.' – Lucy Caldwell, author of *Multitudes*

'A beautifully crafted tender, evocative collection. Full of wisdom and light.' – Irenosen Okojie, author of *Speak Gigantular*

'Every sentence is both unpredictable and exactly what it should be. Reading them is a series of short shocks of (agreeably envious) pleasure.' – A.S. Byatt, *The Guardian*

'The beauty of Constantine's writing lies in his extraordinary patience and precision with every whorl of consciousness, his unabashed fascination with every leaf and branch of the inner life. His emotional intelligence is as abundant as his linguistic gifts, and as necessary to the story he's telling...'
– *The New York Times*

'Constantine's writing is rare today... unafraid to be rich and allusive and unashamedly moving.' – *The Independent*

'David Constantine is one of Britain's most underrated writers... his balance of the lyrical and the sparse echoes John Williams, James Salter and John McGahern.' – *Huffington Post*

Rivers of the Unspoilt World

David Constantine

Also by the same author

SHORT STORIES
Back at the Spike (Keele University Press)
Under the Dam (Comma Press)
The Shieling (Comma Press)
Tea at the Midland (Comma Press)
In Another Country: Selected Stories (Comma Press)
The Dressing-Up Box (Comma Press)

NOVELS
Davies (Bloodaxe Books)
The Life-Writer (Comma Press)

First published in Great Britain in 2022 by Comma Press.
www.commapress.co.uk

A CIP catalogue record of this book is available from the British Library.

ISBN-10: 1-912697-56-4
ISBN-13: 978-1-91269-756-4

The publisher gratefully acknowledges the support of Arts Council England

Printed and bound in England by Clays Ltd, Elcograf S.p.A

Contents

Living in Hope

1

Dr Wiktoria Okołowicz, Lecturer at the University of Gdańsk, on a year's study leave in Paris, had found a small and affordable flat up under the eaves in the rue Jouye Rouve with a view from her bedroom of the Parc de Belleville. She was writing a book on the Paris Commune, dealing particularly with the women, their active shaping of it, what they wished it to do, and what it was stopped from doing, for women's lives. So: a study of what women gave and desired and of their struggle, defeat and disappointment. The material of this subject has been greatly increased by research in recent years, and day by day with a passionate confidence Dr Okołowicz was realizing her idea of it, her hopes in it.

She had quickly discovered a network of helpful scholarship: other women and men working from a variety of points of view on subjects more or less connected with her own. She had sociable meetings in cafés and bars; one or other of the universities and colleges hosted a fortnightly seminar; she felt herself to be creatively in touch; and when she emailed home they could tell she was happy.

There are such phases of life, if you are lucky. Days, months, when everything seems to assist in the shaping of your self. A purpose clarifies, it attracts what will further its development and flowering. Glorious, such a making! And, if you are lucky, it will be a measure, an orientation, all your life long. It will have settled in you, as a capacity for faith and trust. And this achievement is far removed from selfishness or being self-satisfied. A person living as Dr Okołowicz was living during her first months in Paris will quite unconsciously, never giving it a thought, encourage others.

But then, born in a Chinese wet market and very soon crossing frontiers world-wide, came Plague and with it a gradual revelation of the dealings of people with one another and with the world. And many of these relations soon looked questionable and some, for good or ill, looked unlikely to survive. Anxiety took root. Older citizens looked furtive and mistrustful. They veered away from the smiling faces of the young. They developed a sort of sonar feel, like bats, to swerve aside before collision. Don't come near, don't touch, don't breathe on me.

Waking in her flat in the rue Jouye Rouve, as the year advanced, Dr Okołowicz heard ever more birdsong. From the rooftops, from the trees in the Parc de Belleville, daily more and more and louder, confident, exultant singing. Except for ambulances, the streets had largely fallen silent. In the skies too the traffic had all but ceased. She pushed open her shutters, the whole morning light came in, and she lay a while listening. She knew this to be one of the changed relations. Never in her life before had the earth been so open to listening. The noise of the city seemed for once to be in proper proportion to the rest of creation. It felt for some weeks that even a vast conurbation might be liveable with. Paris with her many gardens, her flowery *ruelles* and *impasses*, her countless cherishingly watered window boxes, her river, her fountains, slowed down for a while, hushed, as if she hearkened and attended now to what had been missing, lost beauties of scent and sound... Might this not be a thing you would never again want to be without?

Fearful at the outset and in continual contact with her anxious mother and father in Gdańsk, Dr Okołowicz before long began to sense some benefit in the state of siege. As an only child, she had developed resources of self-reliance. She was, she said, quite good at being on her own. And besides, she was not a friendless stranger. They knew her by now and liked her in the *quartier*. That network was still more or less intact. You must keep your distance, if asked by a policeman you must produce your permit. But every day in your own locality you show yourself and exchange signs of life. And the workplace, the web, world-wide, continued pretty much as before. She had most of her sources to hand, access to more through links, documents already downloaded and safely stored. When the talks and seminars moved online, with general agreement they became weekly. Being virtually together was a good deal better than being together not at all. And they extended themselves, they crossed frontiers, they managed times and time-zones to accommodate as many colleagues as possible.

Dr Okołowicz's subject possessed her more and more. She would learn, clarify her thinking, write. The Plague would go away or become manageable and by the time the old freedoms were restored she would have finished her book. Meanwhile, good to be *en situation* and face up to what it entails!

The Commune lasted seventy-two days. Adolphe Thiers would have liked by massacre to entirely extirpate it as a social possibility; but he was a realist and knew that in practice, however bloody, he would have to settle for less, a further generation or so of power in the hands of his class. Then more trouble, no doubt, and another restoration of order.

In the chronology of her book Dr Okołowicz stood on the threshold of the end; but she had reserved till now, as a sort of pause in hope, an account of the discussions of the Women's Union, the social laboratory of the Commune, during April and May and the demands they wished to see pass into law.

She would hold this interlude aloft, to be contemplated, on the brink of its drowning in blood.

She began with the fact that the dominant attitude of mind in working-class women *then* was resignation. They believed their situation to be hopeless. In that fatalism they abetted their own oppression. And to give some idea of what women were up against not just in themselves and from the usual enemies (the Church, the schools, the legislators), Dr Okołowicz added a few thoughts from Proudhon, a supposed comrade:

'Though men and women may count the same in the eyes of God, they are not equal, cannot be, neither in the family nor in public affairs.'

'Woman is a pretty animal, but an animal. She is as greedy for kisses as a goat is for salt.'

'It is absolutely necessary that a husband impose respect upon his wife. Strength, foresight and industry are his and in none of these can a woman equal him.'

'A woman cannot have, and look after, children if her mind, her imagination and her heart are preoccupied with political, social and literary matters.'

And after him, in simple juxtaposition, she placed some statements of the basic principle of equality between the sexes.

Louise Michel: 'Recognizing the equality of the two sexes would be a glorious breach in the wall of human stupidity.' And: 'The struggle in defence of the Commune is the struggle for the rights of women.'

The Hungarian Léo Frankel, the Commune's Delegate of Labour and Exchange: 'All the objections produced against equality of men and women are of the same sort as those which are produced against the emancipation of the Negro race [...] First people are blindfolded and then they are told they have been blind since birth.' (He was wounded defending the barricade in the rue du Faubourg Saint-Antoine and saved there from capture and certain execution by the founder of the Women's Union, Elisabeth Dmitrieff.)

The Union of Women discussed and announced its priorities:

The right to work, and for equal pay.
(Eugène Varlin, four years before the Commune, had stated as incontrovertible: 'No one has the right to refuse women the only means of being truly free.' That means was work. Equality entailed the right to work. To women as to men should go the honourable appellation: worker.)

The right to take a full part in the Commune's combats, including membership of the National Guard. (This right was inherent in the full title of their organization: The Union of Women for the Defence of Paris and the Care of the Wounded. And how they fought! A hundred and twenty of them held the barricade in the Place Blanche. And they served as field-nurses, *cantinières*, dressed as ordinary working-women. Citoyenne Lachaise is remembered: attached to the 66th battalion, at Meudon 3 April, she was all day in the fighting, alone, tending the wounded, without a doctor.)

The right to pensions for the widows of soldiers killed fighting for the Commune whether legally married to them or not and similarly for their children legitimate or not.

Free and complete education for children of both sexes.

Immediate and total suppression of all faith and religious teaching for boys and girls in state schools. (The Union wanted rid of the 'vile and malign teachings' of the black brotherhood of the priests, who, when order was restored, as consecrators of massacre, led the monied classes in thanksgiving.)

The opening of schools for the professional education of girls.

The opening of public crèches and kindergartens.

Equal suffrage.

Initially Dr Okołowicz added that it was 1945 before French women first voted; then deleted that comment. She would leave it to readers themselves to hold up the Union of Women's demands against present realities in France and Poland and other more or less developed democracies. Altogether she wished her historical account of the Paris Commune to make for a continual juxta-positioning of then and now, of the women's revolt then and now, in my country and in yours. How far have we got? How far still to go? Writing in a locked-down city, the pandemic going from strength to strength, no vaccine in sight and the scientists already warning that the virus was clever and would mutate, Dr Okołowicz felt sure of herself. She had amassed the evidence, she would present it to her audience with all the force and clarity at her disposal, and rest her case. How will you live now, knowing this?

Asking that question, she rose from her desk and went

into the bedroom to look down over the park. Much of the last days' fighting had been in Belleville. In the rue Ramponneau itself the last barricade fell. Through the half-open window she heard birdsong from among the trees in the park empty of humans. The shrubs and the clumps of flowers in the neat borders seemed to be wondering what degree of disorder, what blooming for the sweet sake of it, they might get away with. Then turning to go back to work, Dr Okołowicz caught sight of her face in the dressing-table mirror and it halted her. A small face, the pure oval shape of it framed with close black hair. Around her throat she wore a thin red scarf. If asked, Have you not become rather self-regarding? she would have thought seriously about the question and answered, No, I don't think I have. But meanwhile the first look of the face in the mirror, thoughtful, calm, had vanished and now what she saw was an anxious puzzlement. Rising from her desk after her rhetorical question – How will you live now, knowing this? – going through to the bedroom window and viewing the self-delighting trees and flowers in the locked park, she suddenly felt that she had asked in a public and grandiose sort of voice a question she had no right to put to anyone but herself. Oh well, she thought, it doesn't matter. I'll delete it and nobody will know. And she took up her bags to go shopping for lunch and supper.

On the street, however, where everything was familiar and friendly and people were making the best of a bad state of affairs, Dr Okołowicz, first in a wondering but then in a more and more troubled fashion, began to feel, so to speak, shadowed by all that she had learned of the events of a century and a half ago, she felt with a stirring of dread that in every savage detail they had settled and rooted in her and lifelong they would infest her, she would never be free of them. And before she returned and let herself in again and climbed the stairs to her safe little flat, the shadow had become a presence, something palpable, and the easy rhetorical question, addressed to the putative readers of her account, was hers and nobody else's to answer first. Indeed, it shifted into something clearer and more fundamental: Will a life of your own survive now, knowing this?

Dr Okołowicz had signed up to give the next talk but one, which left her ten days. Next morning early, still uneasy, she resumed her work. She must write about the end and the aftermath. All the material for it was marshalled in accessible notes and references and even more so in her head and around her heart, in her waking and sleeping life. Every morning she woke travailed by it. In deep sleep it worked in her; surfacing, she felt herself borne along in the rapids of it; sitting down at her desk, she felt the shadow, the onus, of it. She must pace herself, not too much in one session, walk fast and as far as possible in the daily hour allowed. She was still prepared to believe that by writing and speaking to others about it, she would cease to be at its mercy.

Three days later, having observed her own rules of moderation and got on pretty well, Dr Okołowicz logged in to hear a paper whose author and topic she had been too preoccupied to take note of. So it shocked her to discover that the speaker, a young man, was a compatriot of hers who introduced himself, neither apologetically nor polemically but 'just by way of a premise', as a devout Roman Catholic. In his talk, he said, he would bring new and compelling evidence that only by expunging the Commune could Thiers establish the Third Republic. The bloodshed – in the view of several modern scholars (including the present speaker) greatly exaggerated by the subject's partisans – was necessary and justified. The building of the Sacré Coeur was not an act of expiation but a celebration of the glorious triumph of the Church.

Dr Okołowicz felt her chest tighten. Her breathing quickened. She felt she must quit the meeting at once or become very ill. She stood up, drank a glass of water in the kitchen, walked through into the bedroom and stared at her face. Partisan, she said. So be it. Seating herself before the screen she faced the plausible young man in Warsaw and gave him her cold attention. She heard him out. He had an elderly, patient manner. He seemed assured that his audience would agree with him, if not at once then after mature reflection. As soon as he was done, not waiting for the questions, certainly not wishing to ask any or enter into any discussion, Dr Okołowicz logged off.

She would work; work late; answer back quickly and with the needed edge. The elderly young man had clarified her purpose. She set the small kitchen table, lit her candle, prepared her supper, as she always did, with due love and care. And seated at the open window, scents from her herbs on the sill, birdsong from the rooftops, dusk, a pale-green sky, slowly she ate her simple meal and sipped the red wine with her usual feeling of ceremony. She had grown to love her solitude and her rituals. They helped. Daily she kept up with the world-wide toll of infections and deaths. She heard men and women expert in such sickness admit the limits of their knowledge. Often she phoned Gdańsk to give and receive reassurance. And that evening more than ever she was glad of her own undertaking: what she had taken on, what she must do. She sat longer than usual, listening to nightfall; and suddenly very tired, with no feeling of guilt, she cleared away the supper things and went to bed. Slept better than she had during all the weeks of the Sickness so far, and woke wondering at this passage through the night without dreams or travail. I can do it, she said to herself. I shall be able to write what needs to be written.

Day after day she wrote pell-mell. Mornings, she scribbled

it fast in a script only she could read; late afternoon and early evening very slowly (chapter and verse for every assertion and illustration, should she be asked) she made it legible and intelligible in Times New Roman on the screen.

Her occasion came. She began by thanking last week's speaker, her compatriot, for clarifying her responsibility. She would be the antithesis to his thesis and would not be suggesting any synthesis, compromise or middle way. It was her view or his. Marx got it right, she said: 'Thiers, that deformed dwarf, has spellbound the French bourgeoisie for more than half a century because he is the most perfect expression possible of the depravity of their class.' Only once, she continued, did he speak truthfully, and that was when he announced that he would be merciless. Otherwise he lied and lied. His soldiers followed suit, promptly executing *communards* who had been told they should surrender and would not be harmed. One officer, when the boy he was about to shoot begged three minutes reprieve, to take his silver watch to his mother (so that she would have something she might sell for food), and promised to return, was touched and let him go, not expecting to see him again. But three minutes later the boy returned, placed himself quickly against the wall, and was shot. These anecdotes, she said. You might make 'teaching plays' from them, view the matter this way and that, distinguish better and worse behaviour. Bismarck and Thiers are an ugly but instructive couple, she said. They had a common interest: the suppression of the labouring class that was beginning to make demands. Thiers would lead in his country. Bismarck would aid and abet. He released thousands of French prisoners-of-war to fight for Thiers. His own troops, after the cease-fire still encircling Paris, held the ring; which in practice, once the struggle was well begun, meant penning the Commune in at the mercy of their merciless compatriots. The class war was more urgent than war between nations. Wars between nations could be postponed.

She spoke of the modernity of the Commune and its repression. Thiers advanced his troops along the railways; iron-clad locomotives brought both sides' guns to bear. The Freemasons, declaring for the Commune, scattered manifestoes from a hot-air balloon. Newspaper correspondents, and they were many, could send in their reports to London or New York by telegraph. Thiers himself made great use of this resource: to send false news into the French provinces, to defame the Commune, deny its few victories. At a time when the first attempts were being made, in Geneva, to agree some few conventions for the conduct of war, this between the classes was fought by Thiers with all the licence of Saint Bartholomew's Day. Yet he was forever publicly denouncing the Communards for acts 'contrary to the laws of war'. His soldiers fired at the ambulances; and at the *cantinières*, killing many, as they tended the wounded. His firing-squads, having an exhausting amount of killing to do, might use machine-guns, newly invented and inefficient (being only several rifle-barrels fastened together), for a change. Some executioners became so weary they could scarcely lift their weapons and would support the muzzles actually against the chests of the condemned. When it was over, Thiers announced: 'The cause of justice, order, humanity and civilization has triumphed.'

She paused. Addressing a screen and some few of an audience in rows in little boxes, though she had done it several times before, suddenly seemed to her strange beyond belief. Continuing, she felt her voice to be almost a thing apart from her uneasy self. I want us to look more closely now at the reality of this triumph, she said.

True, she said, besiegers in the past have not cared much for the civilians locked in behind the walls. Since Troy, getting in has brought with it slaughter, rape and looting and Thiers' men did all three abundantly. From the heights around Paris first Bismarck's forces then, as they advanced towards the centre, Thiers' bombarded whatever they pleased with their artillery. Whole *quartiers* on a small and local scale looked much like Mosul. The village of Neuilly was reduced to rubble. When it was over, many who came up from the cellars after three weeks hungering in the dark were raving mad. Long cannonades caused the atmosphere to thicken, darken and pour with rain. Much street fighting was done in a noxious fog among black trees with broken limbs. And Paris has a city beneath the streets. Retreating *communards* fled through the Montrouge quarries. The tunnels in there were packed with corpses. A couple of thousand fighters were never accounted for. Weeks later, stray madmen appeared in daylight and seemed, witnesses say, to be looking for something. Further north Thiers' soldiers hunted with dogs and bayonets down the skull-lined alleys of the Catacombs, for any survivors.

I speak of the city's subterranean life and death, she said, but must not forget her heights and cleaner air, her sunny places from where the gunners, stripped to the waist, launched their explosives into the narrow streets and the lower cemeteries. Quite a ploughing up of the already dead was done in those final days, and the still living, the about-to-die, mangled and broken, hour by hour were added to their number. But chiefly those heights, Chaillot, Mont-Valérien, Passy, in those days of May will be remembered as platforms at the disposal of Thiers' bourgeoisie, the class this war was *for*, to watch the infliction of death and maiming on fellow humans down below. Yes, they drove up there with picnics, spyglasses and the necessary servants and viewed with glee or shivers of delightful horror the entertainment, he, their compere and epitome, day by day laid on. It was theatre – better than theatre! The dying were really dying and the dead were really dead.

In the wealthier arrondissements, in the south and west, which Thiers' invaders cleared first, the lights came on again and in cafés, restaurants, clubs and brothels the capital resumed its amusements. Long before the cobbles dug up for the barricades had been replaced and the corpses had been removed, the liberated wealthier citizens were out en masse and enjoying themselves. If they paid attention, they could hear the bombardments continuing in the north, and must nearby, whether they attended or not, hear surrendering or captured fighters for the Commune being shot. Beginning to prepare this talk, she said, I was at first astonished that even *those* people could be amid such irreconcilables and not disintegrate. But then, collecting countless instances of bourgeois delight in the vilification, torment and mass killing of their class enemy, I saw that their hatred was implacable and their desire for vengeance beyond all measure. *Vae victis!* Woe to the defeated! Now the victors will do as they please with them. Dead *communards* left at the barricades with their *képis* covering their faces had these masks of pity and respect lifted on the points of parasols by well-dressed perfumed ladies who wanted to take a look. Dead *communardes* were exposed. Having *de-natured* themselves they had got what they deserved. *Le Figaro* countered any pity for them by asserting that most before becoming insurgents had been whores. Their betters lined the narrow streets to mock and beat with canes and spit at prisoners not yet shot being conducted to the designated wall. Later when the summary executions ceased and the many further killings were being decided by the bourgeois courts, those people flocked to the trials with opera glasses and lorgnettes as to the theatre. They were a noisy audience. They applauded good performances. And when the time came they screamed their verdicts: The wall! To the wall! And the judges nodded. Occasionally, it is true, there were complaints that the judgements were too *summary*. Spectators wanted the proper to and fro, the for and against, a bit of suspense, a passage of courtroom drama. And indeed the prosecution had so many lives at their disposal they could allow a surprise or two now and then. Defence and prosecution counsels dined together, needless to say.

The bourgeois *mind*, she said, was well expressed and is preserved for ever in the diaries of one J. Audéoud. 21 May he watched eight *communards* being shot: 'What hovels, what sewers, what jails could have spewed forth these ferocious brutes? How the honest man's heart delights to see them lying there, riddled with bullets, befouled and rotting! The stink of their corpses is an odour of peace, and if the all-too-sensitive nostrils revolt, the soul rejoices...All of us wish to see them die in torment.' And the daily press was the public voice of that hatred. It is the usual way: hating, deny the people you hate are human. Speak of them as 'the most frightful monsters ever seen in the history of humanity' (*Moniteur universel*). The rest follows: 'Hunt them!' (*Le Bien public*). 'Make an end of this international democratic vermin' (*Le Figaro*). And a British publication, the *Naval and Military Gazette*, 27 May 1871: 'We are of the opinion that hanging is too good a death for such villains to die, and if medical science could be advanced by operating upon the living bodies of the malefactors who have crucified their country, we at least should find no fault with the experiment.'

At this point whether by some interference in transmission or whether, unconsciously, she had changed the settings herself, all faces vanished from the screen except her own. She was staring at, and for all she knew addressing, only herself. Then something gave way in her, a barrier of resilience perhaps, and she saw that what she had exposed herself to she could not bear. Quit now, at once, that would have been sensible. Switch off, leave the room, go to bed. But a voice, good angel or bad, said, Do what you said you'd do. Tell what you have learned. Unclearly she felt the injunction applied whether she still had an audience or must finish the commission anyway just for the mirrored face.

Faces, she said, here are my present thoughts on faces in the context of the Paris Commune's *Semaine sanglante*. Many condemned walked proudly to the wall and turned to face their compatriots about to kill them. Many unbuttoned their tunics and their shirts, baring the breast. Aim there, they said. Try not to hit my face. For the face, she said, is where the living soul of man, woman and child is shown. Your face speaks for you whether you move your lips and tongue and utter words or not. Disfiguring a face is an offence against the holy of holies. So the *communards* upright against the wall and about to be silenced asked as the last request of one human being to another that their faces be left unharmed to show what they had been and thus to speak for them a brief while longer. Eugène Varlin, that decent man, born into a peasant family, becoming by his own hard work a master bookbinder in the capital city, organizer of resistance among the labouring poor, passionate advocate of the rights of women, by the time he reached the wall he had no face, civilians and the military, his fellow human beings, having hacked it to a pulp along the way. One eye was hanging out. At the wall he could not stand, they had to shoot him kneeling. They battered his dead body with their rifle butts. Male and female citizens came to spit on it. Many at the wall had been made unrecognizable when they fell. Or an officer would kneel and blow a head to bits with his pistol. Was it always a *coup de grâce*? Or was he censoring the telling look of a dead man's face? One captain is reported to have stirred a man's spilled brains with the toe of his boot. This is what they *thought* with, he observed.

In Père-Lachaise, the Communards' last cover was the tombs. Street fighting of a sort, being driven back from house to house, hand-to-hand inside sepulchral vaults roomier than their lodgings in Belleville. Their corpses made a new stratum upon the long-buried dead. So many dead, she murmured, they were two metres high on the floors of cellars, dumps of them in public gardens and in the ruins of the cobbled *impasses*. Much blood. Half a dozen women fighters, corralled at the foot of their fallen barricade, at dusk, thirsting, begging their captors for water, were directed to crawl to a nearby puddle. The first, kneeling, lifting her cupped hands to her lips, spat the liquid out. It was their comrades' blood they were given to drink. Strange sacrament. Blood ran from under closed doors across the streets, the officers' horses slipped and skidded in it, by gutters and sewers it found its way into the river. *La Liberté*, 31 May, reported: 'On the Seine may be seen a long trail of blood following the course of the water and passing under the second arch from the side of the Tuileries. This trail never stopped.' Carters with muffled faces transported the dead (and among them the not-quite-dead) to holding places. If they hadn't been robbed before they were robbed there. Looting the outlawed dead was allowed. Their boots were prized. How white the bare feet of corpses looked, so forlorn. The poor, still poor, in the filthy trade of shifting corpses, took what they could, to sell and live off for a while. But often the better class, present at the killings, were given first pick, took what they liked and not for the market value but as souvenirs. An editor of *Le Figaro*, for example, having watched the execution of Émile Duval (he stood against the wall beneath the caption 'Duval, gardener') took away his bloodstained collar. Mementoes, trophies, relics, to put under glass in a sunlit lounge and show to visitors and educate the children with?

When the shooting had nearly ceased, she whispered, and really it should have been possible for the victorious to get back to normal and enjoy life again, a pervasive and increasing stench became annoying and disquieting. The restored authorities were instructed to do something about it, quickly. But it was hard labour. The city demanded to be disburdened of thousands of cadavers, many losing all solidity. Masked men walked with sacks meanwhile and broadcast chlorine, like sickened blossom, on them. Thorough search of doorways, stairways, cellars, and ruins, the feeding places of countless rats. The weather, hot, favoured the exponentially breeding flies. Swallows fell from the invisible blue sky. The summer sun warmed the earth and the dead in the earth. The shallow earlier and hurried interments were heaving their contents into the daylight. It was an audible phenomenon, a sort of groaning. An arm, a leg, a head of hair appeared. Some had been covered over still alive, their faces showed it. Crows perched on fragile walls, waiting. Dogs, disowned, ran hither and thither in starving packs. The stench grew closer and closer to that of pestilence. Three hundred defeated men and women of Buttes Chaumont, a neighbourhood of last resistance, had been flung into its lakes and rose now bloated and making noises. They were salvaged and mounded in a vast pyre, doused in petrol and set fire to. This hecatomb burned for days, its stinking smoke lay over their former dwellings. Much of Paris inhaled the stink of massacre. For the ladies, pretty masks became available.

Prisoners still awaiting trial outside the city were confined underground, a barred aperture above them letting in less than the bare minimum of light and air. There they were compressed into one dense tangle. The living and the dead together coagulated. Same, and worse, in hulks at the ports. Same in the pens and cages for those to be transported. It was housing more crowded than anything in the city's slums. Comes a point, I suppose, she said, when the judges, the priests, the generals, and even the common soldiers ordered to thrust with the bayonet or fire at the least disorder, comes a point when these more or less sentient agents cease thinking of their captives as fellow human beings. The filth, the stench, the sheer mass and inchoate pile of them, all imaginable distortions of limbs and facial features, speechless, muttering, screaming in tongues no person who was free and clean could understand. Worse than animals, screaming. Worse than clods of muck when they gave up making sounds and lay or stood or squatted as allowed in a mute apathy. The faces, the faces... No one in charge wanted those faces lodging in his brain, visible for ever in the mind's eye dreaming, there for ever as spectators when your pretty children run to you for kisses in the morning. But I do them a kindness if I suppose they were ever haunted by those faces.

She had intended to finish her talk with a few brave, glorious and hopeful things but her voice deserted her. She gazed mutely at her own face in the mirroring screen and had in her head – saw them – the numberless faces of men and women and their children, disfigured, made unrecognizable, pleading for recognition.

She closed her laptop and went to bed. Slept at once, on some deep level fearing that if she contemplated her experience it would undo her. In the small hours she was woken by sirens and saw the blue lights travelling across the ceiling of her room. Just past her tenement, they turned right into the rue Ramponneau and were gone. In the restored quiet she heard voices, shouts, footsteps, a crowd running, but her self-defence, her exhaustion, fended off even that and she slept.

She woke knowing what, for the immediate *now*, she must do. Made coffee, broke off a fistful of yesterday's bread and opened her laptop. Her emails were numerous, several names she recognized as members of the study group. Did that mean they, invisible, had heard her? No matter. Quickly one after another she deleted them. There was a message from her mother which she saved without reading to answer cautiously later. Next she withdrew herself from all social media. Still she was trusting an instinct to act from one step to the next. She showered, dressed in clothes she had not worn for some time, put aside the thin red scarf that had been the mark of her allegiance for so many weeks, and went down to the streets for fresh bread and provisions enough to get her in solitude through the day. Shocked to see that many buying and selling were masked, she bought a supply and there and then covered her face.

2

Fine weather, and daylight lengthening, Victoire (as her mother called her) shopped early, breakfasted, packed a frugal lunch, emailed home, and went down the many stairs to the streets. She loved her lodgings under the eaves but was fearful of being there too long thinking. So she walked, great distances, her *Plan de Paris* handy by, but only to orientate herself when it was time to halt, eat, then slowly, hoping not to be stopped and questioned, made her way back.

Of course, this strategy would not get the Commune out of her head. To quite a large extent her map of Paris was a map of the first six months of 1871. Outdoors she did not mind that. She noted plaques and memorials new since her last visit; quite often she could have told you where on a particular street the barricade had stood, who had fought and died there and when it fell: on la rue des Dames, Batignolles, Blanche Lefebvre, laundrywoman, 23 May, executed, aged 24, for example. She didn't walk the streets in search of these places, but came upon them, paused, and set off again.

Walking, Victoire thought a great deal about her mother and father, how proud they were of her and how she would disappoint them. She knew when she spoke to her mother there was anxiety in her voice, once or twice she had been near to saying she might come home. But anxiety was in the air they breathed, in Paris and in Gdańsk. The virus was her cover, so to speak. Stay put for now, among the regulations live as best you can. Friends these days, lovers, families, have frontiers, seas, hemispheres between them. In that situation her crisis was a small circle within the larger one. Masked, with her permit, she sought the freedom of the streets in the city she loved and if she walked them like a ghost, like a spirit in thrall, some days enclosed in a reducing space in the *cachot* of her thinking head, other days it enlarged, the roof became the infinite sky, the heights around the city were in sunshine, the river ran strong and clean, even the long boats now and then with their bicycles, children, dogs and geraniums passed through serenely going about their business. So faith in life opened and contracted. Some nights waking high above the streets, nearer the constellations, she could believe that for now it was a necessary rhythm, a natural pulse, opening, closing, hope expanding and being confined again in a dwelling no more hospitable than a clenched fist.

But then, middle of May and copious birdsong very near her in the early sun, Victoire woke with terror clutching tight around her heart. She felt for sure that her life in hiding in the safest place had been discovered and surrounded and now in an instant would be bayoneted. True, breath re-entered her when she sat up; true, she could get out of bed and shower and prepare her breakfast with an automatic attention to the ceremony; true, she packed her bag and descended like a living person to the streets – but it was all in a mortal certainty that the crisis had opened fully and that she walked abroad in Paris at its mercy.

Viewed from above, say by a sympathetic angel, Victoire's walk that day would have been hard to fathom. For it was, quickly and without a pause, a laborious spiralling around a centre – laborious because the wish to coil ever closer to that centre was difficult to pursue through the grid of streets. She was circling, but in a jagged and impeded fashion, almost as though her unconscious intention (she consulted no plan, nor

20

was there any uttered directive in her head) was being benignly thwarted, as though some counter-instinct wished to deflect her towards, if not escape, at least to a postponement. But the spiral pull to the mid-point was the stronger. With no surprise, no relief, no increase of fear, through a monumental gate she entered among the tombs and the criss-crossing avenues of that city-within-the-city Père-Lachaise. A few minutes later, in a dumb accomplishment of the day's first purpose, she seated herself on a slab opposite the Mur des Fédérés, took off her mask, folded her hands in her lap, and waited.

Is it possible for a human being even for an interlude to have no thoughts? Facing the wall, Victoire came near that vacancy. There were wraiths or miasmas in her head, rising out of some frightful depth, curling, shaping towards things that might have been articulated, but recoiling into the fog. Her eyesight functioned in much the same fashion: all along the base of the wall she could make out the sprawling dead, but unclearly, in the sort of mist you see over meadows and marshland some early promising mornings soundlessly, in lovely slow whirlings, shaping, unshaping, in a movement that had only the appearance of progressing, the motion all being upwards, out of the earth into the air's lowest stratum where they rolled like surf but in silence and not advancing. She saw the bare feet of the dead, their soiled pallor, as in dreams and in too much meditation she had seen them often before, so wanting comfort and so beyond all comfort. Then was it nothing new? She had spiralled as though summoned to this centre and for nothing new? Hopelessness rose in her. She felt herself to be a living thing rooted in harm, forever drawing up not sustenance but malefaction which through the bloodways and their infinite small branchings infected her body and soul. She shuddered, and clutched with both hands at her heart.

The wall cleared. It stood in sunlight. Victoire became aware of the singing of birds. Two children came onto the set, the stage, a boy of perhaps ten or eleven, a girl about half that age, hand in hand they entered from the left. This was a theatre she had not seen since childhood. She watched spellbound, wholly believing. At first she supposed them to be brother and sister – both were black – but soon noticed their difference in complexion and facial features and hair. Red roses, as almost always and especially in May, were lying along the base of the wall and wreaths of *immortelles* hung on the face of it. Midway the little girl, in a white dress and her hair tied back in bunches with red ribbons, stooped and picked up a rose. Only then did Victoire realize they must for some while have had her in view. And now they turned to face her. The girl was serene and smiling over a secret intention. The boy, in soft blue-grey trousers and a long-sleeved shirt, had a face which was helplessly open, nothing he thought and felt would be kept from exposure in such a face. The girl handed him the rose, glanced Victoire's way, and nudged at him with her shoulder. He shook his head. She nudged him again, harder, and signalled with *her* head what she commanded him to do. It seemed he would have to screw up all his courage and the little girl knew that and for his own good she was putting him to the test. He drew a deep breath and almost at a run came before Victoire sitting there entranced on her sepulchral slab. Bowing his head, so as not to show his face or look into hers, clumsily he held up the rose for her to accept. She took it, he stepped three or four paces back, she began to smile, began to say a fit thank-you to him and the girl who stood still at the wall radiant with delight at the courteous brave thing she had made him do. But holding the rose, regarding it in wonder, the rose and the children, the so serious boy, the so delighted girl, contemplating the flower, the children, the wall, very suddenly as never in her life before, never in any desolation in childhood or girlhood or in her adult life, she was broken open by weeping, she shook with it, and dropping the gift and not covering her face with her hands, she clutched her own shoulders tight, rocked to and fro and wept, wept, as if become the source into daylight and lovely sunlight of all the bitter waters that lie in a lake of cold blackness under the earth. The boy's face showed an unmanageable terror, he turned and ran back to his companion who was staring in blank incomprehension at the rose on the ground and a grown woman, an adult, a creature there to look after you, weeping without end, shuddering and clutching her own shoulders as though if she let go she would fall to bits, weeping and showing the children all her horror and sadness and shame in her far too open face. Hand in hand, they fled.

The terror left her, the shaking ceased, she sat in the May sunshine as cold as any stone monument and the one feeling in her, so thoroughly in her she felt it would be her one state from now on, was shame. She masked her face. The rose lay at her feet. She reached for it and went and laid it back among the others under the wall. She was not a fit person for the children's gift. Then following that wall, which was the vast cemetery's eastern perimeter, very slowly and fearfully, guilty fugitive seeking escape, she came to the southern gate.

There stood the children and between them, holding their hands, a woman of about Victoire's age, Middle-Eastern in her appearance, her dark eyes showing above a pretty mask. The three stood facing her in silence. Victoire showed the palms of her hands. Je vous demande pardon, she said. The woman answered, with smiling serious eyes, Ça ne va pas, tu souffres. Her French was accented, as was Victoire's, being that of a native speaker in another country. Victoire shrugged. She said, I have no excuse. I frightened these children. I am more sorry than I can say. Forgive me. The little girl was smiling. The boy had a wariness in his open face which seemed to Victoire the very mark of her fault. We have to go now, said the woman.

This is Donatien, this is Félicité, my name is Jiyan. Will you come tomorrow where the children found you today? About 12? We can talk if you like or just stroll around if you prefer. Agreed? Victoire nodded. My name is Victoire, she said. But lately I have wished it was something else.

See here, Victoire said to the children, see what I've got for you. She opened her rucksack. Félicité came close, Donatien kept his distance. Now cup your hands and close your eyes. The girl did so, the boy hid his face and peeped through his fingers. Victoire tipped seven black-red cherries into Félicité's trusting palms. Now you can look. The gift showed in her face as a flare of joy. She turned to the boy behind her and said, Close your eyes, Donatien, and cup your hands. And for her he did and she let loose the cherries into that proffered bowl. Proud of herself, Félicité turned smiling to Victoire – who selected two pairs from the bag and fitted one and then the other over her ears. There, she said, that looks pretty. But you'll have to walk like a princess or they'll fall off. And now let me fill your hands. With caution and ceremony then the children walked to the far end of the wall and sat down in the sun.

Perhaps he'll never quite trust a grown-up, said Jiyan. Even if he makes it to being one himself, I can imagine him always wanting to be only with children. I don't know much about the Commune, she said. Nearly nothing, in fact. And I know too much, said Victoire. Some days and nights it seems to me that's all I know. The women were masked, sitting where Victoire had sat the day before, turning to face one another across a little distance, the open bag of cherries on the stone between them. I got it from my mother and father, she said. A lot of Poles fought for the Commune. They had a history of fighting for freedom, their own and other people's, by then. My father claimed to be a descendant of Auguste Okołowicz, best known for climbing the July Column on 26 March 1871 and planting the red flag in the hand of the Spirit of Liberty, left or right, I'm not sure which. He's buried against the western wall, behind us, scores of tombs between us and him. He lived twenty years after the bloodbath. My mother – she's French – named me after Victoire Tynaire who married a businessman and had six children. The education of children was her passion. Under the Commune, briefly, she was an inspector of schools, very set on ridding them of the priests. In the last week she and her husband went from one barricade to the next, tending the wounded. When it was finished, her concierge betrayed her to the killers, her husband came looking for her, they let her go and shot him instead. She also wrote novels. Tell me, where did Félicité come from? She came to the Foyer six months ago, Jiyan answered. The Sister who brought her couldn't or wouldn't say how she got to be with them. But they named her. The Sister said her radiance was a miracle and our Director said, Well, that's very nice, I'm sure. And so it is, said Jiyan, very nice. I'll tell you properly about Donatien when you're a bit stronger. But for now I'll just say that a policeman brought him in – from the Catacombs, he said. I think we should be going now. And you'll have things to do. I'm not sure I have anymore, said Victoire. Where is the Foyer? Métro Jourdain, said Jiyan. That's very near me, said Victoire. Would you like to come to the Buttes Chaumont? And let me make a proper picnic. Tomorrow? By the lake? Around noon? Jiyan nodded and smiled. That gives me time to help the children with their lessons. I'll go now, said Victoire, suddenly anxious. Say goodbye to them for me. The cherries are for the three of you.

The children were down by the water sitting closely side by side. The women, masked, sat the yard or so apart a little way up the slope, behind them. Sunlight and a slight breeze were causing a continuous sparkling over the surface of the water, infinite resources they had of movement, dance, aspect, every glance and instant being as unique as snowflakes. That pair, said Jiyan. Donatien won't say a word and often Félicité sits with him in silence. Other times – and I think it's when she feels he is frightened – she begins a very quiet singing in a language I don't know. It might be one from before her French, or more likely she just makes it up. And if I'm studying or sewing with my back to them I pause and listen. It's the loveliest sound, under her breath at times, and then coming up again, her singing, like nothing I've ever listened to in any other place. Perhaps she's a changeling and has lived somewhere else, in a land with that native tongue. I do hope she won't grow out of it and most days I don't believe she will. This place, said Victoire, for centuries was the foulest place in Paris, they did their torturing and killing and the mouths of their cloaca were here, it was their plague pit, mad and starving people lived in the quarries and underground. You know those things, said Jiyan. Myself, I know that once I lived in a village among olives and vines and all manner of blossoming and fruiting trees. Irrigation was very necessary and for centuries people had managed it with skill and tact and beauty. Going to sleep and in my sleep I could always hear the channels of clean cold water hurrying to keep alive the fruits, the vegetables, the flowers we needed for our lives. And west not very far away was the sea and south, no further, the town with its towers and arches, stairways, minarets and souks and marble lanes and fountains, oh so many graceful marble splashing fountains! And much of that town is rubble now and people house in cellars to try to stay alive and muffle their mouths and noses against the smell of the dead. My village is commandeered by men with guns, who live by terror and extortion and they took our house and our neighbours' houses and billeted their killers in them who pray five times a day. And the sea is out of bounds to all who are not their kind. I was a doctor in my previous life, just qualified and working in a hospital. My brother phoned a week ago and said that hospital got bombed. He is still working there. If they will let me stay in France I hope I'll work in a hospital again. Go down and tell the children it's time to eat, will you? What a feast it will be! How kind you are. I am so glad we met.

Walking along the avenue de la Cascade to the exit where they would part, the two women were mostly silent, watching the children hand in hand some way ahead. Once or twice Donatien glanced over his shoulder, just to be sure. Victoire said, I know very little about children. In fact I feel I haven't paid much attention to anything except my work. I shall be at a loss if I give it up, which I suppose might be good for me, for a while. Why should you give it up? Jiyan asked. Victoire shrugged. It moves me more than I can tell you that Donatien who is twice her age depends on her – on you also, of course, but that is as it should be. I soon learned with those two, Jiyan said, that I wouldn't get very far with 'how it should be'. In your situation I would be afraid, said Victoire. Each in each, the three of you, you have invested so much love. Jiyan answered matter-of-factly, We can't not love, or love less, because of that. The fault is in me, said Victoire. It won't be, said Jiyan. I haven't known you long, but long enough to feel sure that what you call the fault won't be in you for ever. I see you are not well now. But I also see that you will be soon.

At the gate the two children lifted their faces towards her and Félicité said, Thank you, Victoire. Both seemed to have forgotten the spoiled gift of the rose.

Leaving them, Victoire bore away west to the canal and via Bastille, in a long detour (needing to be tired), came home. There at the window high under the eaves in a trance or absence she watched the swifts and swallows ferociously hunting invisible specks of life, to stay alive. She opened her emails, deleted all but her mother's, and answered that one saying she had spent the day very happily with a new friend.

She woke hearing ambulances and having dreamed again of Tissot's wall. She was one and then another and another of the executed falling like rag dolls from the parapet through thin air to land as deadweight among the comrades far below. She switched the bedside light on and sat up. Once the shaking with terror had passed, she felt ashamed. She thought of Jiyan and the children and the vast hinterland of atrocities they had emerged from. My equivalent is partisan scholarship, she said to herself.

Next morning, having showered with especial thoroughness, she went down to the streets for bread, yoghurt, honey and a peach; returning, set the small table in the window very carefully; and observed a moment's silence before she drank and ate. The sky was entirely a pale pure blue. Swifts criss-crossed it, shrieking. Victoire sat a good while there. She was in no hurry.

She wrote to Jiyan:

My dear friend, I will copy out for you a declaration by one of the women of the Commune I most admire. Her married name was Léodile Champseix but when she began her public life as a novelist, journalist and agitator she called herself André Léo after the twin boys she had just given birth to. Her motto was, We can do nothing without hope, however faint that hope may be.

So long as children are born with no angels present but Death who will end their frail lives at the start for want of care; and Poverty who, if they live, will malform their limbs with rickets, stunt their faculties and condemn them to the unceasing pains of cold and hunger and often, alas, even to harshness at home; so long as, on the streets, in the slums, in misery, children are denied even their innocence; so long as their minds receive, at most, the superstitious and dogmatic education that makes our primary schools so sterile, cold and harmful; so long as they grow up with no future but drudgery day after day – most of humanity will be denied their rights; society will live poorly, narrowly, corrupted and defaced by selfishness; equality will be no more than a false hope, and war, the most horrible and savage of all wars, whether unleashed or forever brewing, will dishonour humankind and lay the world to waste.

It is the last paragraph of a speech she gave, by invitation, at the Congress of Peace in Lausanne in September 1871. Having fought from one barricade to the next during the Days of May, she had escaped to Switzerland. Her audience in Lausanne shouted her down, she was forbidden to continue, no one there heard her speak those final words. But her address was published in Neuchatel that same year.

Shall we meet again soon? I do hope so. Where would the children enjoy themselves most?

Je t'embrasse

Victoire

One day I will hug you all tight.

They met quite early at Jaurès, from where it is straight through to Porte Dauphine. Victoire and Jiyan sat masked with a distance between them facing the children, Donatien tightly gripping Félicité's hand. So on view, it must have been obvious to other passengers and a cause for wonder which child needed the greater encouragement.

Once in the Bois, all four in their different fashions and degrees took heart. They felt an opening into a dedicated space – not a wilderness, to be sure, but a zone unlike the streets, a borderland of waters, lawns, avenues and trees, outside the ancient walls and large enough for citizens to disperse into and go their own ways. This is new for us, Jiyan replied. Though not for you, I'm sure. Victoire hesitated, but then she said, I spent a whole day here once following the course of the old fortifications. Thiers built them, they were demolished in the 1920s. I had a copy of a sketch done by James Tissot, 29 May 1871, of executions. I think he must have witnessed them from a hiding place and I was trying to work out where but of course I couldn't. He had driven a Commune ambulance so they'd have shot him, had they found him. The dead were falling backwards off the parapet and landing in a heap at the bottom. Like rag dolls, he wrote. He was a society artist and had done very well for himself painting ladies and their pretty children. He got away to England and carried on doing that. Have you told your mother about your talk and what happened and how you have felt since? Jiyan asked. No, said Victoire. I email her every day and phone as well and speak to both of them two or three times a week. But I haven't mentioned what state I'm in and I don't think they guess. *La machine*, said Jiyan. Once I did three months acting my life, doing it mechanically, and although it was arduous and very eerie and even slightly annoying that nobody seemed to notice, I'm glad I stuck it out because in the end it worked. I'm not acting now, with you, not in the least. True, I have the children. They strolled along, they would have been arm in arm were it not for the Sickness, but perhaps the masks and the distance, like formality, like courtesy, also in some measure helped. I haven't told them, Victoire said, because my truth would disappoint them and they deserve better than that. After a silence Jiyan said, I don't believe you will disappoint them, or anyone else for that matter. Eyes meeting over masks may be very eloquent. My mother and father, said Victoire, met at a demonstration at the gates of the Lenin Shipyard in Gdańsk. He was a welder there, she helped in a primary school nearby. I almost believe the only pet-name between them was 'Comrade'. They were in at the beginning of something youthful, glorious, one of those eras when the people see that unchanging things can be changed and a whole new perspective opens up. They were – still are – International Socialists. They read Marx on the Commune, they believed with him that the Commune's martyrs are enshrined for ever in the great heart of the working class. Lately, of course, they have lived in bitter disappointment. But they were there at the start, at the gates, in St Brigid's Church, from the balcony of their flat they counted the tanks rolling by to impose martial law, they were both imprisoned and came out strengthened, they were on the streets among the quarter of a million in rage and grief at the murder of Father Popiełuszko, they were there at the declaration of the Republic in December 1989, I was born the following autumn. And in their disappointing country now they look to me, their only child, a teacher at their city's University, they look to me to keep at least a flicker of hope alive. They had tears in their eyes when I told them I would write a book about the Commune. They are proud to say to people, Our daughter is in Paris. They worry that I might get the virus, but it won't have crossed their minds that I have hit the wall and can't go on with the brave women of 1871 nor with anything else, it seems. Let's sit down, said Jiyan. Or why don't I get the picnic ready while you take the children for a little walk?

Victoire's face behind her mask expressed a fearful shock. Enough of it showed in her eyes. After a silence, during which she was looked at wonderingly by Jiyan, she said, But would they let me? Go and ask them, said Jiyan. They were sitting a little way off on the edge of the open turf where a path went into woodland. As Victoire approached they stood up, watchful. She halted and said, Shall we go for a little walk while Jiyan gets the picnic ready? For his answer Donatien looked at Félicité, who for hers reached out her hand. Donatien followed suit. And waving with their free hands they turned and let themselves be led by Victoire in among the trees.

For a while nobody spoke. Then Félicité said, Are there

some cherries again? Yes, said Victoire. Some for now, some to take home. Donatien kept glancing up at her masked face, and across her to check what Félicité was making of it all. We shan't go far, Victoire said. Just to the stream. What is your home like? Félicité asked. It's a flat, Victoire answered, quite small, a bedroom, a kitchen, a *very* small bathroom. And it's high up and no lift. I have to climb five lots of stairs, fifty-five steps, and you can't go any higher than where I live. It's right under the roof. From my bedroom I can see down into a park and from my kitchen over hundreds of rooftops. Swifts and swallows come very close past both my windows. On the kitchen side, other birds come to the sill and I give them crumbs. Donatien looked towards Félicité and she nodded. Can we come and visit you one day? she asked. Of course you can, said Victoire. Again, for a different feeling, her mask was a blessing.

Near the stream she let them go and they ran to the bank and knelt and paddled their hands in the fast clear water. Her own childhood came upon her, it entered her, erasing the adult.

Victoire stepped forward and touched the children's shoulders with her fingertips. Picnic time, she said. They turned and unbidden reached for her hands. This time she held Donatien's right and his white sleeve there slipping he became suddenly troubled and pulled free of her grip. Félicité shook her head at him, and then also pulled free. Please can we change sides? she asked. And so they set off. His right sleeve dangled loosely, his left stayed buttoned tight. Emerging from among the trees, they saw Jiyan sitting on the picnic rug and looking out for them. Run, said Victoire, letting them go.

The rug was a spacious square of dark red woven in lighter colours with flowers, birds, a hare and an apple tree all within a circle whose circumference was an entwining of tendrils in bud. This is one thing I rescued, said Jiyan. I slept wrapped up in it on our journeys. She had laid out the food and drink like a rich still life. But first your hands, she said. The ceremony of protection. She squirted the sharp clear liquid into three cups of hands. Then noticing Donatien's loose sleeve – a button had gone missing – she rolled it up to the elbow, and since that looked odd she rolled the other up as well and when she saw dismay and shame on his face and that he glanced repeatedly at Victoire, My darling, she said, it's alright, nobody minds, everyone here loves you. Victoire saw the grey-white markings, the cicatrices, across the boy's forearms and once more she was glad of her mask. She reached for the cherries, smiled with her eyes and said, Cup your hands again.

They walked back together as far as Porte Dauphine. There Victoire left them. She would make her way home in a long arc by the boulevards: Courcelles, Batignolles, Clichy, Rochechouart, passing below Montmartre and the hated Sacré Coeur.

Victoire lay on her bed with the window open and listened to the carolling of a thrush. Now and then she heard ambulances. She thought especially of Donatien's arms. Or rather she *saw* them, in terrible clarity; and all around that image was a haze in which starts and failures of thinking drifted. But there had been so much good in the day that she felt, if not hope, at least an alteration of her spirits and that from one quarter and another incidents and visible ideas were gathering in a sort of holding place and in due course if she had faith and patience this would amount to hope and with hope would perhaps come the necessary resolve.

She went through to the kitchen, opened that window and sprinkled seed and crumbs on the small table that took up most of her balcony. Then she stood to watch the birds arrive. My rituals help, she said aloud, softly. Next came her own meal, its simplicity, the ceremony, the magic intended less to ward off ill than to beckon close the good.

Emails. She hesitated – but then, as had become usual, deleted almost all unread. One from her mother, to answer. And this from Jiyan:

My dear Victoire,

I wasn't going to tell you about Donatien for a while yet but after yesterday and you seeing his arms I think I must. Forgive me, dear friend, if it burdens you.

He's from the Congo. There are worse places no doubt but not many. He was playing football after school and with his best friend and several other boys he was abducted by one of the many militias that have been fighting it out round there for the last twenty years. He and his friend were about as old as Félicité is now. There was a lot of screaming and gunfire. He struggled and shouted so they hit him on the head. Next he knew, he was in a truck with a lot of soldiers with their guns and they were laughing. They drove for hours to a camp. The first thing he saw there, on the ground as he got out, was a human skeleton. They said they were going to make a soldier of him. They cut him across both forearms and rubbed cocaine and gunpowder into the wounds. Then they blindfolded him and put an AK-47 into his hands. It was very heavy, he could hardly hold it. They put his finger on the trigger and told him to fire. He did. Then they took his blindfold off and showed him his best friend lying dead in a pool of blood. You killed him, they said. Now you are a soldier. Some weeks later they were taken to a village which they were ordered to attack. In all the confusion he ran away into the jungle and ended up three days later in a town not far from his home. He found a mission house and a priest there got him to say what had been done to him and what he had done. This priest wrote it all down. He had seen arms like Donatien's and heard the story often before. It was a common atrocity. They made enquiries and found that his village had been attacked and mostly destroyed. They were told his father was dead and his mother and older sister had been abducted. How he got to France I don't know. He was brought to the Foyer by another priest who left a dossier with our Director which I read when I offered to look after him. He was mute by then. Five or six weeks before you met us he had some sort of crisis and ran away. Seems he hid in the Catacombs, as I told you. Since then he has been better. Félicité had arrived in the meantime and she befriended him at once. She knows what he wants to say. And now he has you as well. So all in all… Félicité said you said we could come and visit you in your home under the roof. What a treat that would be!

With my love

Jiyan

Thursday 28 May, early, Victoire emailed Jiyan:

I think because of my mother I'm a French citizen! I wonder if that might ever help us? In the Bois when I walked with Donatien and Félicité a little way out of your sight we halted at a stream and when they knelt down there and paddled their hands in the water I suddenly thought of myself Félicité's age on the beach at Sopot and the white waves coming in and swans riding them and left and right it stretched for ever and invisible ahead across that water were foreign countries. My mother and father did much of their courting on that beach and in the woods along it. They spoke of it as a paradisal place. I know now how foul much of it was back then – half the trees dead of acid rain, the water so toxic it would take the skin off you… And the stench! The bay is very shallow. All the filth flowed into it and couldn't even disperse. But I grew up thinking of white swans, white breakers, voyages in freedom to other lands. And of amber. That coast is the amber coast. You find bits along the tideline and beautiful things made of it not very dear in the shops. And throughout my childhood and girlhood the sea and the forests, being cared for, were recovering the beauty that belonged to them. And we went there on Sundays, I stood securely between a mother and father under the infinite blue heavens and from an infinite store the sea waters advanced at a gallop, blue, green and streaked all across from end to end with pure white. And there were white swans, riding in close. I'm writing this thinking of you, Jiyan, and Félicité and Donatien, and wondering whether perhaps one day, who knows…?

I'll see you very soon.

With love

Victoire

PS I checked with my nice concierge and she said of course your visit is all right. And anyway a bit of company will do me good!

That dispatched, she went down masked for an outdoor coffee and croissant, crossed then to the florist's opposite for six red roses, and carrying these arrived at Père-Lachaise just as the main gate was being opened. She assumed there would be the usual commemoration later but wished to be on her own. She placed her roses under the wall and, uncovering her face, seated herself opposite on the sepulchral slab. Few people think sequentially, one particle of thought being joined by the next and progressing to a conclusion. Facing the wall, Victoire did not sit there *reasoning*. She looked along its base and again in the mind's eye saw, or, by that way of thinking-seeing cast, the barefoot dead in their sprawl and intermingling where the bullets had flung them. So she could say, I remember you, I will not forget. And from that stock then sprouted things her mother and father had seen, the tanks smashing down the gates of the Lenin Shipyard, for example, and things they had not seen but which had been critical in their education, such as the massacres ten years earlier in Gdynia. More and more out of Victoire's kitty of such things put forth and ramified and would not end but pushed into further and further branchings. So she stared at the wall and saw Donatien standing there quite alone and turning up his palms and extending his arms for all the world to see his hurts.

Back home she set the table in the small kitchen. Laid out the feast, the bowl of cherries at its centre. She was as happy as she was nervous. Nearly time, she put on a summer dress she had not worn before, light blue, and an amber necklace, and the thin red scarf as a *bandeau* around her black hair. Stood then at the bedroom window, holding her phone for Jiyan's call. When it came it shocked her with a fearful joy such as for years nothing had.

Victoire had invited people before, not many, it is true, and of those some baulked at the stairs so she took them instead to her regular café-restaurant. And in none who made it to the top, in none of their faces, did she realize her good fortune so thoroughly as when Jiyan and the children in wonder surveyed her home under the eaves. Donatien, in a white shirt buttoned at the cuffs, long red shorts, bare feet in sandals, more visitant than visitor, showed a face for a while quite rid of nightmare. Félicité hurried him hither and thither, pointing and describing as though she owned the place. We wash our hands in here, she said. Altogether the four of them were *jolly*, a word she had not till then ever associated with herself.

Later they were down in the park among solitaries, couples and families, and Victoire counted their quartet among the last. The children, Donatien not *very* often turning to check where the grown-ups were, went ahead hand in hand as far as the cascade. Jiyan and Victoire, continually glancing their way, found a bench and keeping their distance, through masks began to say what needed saying, the urgency of it showing in their eyes.

Marx wrote after the Commune (Victoire said) that henceforth there could be no truce or peace between the class who worked and the class who expropriated what their work produced. Social war then, for as long as need be. And war entails hatred. When I was writing, I filled with hatred. I told you I was partisan. I *hated* Thiers and his murderous captains. Do you know he is buried in the very heart of Père-Lachaise? His tomb squats there gloating. How I hate whoever thought it fit that he should be buried in this place! That's why you got ill, said Jiyan. Hatred even of injustice distorts the face and harms the body and soul, if you let it. Victoire looked at her friend and was ashamed. Jiyan, she said, I wasn't there, I saw nothing, I only read about it. When we were just getting to know one another, said Jiyan, I almost pointed that out to you, I almost asked you what exactly you thought it meant to hate people who did abominable things a century and a half ago, but I forbore to. Times have moved on, she said. There are new wars. Atrocities once unimaginable in kind and degree have come on ceaselessly in multitudes. I might have mentioned that, but wasn't ready then to say to you what I must say now. I hate the men who cut Donatien's arms and made him kill his best friend. I hate whoever cast Félicité out like wreckage on the waters. I hate those who drove my mother, my sister and me from our beloved land and those who at any hour of any day may bomb my brother's hospital again and bury him alive. I don't want ever to be reconciled with them. But also, and more strongly, I don't want my life – my rescued life – fouled and constantly wounded by my hating them. I want rid of them out of my head. I don't forgive them. I just don't wish to let them harm me even more than they already have. I just want rid of them so I can continue doing, like my brother, the work of healing. I see what has been done to those children – and to countless others whom I have only read about – and I want them to get well and if possible whole again and to manage better and better, to love, to make happiness in themselves and in others. I can't even wish that properly if all the time I nurture my hatred for the torturers and the killers and their deeply evil lords. Her voice was quiet and level through the pretty mask. Her eyes were calm and beautiful above it. After a while she said, You'll keep your job, Victoire, won't you? It's your duty to keep it. Teaching is vitally necessary. I'm partisan, Victoire replied. Even so, said Jiyan. Teaching and writing, tell the truth. Say to your students, This is what truth looks like from my point of view. Answer me from your slant, please.

Victoire stood up. Shall we walk a little? she said. And then: You never mention your father and until this minute I have never wanted to ask. They walked as far as the water and there, quite close to the children, sat down on the low stone wall, turning to face one another at the usual distance. My father was a writer, Jiyan said. A writer of poems and stories. And a journalist too. In both kinds of writing he told the truth. I say 'was' and 'told'. Some days I say 'is' and 'tells'. He's one among the countless missing and alive or dead is most likely still in our wasted land. I thought of him often when you were telling me about your work and the talk you gave that so upset you. And just now when you said 'I wasn't there'. Don't suppose those who weren't there must always hold their peace. You weren't there at the shipyard gates but your mother and father were and perhaps you may speak for them or, better, alongside them. And what you learned or strengthened from studying the Commune is the love of justice, the desire for it, the rage for justice. And now you know me and those two children, one of whom is mute. You extend your sympathies. That's not nothing, Victoire.

Victoire looked away, and after a silence said, My mother told me a good story about writers. It was after the imposition of marshal law in 1981. The government persuaded a few well-known ones to appear on television and express their approval of the measures taken. Next day and for some weeks after, these writers when they opened their front doors in the morning found copies of their books which during the night had been returned to them by readers who now held them in contempt. Yes, that is a good story, Jiyan said. But now Donatien is looking anxious. – He watches our faces, doesn't he? said Victoire. What he can see of them. I'm a poor beginner in the art of reassuring. Would they like ice creams? There's a kiosk quite near here.

All four strolling along then, the women with their masks down, licking, Victoire said, Thanks to you, it is decided: I resolve to finish my book, keep my job, write to the organizer of the seminar and say I have been unwell but will be 'there' again next week. I'll go home for a week or so in June. My study-leave here is supposed to finish at the end of October but might be extended till Christmas if I ask. The Plague will be gone by then. And I've been thinking – she halted and turned to face her friend – I live cheaply because of the Plague, no cinema, no theatre, concerts, no shopping to speak of, so please may I give you my spare cash to buy things for the children and for yourself also, the books you need for your studies, for example? Please, for love and friendship, let me do that. Jiyan bowed her head. Good, said Victoire. That's another thing decided. – I've been thinking too, said Jiyan, as they resumed their walk. I've been thinking that I live in a cloud of unknowing. I don't know whether my father is alive or dead, nor when or how I'll see my mother and sister in Germany, nor whether I'll be allowed to stay in France and become a doctor again. I don't know where Félicité came from nor how she got here. Nor how the priest got Donatien to the Foyer. I am told his organs of speech are in perfect order, he *elected* to stop talking, I don't know and nor does anybody else when or if ever he will choose to speak again. I don't know whether they'll be allowed to stay in France when they are older, nor whether – this worst of all – I'll even be allowed to continue looking after them while they are here. And when I put it all together like this – as I have never done in speech to anyone before – I don't know how I can bear to live in so much unknowing. Such possibility, even likelihood, of unbearable pain. But you have come into it now – Let's catch them up, shall we? He keeps looking back – and it is more than bearable. It's not a fatalism, it's not like saying, Oh well, what will be will be. It's more active than that. It's love, faith and hope. Yes, Victoire, dear friend, I live in hope.

Our Glad

COME IN, SHE SAID. Start talking! Start listening, more like. Let the asking and the telling and the listening begin where we left off. Or before that, if you want. Listen to me remembering an early part again, the same only different, again. And tell me again or for the first time what you have known for years and what you have just found out. Tell me how you see things now. But come in here first while I make the tea. The eats were ready and waiting on a trolley so there was hardly room for the two of them in the kitchen. He would stand at the window, looking down the little garden to the fence. How's your mum managing, she asked, without your dad? Turning, he answered her. She wanted to know, he answered truthfully. She sometimes thinks I *am* Dad, he said. She thinks I've come home on leave. She asks how long I can stay. I don't mind her thinking I'm him, he said. Not really. It's someone she loves and who loves her, that's what matters. Through the half-open window he could hear the children in the school beyond the fence and the little stream, the children yelling in the playground among the trees. I like that noise, she said. Cheers me up when I need cheering up. I had a burglar last week. A man rang the front door bell and kept me talking about Salvation while his pal came over the fence and down the garden and took my purse and my pension in it off the table right where you're standing now. Keep the chain on your front door, love, the nice police lady said, and keep your back door locked. Oh well, she says, a bit shaky telling it, worse things happen at sea. And two little girls from the school brought me that bunch of flowers. Our class is very sorry for what happened to you, Mrs Gregory, they said. So that was a happy ending, wasn't it? And she set the teapot in its cheerful cosy on the trolley. Push that lot through, will you. I've found some more photos. They were in another box under the bed.

Sit down, she said, handing him his tea. And help yourself, here's a plate, I got some of that cheese you like. On the trolley, besides that cheese, were some little meat pies and piccalilli, lettuce and tomatoes, a couple of barm cakes sliced for rings of tongue, a packet of cream crackers, tinned peaches ready in dishes and next to them the little can of evap. Where were we? She sat up on a cushion like an oracular bird, a Sibyl, infinitely wrinkled, Mnemosyne herself, chirpy and ever more animated, in thick crocheted socks like a baby's bootees, with a neat scarf at her throat. He pulled his chair so close his knees were touching hers on which she held an old Clarke's shoebox full of photos in shades of sepia and black and white. Here's me, she said. An infant in a pretty frock sitting up between Father and Mother and looking out as though reserving judgment on what she sees. And look at them, she said. What they know and she doesn't! And here I am even younger with a rusk in my fist. That can't be the mantelpiece they've put you on, can it? he asked. I doubt it, she says. But you never know. Well you look very eager, he said, very hungry and interested. So I was, she said. From the word go. And that reminds me: I've been in the *Stockport Times* since I saw you last. There's a cutting in that dresser behind you, top righthand drawer, where my purse should have been when Burglar Bill paid me a visit, but it wasn't, it was on the kitchen table, God knows why. Have a look if you like. What a picture! Three ladies, with a combined age of 258, a sprightly trio, as the caption says. The Three Graces. And I'm the oldest. And Ev dropped dead last Sunday after church on her way to the Lord Nelson. And then there were two. But what a thing to tell Saint Peter! Walking for Wishbone, right round the park, Ev with her hip, Betty and me with our knees, and at the finish none the worse for wear. Around a hundred taking part, but we three got the standing ovation and our pictures in the *Stockport Times*, being the stars.

He said, Coming here from seeing my mother who cannot rightly tell who's who, I was thinking of you telling me when you were a little girl, them sending you by train all on your own, in the Ladies Only compartment with your name on a ticket tied to your waist, to stay with the aunts in Tadcaster in hopes you'd get into their favour and they'd move some of their money our side of the family's way. It was during the war, this visiting, for as much as a month at a time, and if it wasn't in the holidays then she, our Glad, had to go to classes with Aunty Minnie who ran a little school in Clarence House itself, on the ground floor on the left as you went in. And one time, all alone, trespassing, she climbed the stairs to the topmost room in the house, pushed open the door, and there was Granny Gilchrist sitting up in bed with small spectacles on her nose, a crocheted shawl around her shoulders, and a crinkly white cap on her grey head. She almost seemed to have been waiting for the child. Come in, little girl, she said, and beckoned with a thing more like a chicken's foot than a human hand. She grasped me round the wrist, said Glad. And with the other paw lifted up a golden ear-trumpet. And another time they were ordered by Uncle Bert, who was an air-raid warden, to go down into the cellar for safety during a zeppelin raid. They huddled in down there, it was a cold place like a crypt, full of junk and the plaster falling off, it smelled. Then after a very long time Uncle Bert appeared in his tin hat and shouted: All clear! Several such missions to Clarence House her father sent her on, and all in vain. Because, as she said, they had religion in Tadcaster but they had not charity.

Who's telling this? she interrupted. You or me? You, he answered, you're the only teller of this tale, always have been, always will be, and death will make no difference, it'll still be you, I'll never be the teller, I'll always be only the scribe, our Glad's scribe. And don't you worry, me dying won't make any difference either, it'll be there – I hope – by then, the whole story, the whole truth of it, a selection of the varieties of the truth of it, as much as I could manage, it will be running on and on, like a stream in the Dales, underground sometimes and elsewhere coming up again surprisingly, running on and on, neither you nor I has to be there for that, it'll dive and vanish and surface again, you telling the tale, until Earth is become an unlovely cinder and she carries, for the foreseeable future, no more living waters, no stories, none of our kind of life.

Seven children, she had, that funny old woman with her ear-trumpet in the attic, said our Glad. The first was a Henry but he only lasted six months, he died in the night, poor little thing, Visitation of God, convulsions, they found him in the morning. Help yourself, have another little pie. Or are you ready for your peaches? The other boy was Father, John Willie, your grandfather. The rest were all girls. She rummaged in the shoebox on her lap. Here we are, she said. That's Aunty Minnie. She stabbed with a finger at a neat little woman with round specs, third row, five from the left, in a group photo of the Tadcaster Choral Society. And she ran the prep school, don't forget. Like a thrush on the lawn, Glad stabbed, that quick, intent, a moment's close attending, than stab: that's her, that's Aunty Minnie. Only Annie, named after her mother, married. She taught piano, had three sons and a daughter and died of breast cancer after two mastectomies. She married into money – Uncle Bert, the air-raid warden, was a Smith of John Smith's Breweries, Smith's Tadcaster Ales – but none of it came our way, needless to say. Ruth was another teacher. Edith was stone deaf, she came over to Salford to help with the births. That leaves Christina, called Ina, I got on best with her. She rummaged in the box. Here's me and her and Aunty Edith – stabbing at each in turn – on the prom at Llandudno and here we are again in Southport. When things started going wrong and they had to give up the big house, Minnie and Edith moved to a council estate and Ina and Ruth into Hunt's Hotel, the temperance place, in Mount Pleasant in Liverpool. Ruth had been a receptionist there, Edith joined them after Minnie died. So that's the aunts. How long have you got? A while yet, he answered. Then he said, Last night I woke hearing her in the hall outside my bedroom. She was walking up and down, talking to herself. She was saying, I don't know where I am. Is this the right house? Saying it in a marching rhythm: I dón't know whére I ám. Is thís the ríght hóuse? Over and over again, marching up and down in the hall. I went out and saw her in the dark in her bare feet and nightie, like a sleepwalker but she was wide awake, only lost. So thin her shoulders felt under my arm, so puzzled her face looking up to see who had come for her. Poor Bertha, said Glad. She's missing him to death. When he was alive and she was looking after him she never wandered in her mind, so you've told me. Sharp as you, she was, he said. All the living and the dead she could conjure up and speak their parts. Same as you do, same as her mother did, Gran Gleave, my Gran. Driving over, leaving her again, I could hear the women's voices, and that's a blessing and a strength, believe you me.

Stuck there keeping house for Father, I nearly didn't get a husband, though I'd always wanted one, said Glad. I feared I'd be joining the company of the maiden aunts. All the boys had gone, got married, left home soon as they could, all gone by the time of Dunkirk and the Blitz, and me left looking after Father. For, in their troubles, Mother had delivered him more and more into my tender care and gone her own sweet way, not so very sweet, some might say, but it was her own. I always liked Uncle Norman, he said. Yes, Glad said, I could have ended up with worse than him or, as I say, with nobody at all. Father liked him. Marry him, he said just before he died when the Second War was ending. He's a quiet man and at least he doesn't work in the Post Office. A widower, ten years her senior, with two children, the boy already nineteen. So I did, being nearly on the shelf by then. At family gatherings he stood always to one side, looking on. That was his deafness, I suppose. Sometimes he made a joke but rather as though he'd been thinking of it for quite a while before he dared utter it. And few found it funny when he did. His hobby was photography, a good choice for a shy man on the outside looking in. Once when we were round at Tamworth Street he gave Steve and me some back copies of *Amateur Photographer* to look at, to keep us amused while the grown-ups talked. But he leafed through them first to be sure none of the pictures in them were unsuitable. Norman all over, that, said Glad. The things you remember. I specially remember people ill at ease, he said. To be honest, he wasn't my type, she said. I'd have liked a man a bit more outgoing, a bit more romantic. Saturday nights on the Monkey Run, up and down the Cheetham Hill Road, I was always on the look-out for a feller in a trilby. Yes, I was holding out for a trilby. If I ever made a date I'd ask him to meet me at the end of our street and I'd be spying from the bedroom window was he wearing a trilby or a flat cap. And if it was a cap, God forgive me, I didn't come out and he'd be walking up and down at the end of Heaton Street till he lost hope. Really Jack Buchanan was the only one for me. When he died, my friend Amy sent me a cutting from the *Daily Express*, an article on him by Logan Gourlay and photos from his films. 'Even off-stage he was ageless,' Logan wrote, 'pencil-slim, unfailingly elegant, invariably hatted in a pearl-grey trilby.' Amy asked was I sending red roses or orchids to the funeral. Father was long dead by then and Heaton Street sold, and I'd been twelve years married to Norman. He was in the building trade and I had high hopes he'd use his influence and get us a nice house of our own. But we ended up renting in Tamworth Street, which wasn't even as good as Heaton Street, so that was another let-down but all-in-all I can't complain, he was a gentleman, he never shouted, he never got drunk. Father died in my arms. He had cancer of the larynx that spread to his stomach. And I know it says on the death certificate his wife was in attendance but the truth is otherwise.

2

Thank you, he said, as she handed him his tea. She's a bit worse perhaps but not much. There was a concert on the prom, the Town Band playing. She enjoyed that. We both did, in our different ways. When there was singing, she joined in, very quietly, the words coming back to her. I got talking to an old man who as a boy used to help get everything ready for these concerts. They set out a thousand deckchairs back then. And the boats arriving from Liverpool, landing hundreds of trippers onto the pier. And three or four times he heard Paul Robeson sing – not on the prom, but still in the open air, in the amphitheatre under the Orme, that big voice, and a multitude of people, some paying, some on the slopes above, hearing him sing for free. You got backache again? Nothing much, she answered. They say it's from the stomach trouble but I don't see how it can be since I got that fixed. And I'll get this fixed by the end of next week, I hope. Mr Lee, a Chinaman, is giving me acupuncture. You all right with needles, Mrs Gregory? You know me, I said. Try anything once. Have some of your cheese and carry on talking. I don't mind sitting here listening today. Nothing very cheerful, he said. Tadcaster in the bad old days. I don't mind things like that, she said. We can thank our lucky stars we're living when we do. You being funny? he asked. Anyway, the workhouse your grandfather and that deaf old lady in the attic became Master and Matron of in 1872 was brand new and built on the Brewery's land. It replaced two others, one of which, in February 1865, was brought into disrepute by the behaviour of the woman running it, a Mrs Catherine Leivers. Like you and Ev and Betty, she got herself in the papers, but it was the *Tadcaster Post* in her case and nothing to be proud of. She had a down on paupers, so how she came to be Matron of a workhouse is a mystery. I mean, I can see why she might want the job – to enjoy herself – but not why the Board of Guardians would think her a fit and proper person. At first when the complaint was made – after the death and disgraceful funeral of one Elizabeth Daniels – they said it was all invention and exaggeration, the Matron kept the linen spotless, but at the public enquiry, when the witnesses lined up to tell the truth, the Guardians quickly capitulated and demanded her resignation. Her mistake was the funeral. Seems she hadn't quite finished with Elizabeth Daniels, a local woman, a pauper, formerly in service, and insisted on a funeral that would carry a fellow-creature's humiliation into the beyond. Mother told me more than once she prayed for a decent burial, said our Glad. It annoyed me that she felt she had to pray for it. Elizabeth Daniel's coffin, he continued, was made of blackened deal, unplaned, and had no tire or handles. Tire! said Glad, there's a word I haven't heard for quite some time. It's the metal edging any decent coffin has, he said. Yes, I know, she said. I'm saying I haven't heard it for sixty or seventy years. Some women in that prison of a workhouse, he continued, offered to carry their poor sister to the grave themselves. Ah no, said Catherine Leivers. She'll go as she deserves. So they slid her headfirst into a chimney sweep's donkey cart, roped her down, and another inmate, a lad called Alfie Daws, a vagrant's abandoned son, who was himself as black as cart and coffin, climbed up and drove her to St Mary's. There at the lych-gate this sad cortege was met by the undertaker's apprentices wearing white aprons over their working black. They were ashamed and on their own impulse had come to carry Elizabeth Daniels to her pauper's plot. Her father, a very old man accommodated in one of the town's bedehouses, followed on foot. Persons at the many windows of Clarence House would have had a grand view, like nobs in opera boxes, he said. Before my time, said Glad, a long time before my time. But carry on. I can imagine it. At the public inquiry, he said, the first witness, a Bridget McCormick, pauper, formerly a seamstress, who had been in the workhouse just two months, testified to having seen Mrs Leivers beat Elizabeth Daniels three or four times a day: most often with the rolling pin, but once – on the head – with the poker, cutting a great gash, and once – on the arm – with the coal-rake so she bled. And she saw two little brothers, Charlie and Willy Townend, thrown by the death of their mother on the mercy of the parish, beaten on their bare backs by Mrs Leivers till they were black and blue, for taking a glass of water. The one good thing in all this, he said, is that at nightfall three or four hundred people gathered in the High Street and from there, with torches and led by the Tadcaster fife and drum band and two men carrying a banner on which was written 'He that oppresseth the poor oppresseth his Maker', they dragged an effigy of the hated Matron on a tatter's barrow to the Market Place where Mr Edward Spink, the bellman, delivered a speech against her and her cruelties. Then, under the Workhouse windows, the barrow and its straw corpse were set fire to.

Beats me how you find all this out, said Glad. It's easy enough nowadays, he replied. You don't really have to leave the room your computer's in and where you sit and think about such things. But I do leave that room. I go and see for myself whenever possible and when there's anything left to see. And even when there's nothing to see – in the sense that what you want to see just isn't there anymore – still I do feel I ought to pay the place a visit. What was there but isn't now has quite an effect, in a funny sort of way. We had a night in Clarence House last week. It's become a hotel. The proprietor showed us round. He even took us down into the cellar where you hid from the zeppelin. I felt closer to the story then. Would you like a trip to Tadcaster? We thought we'd take you for a night in the Shann House Hotel – Clarence House as it was in the days when Father sent you visiting. Would you like that? You bet I would, she said. When the warmer weather comes. Yes, he said. Soon as the warmer weather comes.

We had a look round the town, he said. Your grandfather's workhouse has gone. With some modifications – knocking the high walls down between the male and the female quarters, for example – it ended its days as The Beeches, an old people's home, which they bulldozed in 1985, for new housing. The workhouse, she said. Father was born in it. 'Born in the workhouse.' It was a family joke. Except when she turned against him. Then she spat it out. As though he were a pauper, as though marrying him she'd lowered herself, into the muck. More the other way round, said Glad. The old Union still stands, he said. Where all the cruelties were. It's a fine big town house on the east side of St Joseph's Street. There's offices in it now, an advertising agency, to be precise. Funny the past and the present in one place. Where Dad went just before he died, Conwy Hospital for the Aged Sick, it too had once been a workhouse, there under Conwy Mountain. I love that upland. It's the first step up to the Carneddau and

Snowdon, or the last step down from them, down and down into the estuary. Great grandfather, grandfather, father, in a workhouse, it's a strange succession. I wonder if that Mrs Leivers drew a pension, said our Glad. Or got some sort of a golden handshake. People like her often do, so I hear. That's not recorded, he said. Well I'll bet she wasn't unemployed for long, said Glad. After all, as you said, she kept the linen clean. Make another pot of tea, will you?

Nice cosy, he said, coming back in, holding up the pot. Your mum knitted me that, she said, and gave it me, along with a lot of other nice things, when I got married. I was never much of a knitter, never much of an anything in that line, to be honest, and why I ever thought I'd become a milliner, God only knows. Have another Eccles cake. You need fattening up. Funny business, after all, being born in the workhouse, don't you think? he said. Five sons and a daughter born in the Tadcaster Union. In the year your father was born – I've just discovered this – twenty-eight children were in there with him being looked after by his father and mother, five of them were orphans and another four, the youngest two months, the oldest eight years, in with their unmarried mothers, were all, very probably, born there like your father and your aunts, it being the custom back then that the young women, mostly domestic servants, whom somebody had loved and left, vanished behind the workhouse walls. In total, he said, the inmates numbered one hundred and forty-eight, of whom eight, all local, were classed as imbeciles and nine as vagrants who, by breaking stones or picking oakum, could earn themselves a bed for the night in the casual wards. Plus your family and a porter and a nurse, that's quite a gathering, in one establishment, of a few of the lucky and many of the unlucky. Worst almost, is to read what people had done before they became an inmate, what they had worked at until the work was gone or until they no longer had the strength to do it:

sailor, grocer, agricultural labourer, domestic servant, blacksmith, shoemaker, stoker, nurse, tailor, coal miner, dressmaker… Until they were taken into the workhouse and there, till they died, carried on working for their bed and board. There was a man of eighty-four in there, one Thomas Potter, never married, who had been a mason, and another of ninety-four, George Varley, widower, who had been a basket-maker. All life long working and not enough at the end of it to keep you in your own house and home. There were always far more men than women in these places. The women, it seems, however old, however tired, could still make themselves a bit useful in their families just about managing outside the walls, while the men, too done in, too knackered, worked nearly to death, were taken into the workhouse to do that little bit extra, until they croaked. Your father, he said, interests me more and more. Born in the workhouse, in the 1891 census, aged nine, he's living outside, in Victoria Terrace, with his Gran Gilchrist and your aunts Ruth, Annie and Edith, but in 1901 he's back where he was born, inside, behind the walls, working days, and no doubt nights when required to, in the Post Office as a sorting clerk and telegraphist. He'll have left, they'll all have had to leave, five years later when his father died and a new man was put in charge of Tadcaster Union. It will be then, said Glad, around then, just before or after then, that he began making his way towards becoming my father. Funny thought, that, when you weigh up. Yes, he said, the accidents that lead to it and the others that might have prevented it. In the Blitz, the first night – Dad was away on the Mile End Road, with the Pioneer Corps, salvaging what could be salvaged from the wrecked East End – Mum and Gran, still at 57 Liverpool Street, sat on the cellar steps and felt the whole neighbourhood shaking under the bombs. The AA guns, moving up and down the road, made a deafening noise. In the morning when they opened the shutters there was no glass left in the windows and in West Bank Street, just across the railway line, not a quarter of a mile away, a young woman and her three small children were killed in one house, and a young man and two old men in another. So they didn't want to spend another night at home. Mum thought of a friend called Joan, a woman she had worked with in the Telephone Exchange, who lived in Crumpsall, and she set off there, leaving Gran in Liverpool Street, to see if Joan would give them shelter for a while. There were fires in the centre of Manchester and she had to step across the hosepipes lying all over the place. The trains leaving London Road were packed to bursting, people hanging on outside. When she got to Joan's there was nobody in. She left a note and trailed all the way back again. In the meantime – do you remember this? – you'd come from Heaton Street, to say they should move out to Uncle Harry's, in Blackley, for the night at least. So they did, which was a lot of to-ing and fro-ing before dark and the black-out in one short winter's day. Soon after they had a letter from Joan. She said what a blessing she was out when Mum came looking for a safe haven. That night an incendiary fell through the roof and landed on the bed where Mum and Gran would have been sleeping. So perhaps I'd have had no mother and would never have been born. They'd have been in the shelter, our Glad said. You'd have got born all right.

3

He stood at the kitchen window looking out. Close behind him Glad was making the tea. Garden's looking nice, he said. Those autumn crocuses. Who looks after it? Council, she said. All part of the service. There's the tea. Push that lot through, will you.

When they were settled in the other room and he was sitting very close to her with his bag, his cup of tea, and his plate, full of the usual, handy by, she said, How's Alice then? Not well, he answered. And I doubt she'll ever get better. I don't think she even wants to. Everything mithers her. Easy as that: worried sick, worried to death. Her blood's just under the surface of her skin – a very black blood, such a thin skin – on her hands and arms and legs. She bleeds if she gets the slightest knock. And your mum? As she was, he answered, and will be. But we do nice things. I drove her up the steep road behind Penmaenmawr and pushed her in the wheelchair quite a way along the Jubilee Walk. She seems to live completely in the present. It makes her fearless. She seems to have forgotten why a person might be afraid. You're very high up on that walk and I pushed her to where it bends round the mountainside and on your left there's a steep drop and nothing to see but the sea. Her eyes were shining like a little girl's. We're doing all right, eh Mum? I said. Have some more tea, said Glad. And help yourself to whatever takes your fancy. You were going to show me something or tell me something. Both, he said. A while back, a year or two before Dad died, when I was getting more and more interested, already feeling I mustn't leave it too late, when I was over there visiting them, we were in the front room, when he suddenly remembered a book of poems in the bookcase in the front room at 29 Heaton Street, it had a green cover, he said, and gold lettering on the spine, and that evening he phoned you up and you said yes, that was the Bard. Remember? Of course I remember, said our Glad. Father was very proud of that volume. The Coverdale Bard. That's our family for you, he used to say. Though I never saw him reading it. But one night when they were rowing Mother took it out of the bookcase and opened it anywhere and put on a funny posh voice and started declaiming bits, like she was on the stage. Give it here, he said.

He'd gone white. He couldn't bear her making fun of him and his family. Harry and I were there watching. George and your dad were in bed. You give it here, he said. But she put one hand on her hip and pranced around the room reading out bits of the Bard's poems in a lardy-dah voice. He raised his fist to her. Then she stopped. Weak Will, she said. Hit me and you'll regret it. And she tossed the book at his feet, fetched her hat and coat and flounced off down the street. That's the book, she said. I can see it now, lying open and face down on the carpet and him stooping to pick it up, his leg hurting him and such shame and sorrow on his face, said Glad. Well, he said, a couple of months ago I put an advert in the *Stockton and Darlington Times* asking would anyone who knew anything about our family in the Dale, and especially about the Bard himself, please get in touch. And a very kind lady in Bedale, a Mrs S., sent me a bundle of priceless things through the post. One of them was the book. He took it out of his bag and laid it in her lap, saying, He had a high opinion of himself, did this bard of ours. He rode around the place – a small place – on a favourite mare called Tessie, and the local poor saluted him. It was said that in his early youth he had made the acquaintance of William Wordsworth and had been encouraged by him, on long walks in the dales together, to follow the calling of poetry. I've found no hard evidence of any such friendship. I'm inclined to think he made the story up and only put it about once Wordsworth was in the grave and couldn't deny it. Then if anyone asked he would smile his self-satisfied smile and answer, Long ago. What's not made up is that his wife, called Isabella, left him and went to live in Doncaster. Some say that his love of Nature and his frequent long absences admiring it and writing poems about it were the reason why. There was gossip about what she got up to while he was away, which he believed and ordered her out, sending her £1 a month thereafter (in Penny Blacks), for her support. He was in his fifties, very set in his ways, opinionated, fond of himself, and had married in the hope of some home comforts. He died without lawful issue, or any issue at all that I've been able to uncover, and left a good deal of land and property in the Dale to his nephew, Henry, who in due course left a good part of it to John, his son, your grandfather, the Master of Tadcaster Workhouse, who, when his time came, left a fair bit of it and houses in Tadcaster as well, to his only son, John William, your father, who sold the lot when things got bad. So it's not as if nothing came your way out of the wealth of Tadcaster, only that it came a bit late. Early or late, would have made no difference in the end, said our Glad. And we got none from the Brewery, that's for sure. She was leafing through the volume of verse. Very small print, she said. I'd have to get my specs to make anything out. And I don't suppose I'd remember which poems it was that Mother declaimed in her cruel mockery. Well I've read them all, he said, and believe me, it wouldn't matter which ones she happened on when she opened the book at random as you say she did, they're all much of a muchness, all far too long, he couldn't help himself, once he got going, rhyme after rhyme, he couldn't stop. But she was only using his words to upset your father and I agree she shouldn't have done that. And throwing the book on the floor was very disrespectful. A lot of work had gone into it and it was a family heirloom. Your dad tore some pages out of my bible once and threw them in the fire, said Glad. Half of the Book of Revelation, to be exact. Just for spite. I was ten and I'd *got religion*, and Father bought me a bible for my birthday, to encourage me, though he'd lost his own faith in the War, as he often said. I was furious with Bernard but he was only four or five and very liable to fits of devilment, so I forgave him.

Another thing, he said, reaching again into his bag and moving his chair to sit close next to her, really the best thing in that precious package from Mrs S., is this: see here. It was a manuscript book, in which, from 1794 to 1838, the Constables of Carlton recorded the expenses they incurred in the carrying out of their duties. And those duties, he said, were set out for them on this marvellous document – again he reached into his bag – harking back to the days of Good Queen Bess and known as the Fourteen Articles. It's like the Hippodrome, said Glad. It's like that conjuror, what's his name, bringing things out of a hat that cannot possibly be in there. You're the conjuror, he said. You remember things, you set people thinking, the word goes round, Dad thinks he remembers a green and golden book in Heaton Street, phones you, Yes, you say and tell him exactly, and on the strength of that I put an advertisement in the *Stockton and Darlington Times* and hey presto! See here now and hearken to what that kind lady in Bedale sent me through the post a month ago from nearly two hundred years ago, the King's instructions to his local enforcers of law and order, the Fourteen Articles, this from No III, for example: 'You shall certify what Vagabond Persons and Rogues have been apprehended… and who have been sent to the House of Correction…' And this, from No XI: 'You shall inquire and certify what Stocks are provided in every Parish for setting the Poor to work, and by what means the Poor are set to work in every Parish…' Twice a year, he tells them, they must search their patch for vagrants and report on any fellow constables who have neglected 'to punish Rogues and wandering Persons' and any fellow-Christian parishioners who have 'relieved such Rogues with meat'. Small chance in Carlton-in-Coverdale during the French Wars and the uneasy decades thereafter that you would feed and clothe the stranger at your door and so doing perhaps entertain an angel unawares. People don't always do as they're told, said Glad. People are nicer than the ones lifted up in authority over them making the rules and telling them what to do, in my experience. Amen, he said. So many on the road, on that small Pennine crossing in those years of war and hunger and the beginnings of revolt, in every season and in all weathers, sailors dropped on one coast and walking to the other, soldiers and sailors with their families, women and children making their own way, and such distances, from Hull to Liverpool, from Carlisle to Shields, from Portsmouth into Ireland, even from America some landed and on foot then headed further east across the hills, to the next doss-house, common lodging house, unguarded out-house, barn, haystack or thorn bush, lee of a drystone wall, towards the casual ward of a workhouse, towards a house and home. Most of these pedestrians, wayfarers, footsloggers had passes permitting them to be on the roads of the native land for which the menfolk had been fighting, some had none, but with or without a pass they were not wanted in the little townships and villages into which they came, but went to the Constable, got given a dole, more if they had a pass, less if they did not, but never much, and so moved on. Listen to this, he said: 18 May 1800, Gave to a Sailor from Scarbro' to Liverpool sixpence; 19 September, Gave to a Sailor, from Sunderland to Poole in Dorsetshire: sixpence; 6 June 1801, Gave a Sailor's Wife with one child from Liverpool to Durham with a pass: sixpence; 8 July 1808, Relieving 7 Women & 8 Children from Deal in Kent to Carlisle: 3/6; 17 February 1812, Gave a Soldier with a Pass to Haverfordwest: 1/- ; 20 August 1812, Gave a Man & 3 Children with a Pass from Plymouth Hospital to Richmond: 1/6. That's a few of the many in this book who are themselves only a handful in the vast broadcasting of the poor along the roads in that small span of years. Coming here, he said, and while we are here together in your cosy room and on my way home then, the bits and pieces of our family stories teem in my mind and make a restlessness around my heart, which is, I think, the workings of my sympathy with all the living and the dead we ever dwell on or even only glance upon in our talk.

And since the day when, through a stranger's kindness, I got this book all the proud walkers, vagrants, strollers, homesick, homeless wanderers, children, toddlers, babes-in-arms, the sturdy, the footsore, the weary-to-death crossing winter and summer, in fair weather and foul, from west to east and east to west and passing through the dale and the village where one thread of our family lived comfortably off, they are in that multitude too in my waking and sleeping hours, all those transient lives in an age of upheaval. A few have names. 20 October 1813, for example, Constable Thomas Metcalfe paid William Skinner his Wife & 3 Children and, on the same day, Jane Frazer with a pass, a shilling. 11 February 1815 Constable Ingram Thompson gave Ann Comfort & her Child with a pass the same. But most by far are nameless. They are the types: soldier, sailor, a poor man in distress, a poor man with his wife and child, a poor woman in distress, a woman and five children, *a dumb woman* – she haunts me, I can tell you. Yes, said our Glad, I imagine she would. And she added, I worked forty-three years for the blind and married a man very hard of hearing. Silence is all right, I suppose, but speech is to be preferred, I wouldn't like to do without our asking and speaking and listening. So have a piece of battenberg and another sup of tea and tell me more, before you have to leave. Well, he said, Henry Constantine the Elder and his son, Henry the Bard, being among 'the principle inhabitants' of the place, both held the office of Constable at one time or another. From the Elder, 15 July 1803, a poor man in distress got 1/6. From the Bard, 9 May 1834, '3 people going from Hull to Clithero' in distress' got threepence, and on 5 June 'a seafaring man who had been unfortunate' tuppence. He prided himself on his own thrift and industry, did that particular Henry, and distinguished very definitely between the deserving and the undeserving poor. He viewed with suspicion men arriving in the village on crutches who claimed to have been crippled in the service of the King. He paid them the minimum, saw them on their way, and supposed that once out of view they would shoulder their crutches and stride along chortling. I've met a few like him, said Glad. I was up there last week, he continued. I took time off and walked from Kettlewell to Leyburn, over the pass and through Carlton, to get the feel of it. I was lucky, I had the wind and the rain at my back. Also I could afford a night's lodging. We thought when the better weather comes we'd drive you the way I walked over the pass and down the Dale and show you Horsehouse, where one of the ancestors founded a little school, and the old lead-workings that the Bard and his nephew, speculating, put money in, and Flatts Farm on the main street, where the family lived from 1687, a fine big house with some verses on the front of it in praise of the Bard, written and put up there for all to see by the Bard himself, and the churchyard, where the generations of our family lie, and down the Dale to the Wharfe and Tadcaster and the workhouses old and new and the Shann House Hotel, formerly Clarence House, in Kirkgate, where they sent you as a little girl with a ticket on, to remind them of the poor relations in Salford, the dirty old town. You'd like that, wouldn't you, in the spring? You bet I would, said Glad. Some went to Canada, he continued, or New Zealand or Australia. And some moved only a few miles down the Dale, to Exelby near Bedale, and it's no great step from there to the flatlands and Tadcaster. But why the workhouse? Perhaps managing the poor had become a family line by then. And why Salford? I came across a postcard, 1922, of two lovers on the banks of the Wharfe not far from Clarence House and very nice it looks. But the Irwell long before you were there was a very soiled river. We were high above the Irwell, said our Glad, though, I grant you, Mother before they married lived in Reading Street. Yes, he said, no. 23, the whole terrace not long built, but still very close to the river and the weir. I had a walk round there not very long ago. They were pulling a lot down, I can't say what's still standing now. And the first home of their own was only a couple of hundred yards away, on Littleton Road, no. 13, (just past two beauty parlours now, one of them gone bust, and next door to a sandwich bar, also bust) and within a year they moved to 277 – where you were born – and it's true the road back then ran out past the race-course into the beginnings of the country and on a clear day you could see the moors, but you were low down still, in the fogs and the smell of the river. Father was chesty, altogether he was delicate, said our Glad. So they moved again, when they could afford it, to Heaton Street, with a bathroom, going up in the world, close to Cheetham Hill, where the rich lived in big houses with big gardens. And Heaton Park ten minutes away, he said, where Mum and Dad did their courting. There were no parks, or none like that, where she lived, down on Liverpool Street among the works and the railways and the gasometers, so on Sundays she called for him in Heaton Street and they went their own ways in Heaton Park. Another thing, he said, I only found this out last year, on one of my visits, the Pals camped in that park to begin their training, in September of the War's first year, and Mum's father, the other John William, was among them, in the 17th Manchesters. Ours was in the Liverpool Scottish, said Glad. I had a coat and tammy made out of his kilt when he came home. Ours had only a month to live when yours joined up, he said. Being chesty, said Glad, and working in the Post Office and him having five children, he was let be a while.

I'll have to be going soon, he said. I don't like the nights drawing in, said Glad. It's a long time till bed after I've had my bit of tea. I don't watch much television. How's your mum manage? The carers see her to bed, he answered, and come in again first thing. I don't like thinking about it. We go over as often as we can, Steve and I. – And Alice is no use to her, I suppose? – No use. She can hardly manage herself. Pity all that, said our Glad. On foot, he said, over the Vardre, through the ruins of the castle between the two volcanic stumps, it takes me twenty minutes from house to house. In the car it's five. Neither Steve nor I ever fails to visit Aunty Alice when we stay even only a day or two with Mum. Thirty years them living so close and her on her own after Uncle Norman died and never once did she invite Mum and Dad round even for so much as a cup of tea. And every year, once she was on her own, they took her on holiday with them and any number of times year in, year out, Dad was round there doing the garden or the decorating or fixing something for her. She hardened her heart, said our Glad. I wouldn't say that, he answered. It was love, that's what it was. Love stopped in its tracks, love thwarted. And turning it my way, they could never make it up. Their Jack was cold in the earth in a third-class plot in perpetuity in a far corner of Weaste Cemetery that got bombed during the Blitz, being near the canal and the railway line, you can still see the damage done to the tombstones. Gran told me the story in August 1968, when Helen was expecting Mary-Ann, quite suddenly, I remember, she told me the story of my cousin Jack. Born premature, very small and ill, he only lived three weeks. Norman got compassionate leave, went to the hospital, held him, they said he was doing better. But two days later a policeman came to the door and told them he was dead. Norman had to sign for the grave to be opened. I went back there many years ago with Aunty, it was only a mound, never had a headstone, but after some looking she did find the place. Her father was buried there too and two of her aunts who had died in infancy. She couldn't have another baby. They watched me as their own and not their own, doing what Jack might have done, I saw it in their eyes and felt it sometimes like a ghost at my back, as they watched

me going where he hadn't been let, so it felt, at times, that
for them I was living for him as well. I've got a photograph
– I'll show it you one day – of me in my cradle on the
Morrison in our front room. And on that same cast–iron
table top, built not to crumple if the house fell in, he had
rested, barely a year before, in his small coffin, on his way
from Hope Hospital to the plot in Weaste. People get over
worse than that, said Glad. And so much of that kind of
sorrow there was back then. I know, I know, he said. Norman
who had been on the Arctic and the North Atlantic convoys,
then off Algiers, on board the *Broke*, in the wardroom,
helping the doctor with the wounded, saw three men killed,
one of them his best mate, when another shell came in, as
she sliced through the boom. The *Broke* went down, after the
6 o'clock news they read out the names of ships that had
been lost, Aunty was listening, his was first, she thought him
drowned but he was in hospital and did come home on
compassionate leave, as related above, and came home for
good when the war was over with his body, at least, carrying
no worse hurt than shrapnel from that shell, one bit of
which, between finger and thumb on his right hand, he let
us feel, moving under the skin, when we were round at their
house by the railway line, larking about with him. He set us
up on the mantelpiece, either side the fire, and said we were
Gog and Magog. He called us ''orrible ratings', rolled on the
rug with us and tickled us half to death. We loved him, Glad,
and nothing that happened later and nothing that I in my
enquiries ever turned up could alter that. Your mum told me
once they offered to adopt you, she said. It was after they'd
left Weaste and gone to live in High Lane. Both working,
having no children, they had more money to spare than your
mum and dad. I know that tale, he said. It shocked me
through and through with love and pity for them both. They
could with as much chance of success have asked Father

Christmas would he kindly put the clock back to February 1943 and let their baby Jack be born fit and well and live for ever and a day. It hurts me still to think of a wish so utterly without hope. Yet families in those days did, said Glad. One lot doing well might take a son or daughter off their parents' hands if they were doing worse. Give one child a better chance and ease the hardship at home. What saddens me most, he said, is the thought of them discussing it, lying in bed perhaps, perhaps over weeks and months talking it over, and coming at last to believe it a sound idea when in fact it was a thing dreamed up out of their own lack. I was fourteen, I suppose. And one sister puts it to another, Why don't we take your boy to come and live with us? She said a very strange thing to me once. It was not long after Uncle Norman died. He died in the night, lying by her, and she didn't know, she thought that after some difficulty breathing he had gone to sleep and she was glad and she slept herself and woke to find him dying and nothing could be done. Quite soon after the funeral she moved house, and not to a smaller one, as it were for a woman henceforth to be on her own, but to one just round the corner that was actually rather bigger. Altogether, she resolutely embarked on the life of a widow. She joined the Townswomen's Guild. Never very religious, she joined the church. Childless, she joined the Mothers' Union. She entered a circle that kept her busy. And always, close by, she had Mum and Dad, whom she could turn to, who looked after her, and to whom she was determined never to be beholden. All take and no give, said Glad. He shrugged. I don't know. Anyway, I'd gone round to see her in her new house and – I don't know why, I regretted it at once – I began telling her that things hadn't been easy, in fact they had been terrible, between Helen and Mum, even over the baby, there was a struggle, a primitive helpless jealousy, with me in the middle loving and suffering for them both, and Aunty interrupted me and, almost gleefully, almost vengefully – I can still see the look on her face – she said, The trouble with your mum and dad is *they never suffered as much as we did*. I listened for a while and then kissed her goodbye and went and sat on the Vardre, high up and mid-way between the houses of the two sisters, and thought about it, the whole story. As I said, said Glad, people get over worse than Alice and Norman, or let's just say Alice since he was one of her troubles, had to put up with. You're right, he said. But things never worked out for them, and I don't just mean the baby – that's the worst and at the very beginning – but all along thereafter. There was a sort of competition and they lost. Having no children and two incomes they were winning in one way, the car, the washing machine, the television, but in the things that matter they never would win. It's a horrible way to look at it, I know, only now it's over anybody could see that's what it was, a one-sided competition, and not in the sense that one side could never win but, worse perhaps, that only one side – Alice and Norman – felt it to be a competition. They moved to High Lane, like many from the city's back streets, to better themselves, to have a nicer house, to be 'in the country', and the long drive every day back into the city to work exhausted them, they came home and fell asleep, had tea, watched a bit of television and went to bed. They had good neighbours in Salford and most on the new estate on the edge of the Peak District had come from neighbourly back streets too. But on Meadow Lane there was none of that, there were feuds and petty bad deeds – letting next door's tyres down is one I remember – all in all a disappointment. And when they stopped work and moved to Deganwy, to be by the seaside, Norman died within a year, leaving Alice, for a further thirty, maintaining an independence in which she would not admit any suggestion of defeat. Did Mum and

Dad get off lightly, did they not suffer as much as Alice and Norman? True, they were lucky. And Dad's illness, for Uncle Norman at least, never counted as a suffering. He thought it a state any man could snap out of if he tried. I knew he was wrong but his wrong opinion, so common, didn't touch me. I suppose I never blamed him and Aunty, never loved them less, because I knew where I stood, I knew what my blessings were and where my loyalties lay and I knew that their house, for whatever reasons, was far less happy than ours.

4

He stands at the window looking out, the garden rather dank, too much rain lately, the dark sky sagging with it. There's another thing about Aunty Alice, he said to Glad over his shoulder. Another jealousy, or part of the same. I nearly mentioned it last time, when we were talking about them wanting to adopt me and that the reason they thought it might be a good idea was that, being childless and both working, they were getting on very well and already had the car, the television, the washing machine, etc. It was the washing machine nearly made me mention the something else. Bustling behind him, she said almost impatiently, Yes, yes, and Alice said why don't you bring your washing round here, Bertha, and do it in our machine, a lot easier than the tub and you with a good deal of it to do. And when she went round to Birch Grove Alice was never there, only Norman, who worked very strange hours if he ever worked at all. Yes, he said, he worked for the GPO, he repaired the telephone lines and fitted new ones, he was 'up the pole' for a living, he liked the joke when people said, Our Norman's up the pole. Yes, said Glad, he was somehow always home when your mum went round with her washing and soon as she got there he started pestering her. Oh dear, he said, you know all that already. 'Mauling' was the word she always used, he started mauling me, she would say. So she only went round two or there times, hoping Alice would be there or at least that Norman would behave himself and when Alice never was there and Norman didn't behave himself she said to Dad, That's it now, she'd do her own washing at home, thank you very much, and when he asked her why, she told him and he said, That's that then, we'll get a machine of our own, so they did, on the HP, like everyone else, and made a few savings elsewhere in the budget. All that? Yes, said Glad. Your mum told me. Told me too, he said, and still I could never think very ill of him and when I remember it now I pity him and Alice, especially Alice, who had a husband who seemed to prefer her younger sister. I guess that festered long after he was dead. Tea's made, she said, behind his back. Push that lot through will you. I got us some ham for a change. And here's the shoebox in case we need it.

That certificate you've talked about, he said when they were settled, or diploma or whatever we should call it… Yes, she said, handing him his tea, I was going to mention it again last time but you had to be off and in any case I thought perhaps we'd already given ourselves enough to be going on with. We had that, he said. My head was full of it, driving home. Still is, of the more and more of it. And driving over today, I wondered where to start, where to begin again. It hung on the bedroom wall, if I remember rightly? Yes, above their bed. Father framed it and nailed it on the wall above their marriage bed. I stayed in a B & B once, he said, in Bethesda, under the Carneddau, next day I was heading for Conwy along the ridge, and over my bed that night there was a picture of an eye and under it the caption 'Thou God seest me'. Perhaps he meant his diploma to be a bit like that? Perhaps he did, said Glad. It had fancy lettering, in black and gold, and his name bang in the middle in red, from the College of Jesus, to certify that he, John William Constantine, had completed 'with merit' Part I of his training for the ministry. Father himself said 'with flying colours – I passed with flying colours,' he used to say. It hung there till the day he died and soon after that it vanished, Mother must have taken it down, as perhaps she had been wanting to do since the day he put it up. And don't ask me what became of it. Vanished, like much else. If you start in good time, he said, reaching for a piece of the cheese she knew he liked, and talk to the women who remember, you can assemble a great deal of information about a person's life. But there'll always be gaps. I'm sure, said Glad. This diploma or certificate, for example: there it is – or was – beyond doubt on the bedroom wall. And around what it seems to prove, as there was around the thing itself on the wall in 29 Heaton Street, there's an empty space. There was a College of Jesus in Rotherham, founded by Thomas Rotherham in 1483, dissolved by Edward VI around 1550, continuing as a grammar school then on various sites until in 1890 it took over a college for the training of Congregationalist ministers, on Moorgate Road, that had closed and amalgamated with one in Bradford. I've wondered did he go there, to that place in Bradford, though I haven't heard it ever thought of the first College of Jesus as its ancestor. Father wasn't Cong, said Glad. And, he continued, the trouble with the fact that he had such a training (or even just a part of it) at all, and got a certificate to prove it, is that I'm not sure which space of his life it fits into. Because from somewhere, I can't for the life of me remember where, I have a letter he received from the Postmaster General in appreciation of his 'more than forty-three years' of faithful service when, aged sixty, he retired from the Post Office, in October 1941. And another from St James's Palace, telling him His Majesty the King had been graciously pleased to award him the Imperial Service Medal for those years. And that medal's in my collection too. Now, I learned only the other day that he joined the Post Office in March 1899, aged eighteen, so it's not quite forty-three years and it's certainly not 'more than'. In 1901, as we know, he was back in the Workhouse, and employed outside as a post-office clerk and telegraphist. And from then till he married your mother in April 1909 – and on the marriage certificate he appears as a clerk, which must mean a post-office sorting clerk – come what, if he were a rock star, we should call 'the missing years'. And in them – I hope you're following? – there's another fact only very recently brought to my notice, which is that in November 1907 he was appointed to that same job, but now in Manchester. That fits, said Glad. In the missing years, heeding the call to salvation through faith and good works, he went and trained at the College of Jesus for the ministry and that certificate on the bedroom wall, lost without trace, I grant you, wasn't a figment of my imagination – your dad remembered it too and so would Harry and George, if you'd ever asked them – it is the living proof. And besides, she said, there was a trunk on the landing in 29 Heaton Street and once, when Mother had locked my best coat in it to stop me going out, I'd be sixteen or so and I had a date and that coat was my favourite, it had a fur collar and with my cloche hat on I thought it made me look like Vilma Banky, so when Mother had gone out, she was always off out, and Father hadn't come in from the Post Office, I worked the lock loose and when I lifted the lid I saw written on the inside in copy pencil in Granny Gilchrist's handwriting a list of all the clothes and extras Father took with him to the College of Jesus. So that was his trunk, and plus the diploma, what more do you want? And then the story is, she continued, that having with flying colours completed the first part of his training he was sent by his tutors to do missionary work in

darkest Salford and was attached to a church in Lower
Broughton, very likely the Church of the Ascension, and
became engaged to the Vicar's daughter there, whose name
was Gladys, but soon fell for Mother and married her instead.
And I'm called Gladys in fond memory of the daughter of
the Vicar, the Gladys he loved and left. Yes, I had that tale from
Dad, he said, or more likely from Mum who had it from Dad,
who had it, of course, from you. Living in the workhouse,
working in the town post office, who knows, perhaps he
grew weary of it, his life seemed pointless, he got religion, he
desired to do more for the poor than his father had, so he
quitted his job to train for the ministry, was sent to the valley
of the Irwell, became engaged to Gladys, daughter of the
Vicar of the Church of the Ascension, but left her for
Gertrude Adelaide, your mother, my Grandma Con, and
through her father, himself a town postman, returned to his
old employment but now in Salford, as the easy option and
with a decent pension, and stayed put there till he retired at
sixty and won a medal from King George VI. So he'd be a
student, a trainee-priest, at the College of Jesus maybe 1904-
05, and felt he couldn't continue there, or didn't want to,
thought they'd never have him back, once he had blotted his
copybook by betraying the trust of his mentor, the Vicar of
the Church of the Ascension, and thrown in his lot with your
mother and the Post Office. How's that sound? Pretty good,
said our Glad, pretty near the truth, I'd say. And if it's not the
whole truth perhaps it's as near as we'll ever get. Keep your
eye on the time, she said. I don't want them worried at home.
But this Gladys, he said, the one whose name your father gave
you in remembrance of an earlier passion, I've heard a version
of the tale in which she was the daughter of a Weslyan
minister in Tadcaster, she lived on Station Road, very near the
Workhouse, he knew her around 1902, loved her, got
engaged to her, but for one reason or another they went their

separate ways, she married a man from Liskeard and John William, still a sorting clerk, hung around in the Workhouse till 1906 when, on the death of his father, facing eviction, he got a transfer to Manchester, that being as good a place as any. News to me, said Glad. And most unlikely. No, take my word for it. We might quibble about the dates, and perhaps he got leave from the Post Office or maybe he never told them, or perhaps after one war and in the middle of another the King and the Postmaster General didn't trouble to be too exact, they erred on the side of generosity, Father having served his country in some terrible places, and they granted him the forty-three years and a few extra. There's one or two maybes and perhapses, I don't deny. But the College of Jesus, the missionary work in Lower Broughton, loving and leaving that Gladys, believe me: all gospel. Father being the only son, she continued, the family hoped better than that he'd end up by the Irwell married to the daughter of another postman, granddaughter of a carter. Running the workhouse, churchgoers, very respectable, they had surely raised no objection when he told them he'd felt a calling. And no sooner arrived where he would begin his labours, he becomes engaged to the daughter of his Vicar! Knowing them, they will have seen the hand of the Lord in this and could easily imagine him, in just a few years, Bishop of Ripon and able to do something for his five sisters, and the whole family definitely on the up. They were like that in Tadcaster. I always felt sorry for Father feeling he'd let the side down. They never liked Mother, and less and less as things went from bad to worse. All the same, she continued, credit where credit's due, when she was expecting our Harry and Father wrote asking could they come over for the birth, they said yes and welcome, so I believe, and told Father off for making her walk from the railway station already six months gone. Pass the shoebox, will you. You'll want to see what they all looked like at the christening. And don't let that bit of ham go begging. She rummaged in the box. There they all are, she said. And looking no worse than most families look on such occasions. That's Granny Gilchrist, the widow, the woman I saw in the attic a few years later with her ear trumpet. And that – jabbing with a forefinger – is Aunt Edith, her third daughter, born stone deaf. For the births of the twins and George, she came over to us in Heaton Street, to help. And that's me, Curly Locks, middle of the front row, scowling, no cushion, no strawberries and cream. They've all gone now, I'm the last. What the blacksmith hit his wife with. Funny things, photographs. I'm not sure I like them really. You'd better be on your way. It's getting dark already. How did your mum take Alice's death? I can't tell, he replied. She's been quite distant anyway, since Dad. I don't think it was any ill-feeling. Just she was remote. And perhaps, he added, forgetting Gladys's age, it starts to matter less. I remember Dad telling me Harry had died. We were meeting them for coffee in Llandudno and he came up with a slightly odd smile on his face and without preamble said, My brother's died – just like that, without even saying hello, in a sort of wondering way, but not in shock or sadness, so that I almost thought he was wondering at how little it mattered. Of course, they hardly ever saw each other, as you know. Only Christmas cards. I really wouldn't have recognized him, nor Aunty Myra, nor the cousins, if we'd met. But when he said so simply, My brother's died, I thought it will not be like that for Steve or me. Yes, I'd better be going. On the doorstep he held her close a while longer than usual. Look after yourself, he said. Mind you put the chain on and lock the back door. I'll come again soon as I can. We're thinking Mum will have to go into a home. At the gate he turned and waved. She looked smaller, facing out less steadily.

5

Cold, sunny. She had opened the window, just enough to hear the children in the playground among the leafless trees. How's your mum doing? she asked, busy with the tea things behind him. He turned. It's a nice place, he said. All the staff seem to be from Salford, everyone who attends to her speaks in the accent of home. So that's one blessing. Another is they like her to be out and about, they've got a wheelchair and blankets ready when I arrive, and off we go. Doesn't seem to matter where we go or what we do. I wheel her on the hard sand right down to the waves, I wheel her round Asda so I can buy something for my tea, both places it is like a special treat. She looks about her and smiles on all things. She's in the present, right here and now, wherever we are, there she is, looking neither before nor after. That really is a blessing, I should say. But we wanted her home, like Gran, who was home till the end and died there, in her own bed in her own room. That grieves us, Steve and me, both families, it grieves us, I can tell you. She put the teapot on the trolley and, not waiting to be asked, he pushed the provisions through. She followed him with the shoebox of photographs.

In her easy chair, perched upon a cushion, wearing a new dress with her pinny over it, a cheerful silk scarf at her throat and white woolly socks on her feet, bright as ninepence, eager, the shoebox in her lap, fixing him with her story-teller gaze, she said, Are you sitting comfortably? Then I'll begin. There's no piccalilli, by the way. Will pickled onions do? They will, he answered, moving close. Well then, she said, another thing in that trunk on the landing was the dress our Edith was wearing the day it happened, a cotton dress, saxe blue, and wrapped in it was the doll she was playing with, a cloth doll with a big smile and golden curls. I knew Mother had kept them, or what was left of them – Father told me – but until I lifted the lid to get my favourite coat out I didn't know they were there. My Vilma Banky coat was lying on top of the dress and the doll, which gave me quite a turn when I uncovered them. I've only got one photo of Edith, I don't know why, her and your dad together, actually, and it's in here somewhere. She rummaged, he watched her hands, how quick they were, not gentle, and her eyes also, watching for the thing her fingers would bring to light, they were fiercely intent. These are all coming to you, by the way, she said, not looking up. If you want them, that is. I do want them, he said. Got it, she said, and handed him the photograph, an oval of sepia-brown cardboard which, clearly, had been cut out from a larger print, the edges were uneven, the picture, like a medallion, had no surroundings, it was the bare heart of the matter, isolated, without mitigation. The twins, three or four months old, sit each on a large floral cushion, with another cushion between them, on a dark wooden settle. Both almost bald, both in white frocks, one shows a hand, the other a hand and half a foot. One sits slumped against an arm of the settle, the other propped upright against its back. Which is which? he asked. That's your dad, on the left, said Glad. They stare out, neither understands what is happening. Edith looks the more unsure, but that may be only how she has been placed, in the angle, and slumping down, as though cowering away. See on the other side, said Glad, what Mother wrote. He turned the card over and read: 'My twins one burned to death the other lived to help me through my difficult time GaC.' Gertrude Adelaide Constantine. Mum told me about this years and years ago, he said. The accident, I mean. It was when Dad first went into his depressions and they were looking for a reason because by then, in his mid-forties, we were doing well and surely he could see it, surely, after his efforts, he could relax. And a doctor he told about Edith did wonder whether it might be that, after all those years never got over, still in him, biding its time. Who knows? I never asked him about it. It was always through Mum, from him to her to me, and from you. Years later, on one of my trips back, my first visit to Heaton Street, I noticed that numbers 2-14 were newer than all the other houses and, you remember, when I wrote to you, you said that would be where the croft had been and a little pond but they filled the pond in, thinking it might be dangerous for families on the terrace with small children, so then it was just wasteland, 'the croft', everyone called it, as we did in our neighbourhood any bombsite or scrap of unused land, somewhere to go out and play on. That first visit, seeing the newer houses, and learning from you that under them was the croft and under it the little pond, filled in for safety's sake, I felt Edith's death more closely. And now this photograph and the writing on the back. Closer and closer, as the years pass. She was born first, said Glad, by fifteen minutes. But Bernard overtook her and talked before she did. They were always up to no good together. People called them the 'Terrible Twins', like something out of a comic. A policeman came to the door one day and said they'd got our Edith at the station. Mother didn't even know she was missing. She had to go and collect her and when she came back Bernard had turned the bathroom taps on and there was water pouring downstairs. He loved fire as well, he was always getting smacked for going too near it in the living room. Was he with Edith on the croft that day? Mum said she thought he was, but you told me you thought he wasn't. Did she? Did I? said our Glad, and shrugged. Very likely he was, Harry and I were at school, Father was at work, Mother was inside cleaning the floor, when Mrs Benson, who kept the greengrocer's opposite the croft, ran in screaming that our Edith had set herself alight, she had got hold of some matches and set her dress alight. The doll was on fire as well. They ran with her to Doctor Jameson, he wanted half a crown before he'd see her and then said he couldn't do anything for her and they must take her to the Jewish Hospital on Elizabeth Street, on Cheetham Hill, which was the nearest, but still a long way carrying a child in that state. That was a Friday, she lived till Monday. The doll was a new one and called Marie, Father brought it back for her from France, he was just demobbed, he'd only been home a month, he brought us all presents. What happened to the doll and the dress? They were in the trunk, said Glad, and every now and then Mother took them out and looked at them, burned black as they were, though on the shoulders of the remains of the dress the saxe blue still showed through and the doll's smile was still there though not much of her curls, as I remember. Father shouted at her, what good did it do? No sense keeping relics. But I believe she took them with her after he died and we'd all left home and she moved to a flat of her own in Whalley Range. Your dad cleared that place when she died. I never asked him about the dress and the doll, he said. I didn't like. He was ill by then. I expect he threw them out if he found them and I wouldn't blame him if he did. I suppose you're thinking if you'd seen them you'd be closer still, she said. Yes, I am, he said. But if Dad threw them away I certainly don't blame him. And perhaps you're close enough already, said our Glad. I got tinned pears for a change. Help yourself.

Why did she call him 'Weak Will'? he asked, helping himself. There's a couple more snaps of him in here, she answered. Time I sorted this lot out. But he was glad of the pause, he liked watching her fingers riffling among the years. Eureka! she cried. Here's one of him in hospital, the wounded soldier. He is sitting up, arms folded, with a pillow not quite supporting him against the iron bed-end. That will be a night-shirt he is wearing, buttoned to the top, a man of thirty-five, 338459 Private John William Constantine, 10th King's Liverpool Scottish, almost bald, full lips, big ears, unsmiling, a bit supercilious in his look which seems to be meeting nobody's gaze. I wouldn't say he looked weak. Perhaps a bit superior, he'd pass for an officer. Yes, said our Glad. He went to that posh boarding school in Harrogate, don't forget, and trained for the ministry in the College of Jesus, God knows where. Mother called him hoity-toity. She was quicker than him, sharper, *very* sharp with him when she liked, brought him down a peg or two, and since that was an easy thing to do, she called him weak, and on those occasions I must say he looked it. Also, though in their rows he called her all sorts and threatened her, she knew there was no real harm in him because in spite of everything he loved her. Here's another one of him, when he'd just joined up. The usual set-piece, millions of them. He stands resting his right arm on a bare wooden chair, his left is smartly by his side, behind him a ghostly antique column. The cap, the bright buttons, the belt buckled high around the tunic. Unfortunately, that bottom corner got torn off, said Glad, so he's missing some of both legs, as you can see. Your dad did that, if I remember rightly. Or Edith. By accident, I'm sure, and not for evil. There in his cap and a year younger he looks almost boyish, trusting, good-natured, wouldn't hurt a fly. There's another one in here somewhere – him at Blackpool on a merry-go-round. Did he ever talk about the War? he asked. All Father ever told me, said Glad, not looking up, was that he didn't enjoy it. His regiment was in some terrible places, he said. Arras, Messines, Ypres. And being sent back again – Somme, Cambrai, Le Cateau – from hospital, that must have been very hard for him, knowing what it would be like. You find out these things, she said. You don't need me. On the memorial at Thiepval, he said, there are more than 72,000 names of the missing on the Somme, and one of them is my other grandfather, the other John William. And when I first started asking my gran about him, in the couple of years before she died, when she came in her account to the moment of his death all she said was 'Blown to bits', and saying that, she shrugged. And that phrase and that shrug and the look on her face have been with me ever since. And all these many years I've been gathering up the bits, of him and her and the others who matter to me. And my way of doing it was first to hear the word, to attend as closely as I could to the living word, and then by reading but mostly by walking, through the fields before Guillemont, through the streets and parks of Salford, over the pass from Kettlewell into Coverdale, along the Wharfe in Tadcaster, up the Irwell to its source on the moors, to make the word, in my sense, flesh. And the word comes from you and the other women who remember and have the gift of saying it. So never say I don't need you. Well then, said our Glad, here's that one of him on the merry-go-round at Blackpool in a little car, wearing a flat hat. Looks quite cheerful there, don't you think? No idea when it was taken. Before or after. Life goes on.

<h1 style="text-align:center">6</h1>

Come in, she said. I was getting worried. Queues, he said, an accident somewhere. Go on in there, said Glad. I've pushed the trolley through. I'll just make the tea. He did as bidden; but then, after a couple of minutes, went and stood in the kitchen, watching her. You not so good? he asked. I'll be right as rain when we get talking, she replied. You fancy coming to us for Christmas? he asked. Helen said to say she wishes you would. Thank her kindly, said Glad. But I expect I'll be with Norman's family as usual, what's left of them round here. And Betty and me will have our seasonal get-together, no doubt. It will be a bit funny without Ev but two's better than one and one is better than none.

Speaking of Christmas, he said when they were settled and drinking tea in the warm living-room, Dad told me once he couldn't remember you ever celebrated Christmas at Heaton Street. Father was working at Christmas, that's why. We had our celebrations at New Year, she said. Bernard wasn't fair about Father. Saying we never had a Christmas is just one example. Mostly I heard it from Mum, he said, hardly ever did Dad say anything to me about such things. But once – a close friend of mine, who was dying, had asked me would I climb Snowdon with him and his small son, and coming from that, staying the night with Mum and Dad, next morning as I was leaving – I had opened the door – and quite suddenly, Mum standing next to him, Dad said that his life had been ruined by Valium and a poor upbringing. The doctor had prescribed him Valium for his anxiety, but the poor upbringing? Unfair or not, in the light of him saying it I saw that our whole childhood, Steve's and mine, so loving, so encouraging, was made by his determined effort, with Mum who had no father she could remember, to give us what he never had. Having no model, or no good model, he got his idea of being a father negatively, you might say. He knew what he wanted our childhood to be like: not like his. Bernard always took Mother's side, said Glad. He never gave Father his due or even much sympathy. Even after the War and the business with Edith he was a good father to us. He used to take me and Harry for a walk on Sunday mornings, as far as Middleton or through Heaton Park as far as Rhodes. It was proper country round there in those days. Father had a pint in a pub and we sat outside with some crisps and a ginger beer. Then we walked back again in time for Sunday dinner, which always started with Yorkshire pudding and gravy. If that's not a family life I don't know what is. And he was a great one for nature. He told us the names of birds and flowers. Once I remember going to Tadcaster with him, just him and me. There were none of the family left in Clarence House or anywhere else in the town by then. We walked along the river. He walked quite slowly and with a stick, on account of his bad leg. He kept stopping and pointing things out. We went and had afternoon tea together, in a place by the river, we were right in the window, we could see people enjoying themselves in boats. I felt very grown-up. He was very attentive to me, as though I were quite the young lady. Mum told me Dad had a mortal fear of that stick, he said. Not that he'd be hit with it, just the tapping of it on the pavement at night, after the pubs closed, his father and mother coming home, or just the father, and her in the house, waiting, the sound of his stick before the sound of his key in the lock. And soon after, the shouting would start and the boy lay awake, ashamed and frightened. Next morning his mother would have to wake the man still drunk, wash him, shave him, get him off to work. Yes, he sided with his mother. He was devoted to her. Mum told me she would ask him to brush her hair, to soothe her. He poulticed a boil she had on the back of her neck, before he went to school and as soon as he came in. When he started doing jobs, he gave her most of his wages. He earned twelve pence making ice-cream and gave her eleven of them. But when they needed money they would pawn his suit, so that once, she told me, when she came calling for a dance they were going to, he was so ashamed he wouldn't come out, he was sitting on the stairs and she had to talk to him through the letterbox. That certainly never happened, said Glad. I grant you, after Edith they drank, but she was as bad as him, worse, I'd say, it's always worse in a woman, the language and falling over with it. Yes, they ran out of money, they pawned things, same as most people did now and again, but never their own son's suit. Or if they did, he had plenty else to wear. And sitting on the stairs and your mother talking to him through the letter-box, never. Have some trifle, said Glad. I made us some trifle for a treat.

He felt sorry, but for what? For telling her another bit of his side of the story? Or for the whole talking and listening and asking and answering, the whole complicity? This is wonderful trifle, he said. Then: I hope our talks don't keep you awake. Old people don't sleep much, she said. And there are worse things than all this to lie awake thinking about. Your dad was a lucky man to find your mum. Her and you two boys, I don't call that a ruined life. And whatever the facts, I don't say he wasn't telling the truth. Father was nicest to me, I don't doubt it, being as I was the one daughter he had left. And I was going to say, that day in Tadcaster, before we had our walk along the river, he had a meeting with the solicitor, just opposite Clarence House, which by then wasn't ours any more, and I waited in reception, he was a long time in with Mr Bromet and I looked through the window and watched who was coming and going where I'd come and gone during the War. Years later Harry and I worked out it must have been then he decided to sell the two houses he still owned in Tadcaster, they were on the main road, close by the brewery, with gardens front and back, and the land and the houses he still owned in Carlton. I was twelve or thereabouts and he treated me to afternoon tea. That would be six or seven years after Edith so I can't say our decline and fall was from one day to the next, but slowly and surely we were going down. And if your dad ever said there was no money left for schooling after Harry and me then that is the truth and I don't deny it and in fact, and to be honest, it didn't even last for me, Harry went to the Grammar School all right and I went to Summerhill, and then passed the exam to go to Bella Vista on Bury New Road with the rich Jewish girls, I wanted to be a teacher, I'd have made a good teacher, don't you think? But Father took me out, intending me for the Post Office, but I'd missed that year's exam by then and he didn't want me months at home bringing nothing in, so I tried as a milliner, but not for long, I was no good at it, time passing, and then, just turned fifteen, I got a job as a packer in the Royal National Library for the Blind on St John Street in Manchester, ten shillings a week, and stayed with them for the rest of my working life, forty-three years, and Head of Packing when I left. And to think all I asked was to be headmistress of the poshest girls school in England and motor with Jack Buchanan to Monte Carlo in the holidays! Bernard and George had no hopes of any grammar school, there was no money left for them. Your dad had ideas of his own but Father said it was the Post Office for him, any objections and he'd kick his backside, so there he was, aged fourteen, signed up as a boy messenger. George first had a job as a clerk with Marwood & Robertson, ship brokers, in Mount Street, just off Albert Square, he was cheerful enough, I remember him coming home on his bike singing 'Cockles and Mussels', but soon as he could, telling fibs about his age, he joined the RAF and vanished and he was our glamour boy ever after. Father was old-fashioned about family life, the Sunday dinner I've already mentioned, we were to be seen and not heard except to say at the end of it, Please may we leave the table and thank you for what we have received, and, I grant you, he was no friend of the suffragettes, he wanted Mother at home looking after the children, but she wanted to be out, she got herself a job at Cohen & Wilks, in Cheetham Hill, but he went and fetched her home, saying no wife of his would ever go out to work, which didn't help the family finances and in fact he couldn't rule her, she wanted to be out, after Edith it got her down being in the house all day, and when the boys had all left home and only her and Father and me in the house and me and him working I suppose more and more she felt released from her duties and, time passing, wanted some sort of a different life, don't forget she was very beautiful when he met her. She had more than a few affairs, all local, she was too old for the Monkey Run and running away, and in the last few years of Father's life, when he retired from the Post Office and got his cancer, she moved in with a Mr Holland, in Wellington Street East, just across Leicester Road, not ten minutes' walk away, she came home sometimes for money and Father always gave it her and though the whole neighbourhood knew and in the shops and the pubs very likely they laughed at him behind his back and they all knew in the Post Office as well, still he wouldn't hear a word against her, he knew what she had suffered and of course she ought to have stuck by him after all he'd been through in the War and coming home to his little one burning to death but he died never hardening his heart against her, I don't blame her, he said, she had a lot to bear and not just Edith. And so to the bitter end, for all their shouting and fighting, he took her side, even against himself. But before the Second War and before the boys left home we did still have some jolly times, we had what Father called 'musical evenings', Harry could play a bit, they'd paid for piano lessons for him and Father liked to think it was money well spent so he sat down when told to and gave us one or other of his tunes, not very lively, it must be said, he had to keep stopping and starting again, I can see him now leaning close and peering at the music, not like your dad, never any question of lessons for him but from somewhere he picked it up, he had the gift, I suppose, which Harry didn't and if he heard a thing on the wireless that took his fancy he'd sit down at the piano and pretty soon he had it off pat, rag-time especially, Mother loved that, couldn't keep still when he was playing rag-time, quite a sight she was, I used to catch Father looking at her much as to say... Himself, he had a fine voice once upon a time, two of his party-pieces were 'Just a Song at Twilight', which must have meant something to the pair of them in their courting days, and 'Rocked in the Cradle of the Deep', which he said his father

85

used to sing to the inmates at the Christmas concert in the Workhouse in Tadcaster, so while Bernard played Father would stand very close, resting an arm on the piano, and sing one or the other of them and if it was the 'Song at Twilight' he'd be looking across at Mother in a meaningful sort of way. But then one day in one of their rows he took an axe to our piano. Better it than you, he said. So that was that. Nice while it lasted. Time you were going, she said. They'll be worried. I'm alright for another half hour or so, he answered. I stopped on the motorway after the accident, told them I'd be home a bit late. Funny the two husbands called John William. I feel I've known the one blown to bits all of my life, he was there as a ghost with my gran at home and when I became 'interested in these things', decade after decade then, I got to know him ever more closely. But the other John William, the survivor, it's only latterly I've begun to know him better, though he was my father's father, only this last year and through you. I feel I haven't given him his due. And that may be because, as you've said, my father didn't either – *couldn't*, I'd say, things being the way they were. Maybe nobody can give everyone, not even their nearest, the attention they deserve, but still it's a loss and you feel it when you know it's too late, you'll never make it up. Same with the two grandmothers, one always there from the day I was born, close in the family, loved and respected, helping bring us up, and the other out somewhere on the margins, almost like a person banished. Gran Gleave, thin as a rake, was rectitude itself, soldiering on and bringing up her three children without a father, very hard in the years between the Wars, but when Mum and Dad married she moved in with them, Dad said she must, right from the start, though, as Mum said, not all men would, so she always belonged, she always had a house and home, she was busy, she was needed and, as I told you, she died at home with children, and, as it happened, grandchildren and a great-granddaughter, there in the house. And our Grandma Con, the stout one, your mother, when I think about it now, growing up it's as though we hardly knew Dad had a mother, she was living on her own somewhere, in a vague disrepute, she was fetched into our house for the occasions in the year, and treated kindly, year after year, and was taken back again to wherever it was she lived, always gently but with a certain note among the adults, a tone, the odd remark, a look, never unkind, but I picked it up, watching, eavesdropping, like hints of the world we were not supposed to know about, like the other Uncle Norman's drinking and carrying on, the embarrassed world of sorrows, illness, faults, failures, disgrace. It grieves me to think of her now. Dad visited her, of course, he cycled out there and once or twice he took me with him, it was a bicycle ride and I loved riding along inside him, I suppose it was to Whalley Range, quite a way, to Grosvenor Road, but I remember nothing of the place or what was done and said there when we visited. As soon as Father died, said Glad, she got herself a job in Lyons, in town, worked there for years, she loved it, all the company, she went with them after work to Yates Wine Lodge and drank port and lemon and plenty else no doubt. Don't grieve too much about Mother, she made her own bed, she lay on it and she didn't complain. I came across a photo of her not long ago, he answered, old lady in a hat and coat as though waiting to leave, waiting to be taken home, and a sadness on her face I haven't seen the like of in any other person among the countless family photographs, she looks absented in the sadness, remote in it, quite beyond knowing or caring what she'll look like in their photograph. Aged 70, it says on the back, perhaps it was her birthday. She died on the street, said our Glad, of a seizure, she was eighty then. I remember, he said. Came a knock on our door late one night, Dad opened, I was standing close behind him, it was a policeman, 'Mr Constantine?' he said, 'I'm sorry to tell you that your mother's died.' And now you'd better be going, said our Glad. It's dark, they'll be worrying at home. Come again, won't you? There's things still want talking about.

7

Come in, she said, I'm glad it's you. I thought it was you ten minutes since but it wasn't, it was a young woman with a little baby, she didn't say anything, only pointed at her baby and looked me in the eyes and held out her hand, Wait there, I said. I see the chain's not on, he said, stepping inside and wrapping her in his arms again, I hope the back door was locked, at least. Maybe it was, maybe it wasn't, she answered. Any road, nothing bad happened. My purse was still on the kitchen table. So you took her something from it? I did. She had no home to go to? None. When I gave her what I gave her she started crying. The baby's eyes were wide open and very blue. Anyway, now you've come. Push the trolley through, will you, while I brew up. I've found some more photos of our George.

Mid-afternoon, already beginning to get dark. Cosy in here, he said, setting down his plate. As I told you last time, I feel I've taken too little care of the grandfather and the grandmother on your side of the family. And Uncle George is another, I didn't pay him enough attention, I missed my chances, and when I bethought myself of him it was too late. He was away, said Glad, always away, as soon as he could, as long as he could, before the War, during the War, after the War, and came home on leave on visits, and for good only when he had to, when they made him, when they gave him a desk job at Luffenham, which he hated and pretty soon got ill, same cancer as Father's, and died, aged fifty-one, soon after your Mary-Ann was born. Yes, he said, we saw him now and then, he blew in from it might be Gibraltar, Egypt, Ceylon or Singapore, he knocked at our front door like a visiting angel, Dad hero-worshipped him, his kid-brother, and Mum I saw giving him the look that women can't help giving to glamour. He was the officer, the aviator, the DFC, the one who really had got away, and not just to the south of England selling carpets like Harry, but far away, flying. He had the aura, but was a modest, self-deprecating man, he held back in our company as though at heart unsure of himself, I never once heard him hold forth and yet on any occasion he might have done and welcome, with every encouragement and giving pleasure, surely for hours out of his hoard of adventures in a different world. Tall, balding, a squashed nose from boxing for the squadron, softly-spoken, with big hands and, as I remember him now, a wryness about him, a sort of shrug in his gesture (whether he actually shrugged or not), as much as to say, Well there we are, and what does it matter? And suddenly then, speaking of the airman, a strange and intense happiness possessed him, a memory came up in him, very present, he felt the heat of the home fire on his face, he was hot in the face from the coals and from the effort and the excitement of his imagining, drawing and crayoning, there on the hearth rug, air battles over a town or out at sea, gun-turrets, anti-aircraft guns, the barrage balloons, the fighters, the bombers, the bombs released and stepping neatly down, his crayons led from weapons to targets, a line of fire, a crippling, annihilating hit, planes fell in a shape of fire, headlong into explosion and extinction, a parachutist drifted like a seed towards a pyre, tall buildings burned and foundered inwardly or like trees being felled, an Austin K2 hit, an ambulance found its way through rubble and black smoke, a fireman stood out black, high up, against the infernal red, two searchlights caught a bomber and held it steady, as if in tweezers, for the retributing guns, a convoy shepherded the merchantmen towards safe harbour, one of their number raising its snout through an oily sea and the flames of it were doused. And close around me, he said, were Mum with my kid brother asleep in her lap while she knitted over him, Dad at the table doing marquetry, Gran reading the death notices in *The Manchester Evening News* and every now and then, in wonder and a sort of triumph, saying, Ee, d'you know who's died? The door was shut, the room was cosy, everything was close and safe. And he lay on his belly on the hearthrug and drew bombs and fire and tracer trails and made the noises in a constant soundtrack. Such happiness, the sea, the sky, the biggest cities in the world, all his violent joyous doing and undoing on the hearthrug in his home. Later, he said, I made air-fix models of the planes, so light, they hung from our bedroom ceiling and moved in the draughts. And do I remember or do I only imagine he stood there, that big man, in the cramped space between the bed, the nearside wall and the door, in our house for some particular occasion or just because he was back in Blighty for a week or two, and despite his height, the years, the colossal strangeness of him cooped in such familiar small confines, I asked him were they right, the Hurricane, the Spitfire and the Lancaster dangling on threads from the ceiling over the crocheted counterpane? To him the models would be at eye-level. I see him leaning over the bed. I can hear him saying, Looks right to me, old chap. The Lancaster anyway. Never was in the others. And he taps the bomber very gently, so that it rocks and swings. And did I dare ask him, Where were you, Uncle George? Here, he answers. And quaintly, with his crooked little finger, he strokes the underside of the aircraft's forward cell, the perspex blister, belly down there he lay on the transparent floor, thin membrane between him and black space and the flailing lights, the hot iron coming up, the smell of oil, the smell of singeing uniform and hair and roasting flesh, and fires below, such fires, night after night, over-rolling the crouched, the curled, the running, the stricken invisible citizens. Here's one of his wedding photos, said our Glad. She was a beauty and no mistake, too beautiful, that black hair, that look, she knows it, and he looks far too young. They got married in Cairo Cathedral. I don't believe she ever came visiting us, he said. Nor us, said Glad. He never brought her with him. Mother had to make do with the photograph. He turned it over and read, 'My son & my Dear Daughter George & Nellie abroad.' Abroad was Heliopolis. Here's one of himself that Mother specially liked. 'My Youngest Son George', it says on the back, and the date: 19.10.38, like a film star, that thirties face and hair, two years before he married. And another, in uniform, with his decorations, on his birthday, and she wrote: 'April 9th You are with me my Son Love Mum 1960.' Funny her little inscriptions, he said. Like on the photo of the twins. Can't be to remind herself who the pictures are of. Here's one of herself, said Glad. On the back she wrote, 'Just me 1938'. As though she were all alone. But Bernard was home still and so was Father and so was I. It's more as if she's telling the children and their children and their children, he said. This is what they looked like, the persons in my story, and this is what I looked like in the passing years. Nelly didn't last long, said Glad, and don't ask me whose fault that was, six of one and half a dozen of the other is the general rule. And the War. Living apart from her, going where his postings took him and where she could not or did not want to go, he kept an album of his wandering life. It came into our house with other things of his when he was dead. You see him at one function or another in white jacket and black tie, wearing his medals, smoking, raising a glass of champagne or a pint of beer, and one woman and another keeping him company or photographed by him, in a room alone and smiling. And here's a thing − a bit like your Norman checking his magazines – by the time I got a look at that album there were gaps among the pictures where those of women wearing too little or nothing at all had been removed by Mum and Dad, for the sake of George's reputation, as she said to me. Not very happy really, when you weigh up, said Glad. No, he said, the survivor, decorated when the bombings were over, wifeless, childless, wandering the world, I see the way he looked at us, his brother's sons, towards the end. The other day, Steve showed me a letter he wrote him on his 21st. It finished, Please have a beer with me and if you have time shed a tear. Six months later he was dead. And I'd forgotten till Steve showed me his that I'd had a birthday letter too, three years before, similar in tone – regretful, wistful – and with it a volume of English Romantic poetry just right to carry in your pocket. So I think of that now and feel I did not pay him enough attention in the time allowed. Lucky he found Pat, said Glad. Lucky for him to be loved by her and cherished and cared for at the end. She saw him through. And Nelly set sail from God knows where to come and contest the will.

He wheeled the trolley back into the kitchen. She stood in the hall while he put his coat on. There's a thing I never told you about Aunty Alice, he said. I haven't liked to. I was sad when Mum told it me thirty years ago and it saddens me again now but still makes no real difference, it's only another part of the whole trouble. Well, go on then, she said, looking not curious but uneasy. Perhaps I know it already. It was a couple of years after Uncle Norman died, he said, when Dad got the job in Colwyn Bay and they decided to move from Salford so he wouldn't have to travel and they were looking for houses and found the one in Deganwy, on Cefn-y-Bryn, which, funnily enough, was the name of the house in South Wales Norman had grown up in. They asked Aunty would she have Gran to live with her while they sold up and moved and settled in the new place, so that she wouldn't be too mithered by it all. It was the first time they'd ever asked her any such favour, and Aunty, on her own in her house big enough for a family, said yes. They moved, Gran's room with them was ready, but meanwhile she had taken ill, the doctor said she was too poorly to be brought even the little way from one side of the Vardre to the other. All told, she stayed with Aunty Alice for six months. In that time she had a couple of falls. Then Doctor Bell said she was fit to move. Dad lifted her into the car and drove her home. She was still in a poor state, her face was bruised from her falls, she seemed to be wandering in and out of her right mind. She suddenly asked, Is that woman still here? Nobody knew what she meant. Then she said, She told me she'd have me put away. She said she'd get Doctor Bell to put me away. So it became clear that the woman she meant was her daughter, Alice. She said, I thought I was going funny. I just kept quiet and didn't say anything and did as I was told. I thought I was losing my mind. Apart from those anxious complaints about 'that woman', Gran never said anything whatsoever about her stay in Aunty's house. She remembered visiting the first house, where Uncle Norman died, but nothing at all about the second where she had spent six months, not the rooms, nor Aunty in them, nor the neighbours. In fact she seemed not to associate 'that woman' with Aunty Alice at all since one day when Aunty and Mum were with her together she said again, Does that woman still live here? So Alice, widowed, living alone, failed her own mother, and it was with Mum and Dad, rightly and properly, that she died. No, I didn't know that, said Glad. He pulled a face and wondered, Why tell these things?

He stood on the doorstep looking down the little terrace towards where he had parked the car. It was dark and raining slightly. Funny that girl and her baby, she said. Put the chain on now, he said, and make sure the back door's locked. See you as soon as possible, but it won't be till be after Christmas. I left your presents on the kitchen table. You OK? Go in now, don't catch cold. There's a thing I nearly told you last time, she said. Father told it me just before he died so I would think about Mother with more charity. They had to get married, she was pregnant, she had a little girl, they called her Winifred, but she had meningitis and only lived two weeks. So that's how they set forth on their married life. Off you go now, come safely home, give them all my love. She reached up for his face, he bowed, she kissed him.

8

They were all old on that ward. He halted at the door, not wanting to go from bed to bed. Some were lying flat or curled, sleeping or sunk too deep into themselves; but others were sitting upright perkily, watching the door, keen not to miss anything. He was the only visitor, visiting time had passed but out of kindness they let him in. Still he couldn't see Gladys. Then a nurse said, Mrs Gregory? Far end on the left. If she's sleeping it's OK to wake her up.

He stood by her bed and almost at once she opened her eyes. Good, she said. I've been hoping you'd come. I'm weary. And murmured to herself, Weary, weary, weary, weary, weary. No, no, he said. Not you. All right then, she answered. Sit me up. Tell me a story. Cheer me up. Coming from seeing Mum, he said... How is she? Glad interrupted. Pretty well, thank you. We had a happy time. I wheeled her along to see the ponies again. I took her gloves off and she stroked them, they nuzzled her and made funny chunnering noises, as though they remembered her, as though she were a pal of theirs, quite big animals with sticky manes, so gentle, three or four of them around her wheelchair, and when she lifted up her hand to stroke them it was as though she were blessing them and she was quite without any fear. Anyway, coming over here after seeing her, I was thinking about the dance. Shall I tell you that story? If you like, she said. Well then, Are you sitting comfortably? No, I'm not, she answered. Years since I did and it's not going to happen in this place. We were at Mary-Ann's, he said, it was the time Mum had her fall and we had to take her to casualty and next morning she didn't know whose face it was in the mirror and when we said, It's you, she said, Well how did I get like that? It was then, but before the accident, we were still sitting at the kitchen table after breakfast, the sun came over the hill and lit up the daffodils in their blue glass vase, the talk was going cheerfully to and fro, but she never spoke, only sat there silently as usual, her eyes following the speaker whoever it was, and though we looked her way from time to time and smiled and nobody was ignoring her, only letting her bide as usual in her silence and her absence, she never spoke and nobody had bidden her, when in a pause, whose sign for me for ever will be the lighted daffodils on the sill behind her in their blue glass vase, suddenly with not a hint of sadness in a brightening way she said, Have I ever told you how I met him? Yes, she had told us, it was one of the lasting stories, one, the most precious, I suppose, that she took with her into the shadowlands and could remember it and could still tell it. Her friend Joan – the one who got married and went to live in Crumpsall – had said, Why don't you come to the dance? She answered, I've nobody to go with. Please yourself, said Joan. I might, she said. It was in a church hall on the other side of town. How far they went in those days, on the bus, the train, the tram, and miles on foot, mostly alone on foot, making her own way across town, fearless on the loud streets. She was just eighteen, it would soon be spring. She found the church all right and a hall by it and in the hall the dance was in full swing. But coming off the street, where it was already dark, and standing in the door, all she could see in the dusty light and the smoke were people she didn't know who were busy enjoying themselves. The walk had lifted her up, and the music and the cheerful din made her want to carry on being lifted up, but she had come on her own and when she looked in among the dancers there was nobody she knew. So having unbuttoned her jacket she had half done it up again, thinking she must be wrong, when he stood in front of her and said, Excuse me, are you looking for somebody? Yes, she said, as a matter of fact I am. And she said Joan's name, and added, But I think I must have come to the wrong place. No, no, he said, this is the right place. There she is over there. And he pointed her out, in the crowd, dancing. Oh, she said. She looked that way, where Joan was dancing, and not at the young man who had turned her way again, waiting. Later she wondered had he not been dancing himself, had he been standing there at the side of everything, only watching the door to see who might come in. And later he told her it was more or less like that, him watching and waiting, except of course he hadn't known it was her he was waiting for. But when he saw her come in out of the dark and stand there in the doorway not sure of herself, then he did know it was her. And when he saw her begin doing up the buttons of her jacket it struck him like a rush of cold in the heart that he had to come over quickly and speak to her or his life would miss its one and only chance. It was cold outside and a bit foggy as usual and the fog was in her black hair where it curled from under her hat and the cold was on her cheeks, still there on her face like a scent but vanishing in the warmth and dust and smoke of the dancing hall, but still there like a scent or aura around her face and hair when he came up and politely asked her was she looking for someone. Then he said, Will you dance with me? And he added, While you're waiting. Yes, she said, I will. Now she looked at him properly. She had a quick appraising look, for her own appearance and for anybody else's. His suit. He blushed like a girl. It was our Harry's, he said. And by the time he got another it wasn't much good for me. Are you the last? she asked. No, I'm not, he answered. There's our George still. But he'll not want my cast-offs. His silence then was hopeless. They looked out for Joan. Shall I tell her you're here? he asked. For answer she undid her jacket again, and gave it to him to go and hang up. That evening neither danced with anyone else. After an hour or so he asked her was she particular about staying any longer. No, she said. Are you? No, he answered. Can I walk you back? Yes, she said. But it's a long way. The longer the better, he thought.

That's a good story, said Glad. Bernard was a lucky man, luckiest of all of us, even though he lost his twin and was ill the way he was. Soon after she told it us, he said, after her accident, before her face was clear of its cuts and bruises, I took a train to Manchester Piccadilly and did the walk he used to do back up to Heaton Street after he'd seen her home but it took me longer than it would ever have taken him because most of the streets round there have gone, the very names of them, the houses, the public buildings, the local landmarks, gone, so I walked very slowly, halting very often, studying the old *A to Z*, puzzling it out, trying to put it all back together again. You and your walks, said Glad. Yes, he said. I get things by heart through my feet. So he left her on the corner of Liverpool Street and Healey Street, under the lamp there, with the gasometers behind her. That smell, she said, Mother says it's good for you, she says we live to be a hundred round here because of it. He kisses her goodnight and walks away quickly, past the Mission Hall, flowers in pots under the Roll of Honour there, her father, the other John William, in the first column, ninth name down, scents of the flowers, dahlias or asters from the allotments, no other flowers anywhere else the length of Liverpool Street, but smells of the pubs, The Live and Let Live, The Union, The Drover's Arms, and cow shit, sheep shit, the poor beasts, the stink of the fear of animals going to the slaughterhouse. Oldfield Road, turn left there, past Cow Lane, slaughterhouse on your right, the smell of blood, then the railway bridge, a whiff of coal and the hot smell of steam, the taste of soot, then it's Albert Mill and the big junction with Chapel Street, din of the traffic, the buses, the trams, the private motor cars, the horses and carts and Salford Royal Hospital opposite, while you wait to cross, so many windows in it, bigger than a factory or a mill, hundreds of people in there lying still and thinking. The hospital's half way, maybe not exactly half way on the map but passing the hospital he has crossed from where she lives and is entering where he lives, where you lived, along Adelphi Street he goes, the river on his left, sewer more like, it goes over a weir just there and the suds fly up like dirty snow, stench of the river where it falls over the weir and all the poisons in it are all churned up and next it's Broughton Bridge, which the river passes under very slowly, so slowly sometimes it seems almost to have stopped, as though it has too much to bear and it's losing heart and giving up the ghost. Then he's climbing the long hill home, Great Clowes Street, Cheetham Street East, to Heaton Street, fearful, what will it be like at home, will Mother and Father be back and what state will they be in? What an ending, she said. True enough, I suppose. But now I'm weary again. Lay me down, will you. He laid her down, ashamed of himself and his so-called truth. She closed her eyes. He sat there, silently begging her forgiveness, desperate not to leave, I could tell you a better story, he whispered, about Mum and Aunty Alice, when I walked round Crafnant Lake with them and they never stopped yapping and I had to carry their handbags, which weighed a ton, and help them over the stiles and it was getting dark. I kept saying, Shall we turn back now? But no, they would not, so on we went till it was as far going back as going on, I got more and more worried, I feared they'd break a leg, every stile took five minutes, the bags got heavier and heavier, and even while we were doing it they were telling the tale of the Circumambulation of Crafnant Lake, to tell Mrs H. and Mrs W. and Mrs Whoever-else and already imagining the amazement of these women and their disbelief, on and on making the story up as it was getting dark. I could tell you that story, he whispered, but with all the details – and the good of it, their sisterly love and the fun, the wit, the recklessness, the life-here-and-now, the life of this minute in this place in these persons now, the great good of it – is all in the details, it would take half an hour. Shall I? Glad opened her eyes, smiling. Next time, she said. But it does sound like something that might cheer a body up. Listen now, she said. Here's a walk for you. Get this one by heart. There are sad things in it but we didn't let them get us down. Our George tried his best to be home for Father's funeral, but in the end he missed it by a week or so. He sent a telegram, I went to meet him at London Road, it was not long after the Election – the posters were still up – but before we got the result, he'd come from near Bury St Edmund's where his squadron was, he'd been travelling half the night, thousands of demobbed men were getting off the trains, the women there meeting them, the men hurrying down the platforms to join in the mixing of the men and the women this side the barrier. Days and nights it was like that, so the papers said. I feared I should never spot our George, but I did, soon as he stepped from the carriage, and in the same second, for all the crowd of people there between us, he saw me. I don't know that I've ever had a happier moment. Her face through the many wrinkles shone with it, her eyes were bright with it. Leaning down, the relief of her goodwill around his heart, he said, I feel I can see him myself, and you waiting and the moment

when you see him and he sees you. He was in uniform, cap
and all, and as soon as he had hugged me I took him by the
arm and marched him away through the multitude, very
proud, she said. Mother was at home, waiting, but I'd told her
not to worry, no telling when the train might arrive, expect
us when you see us, I wanted him for myself, such a long time
we hadn't had a walk together and a natter. I was going to say,
Shall we walk? but he said it first, he needed a walk, he'd been
cooped up for hours in a smoky compartment, so, Let's walk,
he said, my bag's not heavy. It was sunny outside, mid-
morning, a Saturday, Piccadilly Gardens were still boarded off
but you could go in and through, they were in bloom, and
benches close up together on all four sides and every bench
full, four or five people on every single bench, eating ice
cream, feeding the pigeons, nattering, reading the newspapers,
and many doing nothing, as I remember, yes, I'm remembering
here and now that many in those gardens were sitting quiet
with their eyes shut and their faces lifted to the sun. We were
passing through but we stopped and looked round a bit. It was
like being in the Paradise Garden, she said, and the sounds of
people talking and some children running around shouting,
they were like birds, it was as though you could understand
the language of birds, and there were the same old dirty
pigeons around your feet and flying up like an explosion if
something startled them. The other side the hoarding, *outside*,
as you might say, was the din of traffic, the tram bells especially,
at a distance, so it seemed, and not very loud. Behind the bus
station, between Parker Street and Charlotte Street, all the
buildings got hit in the Christmas Blitz and went up in flames
and the rubble of it was still there visible in a big long bank
behind the boards. I don't remember exactly what the flowers
in the Gardens were, only that they were very bright, there
was a lot of red, perhaps they were tulips and salvias, anyway
the beds behind the people on the benches were bright and

beautiful and we stood there for a few minutes, George and me, looking around us and not saying anything. Her voice was low, he bent close to be able to hear, there were silences, she had her eyes wide open and seemed to be looking for what she would remember next, what she would see, and hear the words for, as she paused. He also waited and listened and her voice resumed its story, low, very rapid, like a stream outside the city coming down in sunlight after a night of rain, very quick and full of itself, of the tidings it carried, through the bluebells in Ringley Woods, or over the gritstone below Kinder, or down Cressbrook Dale in winter over the limestone, quick, clear, very fast. He was just twenty-eight, she said, and he had seen dreadful things, some very close, some far far below. I saw his eyes resting on the mounds of rubble, for a minute he looked twice his age, like an old man, like Father dying in my arms, so I pulled him away and we went out of the garden and into Market Street where it was nearly as crowded as on the station. Corner of Cross Street, ruins of the Royal Exchange; Corporation Street, ruins down to the river; the Cathedral, ruins of the Memorial Chapel; Long Millgate, the old Grammar School, the stations, ruins, ruins, ruins... I saw them, she said, and others too, every day, I'd seen them every working day since the day after it was done, and I almost didn't see them, I was so used to them, that's what Town was like, that's what Salford was like, ruins we were used to, but George hadn't been back for a year, he had new eyes to see and also his head was full of sights and full of knowledge that he had, that the men had, like the knowledge Father had carried with him for thirty years, and that I didn't have, but only guessed at, picked up bits of from the radio and the newspapers and overhearing other people's talk. And worse was coming, I know that now, oh even worse was coming that we should have to know and not be able to forget, but that day in the Gardens and on the busy streets, walking home to

Mother, though we saw what we saw, the damage, and couldn't help seeing it, still I had tight hold of our George, he was home, he'd go away again, but his war was over, he wouldn't get killed or wounded or taken prisoner, he'd come back home, I was happy. On Cheetham Hill Road, she said, he asked after Mother. As if he'd better get himself ready for the family again. I told him about Mr Holland and her not being there at the end. He shook his head and was quiet. Then he said he'd heard from Nelly and she was definitely gone for good. No matter, he said. I told him I'd be marrying Norman Gregory next month and that Bernard and Harry were still away but would be coming back all right. Alice's Norman too. And he asked specially after your Mum and you. Got to get genned up, old girl, he said. A lot to take in. Don't know how well I'll cope with the ordinary good and bad. To tell you the truth, I still can't quite imagine expecting to see tomorrow's sunrise. It was then I told him about Winifred. Father said I should tell you, I said. So I have. Her voice went low again, almost down to a whisper, a hurrying whisper, her eyes wide open, so bright, and always the ghost of a smile coming and going over her face, so that he felt her to be, at heart, joyful. Sing me 'Cockles and Mussels', I said to him, like you were always singing it when you arrived home on your bike from Marwood & Robertson before you decided you weren't cut out for the quiet life and took to the skies. And there half way up Cheetham Hill Road he halted, put down his bag, pushed back his cap at a slant and sang the whole song all through very sorrowfully but with a pause after every verse for a jolly little tap-dance, like Fred Astaire but heavier, more like a bear, clicking his fingers and looking down at his feet, and then he'd halt again and raise his eyes to heaven and sing the next verse, very mournful, and people going by stopped to watch and listen, they clapped, they shouted, they were glad for him and for me there with him and – this made me smile and brought tears to my eyes – as he sang, his Salford voice came up in him, through his RAF posh voice, up it came, pure as it had been in Leicester Road Primary, and he sang and capered on the pavement and made everyone passing in the sunshine laugh and clap because they believed him, the airman in his uniform, to be safe and sound and back home and the war was over and done with, we'd clear away the ruins and something fit to be looked at would begin. Elizabeth Street, she said, almost in a whisper, in a hurry, are you listening, are you taking all this in? Yes, I am, he said, you've reached Elizabeth Street, where they took your Edith, Dad's twin, it got hit in 1941, but not very badly. I said nothing when we passed that bit of damage, she said, but I saw him looking, I saw him shake his head, Come and see the park, I said, were they aiming at the hospital, knowing it was Jewish, and they hit the park? Doubtful, he said. They hit Hope Hospital, they hit Salford Royal, I said, they hit the dead in Weaste Cemetery. Bombing is not a very exact business, he said. You're telling me, I said. Enough landed on Cheetham Park to demolish Buckingham Palace. I know, he said. Nothing much to burn in there, I said, but what could burn, did. Incendiaries, he said. They always find something to set fire to and even if they don't, they happily burn themselves. But that's not what I wanted to show you, she said. You've seen all that. Come and see this. Her eyes were bright with it, she held his gaze in hers, he was bending close, hearkening to her whisper, I tugged him by his sleeve, she said, round the corner to the ruins of the park, it was boarded up like Piccadilly but with DANGER KEEP OUT in big letters all over it, but I had found a place, she said, in a corner where the kids got in, and I took him through that gap, the bomb-aimer, my little brother, easy for me but a bit of a squeeze for him, and look at that, I said, what do you think of that? The place was in flower! Since there had been no big buildings there wasn't much rubble, it was mostly earth, the flowerbeds, the bowling greens, mounds of it and craters with bits of iron and woodwork sticking up that had perhaps been the bandstand or the swings and roundabouts or the ice-cream kiosk and some carved stone from the fountain and bits of a nymph and a dolphin and heads, arms and legs of the statues of local philanthropists and Queen Victoria, but in all that, over all that, were the weeds, the dock, the dandelion and the couch grass, the nettles and thistles, buttercups, daisies and forget-me-nots and even some lengths of the limbs of trees that had survived or taken root again and were risen again in leaf and blossom, but best of all, she said, in a voice that was rapid and continuous, like a susurration through foliage or grasses, the crowning glory of that place, she said, thriving like nothing else, was the willow herb, the pink-red, purple-red rosebay willow herb, climbing all the mounds, going down into all the craters and up out again, up the slopes, and overflowing. And close to where we had crept in, she said, I guess near where the main entrance had once been, quite undamaged, stood one solitary wrought-iron seat with fancy legs in the shape of snakes curving up for the arm-rests, and there we sat ourselves down, George and me, with the length and breadth of the ruined and flowering park, the victorious willow herb, before our eyes. They say it comes in with the bombs, I said to him. The bombsites have flowered every summer. But more likely it's there in the ground all along, under the lawns and the concrete, under the trams and the offices, the avenues and the cobbled alleys and the little backyards, and the terrible upheaval, and especially the fire, gives it its chance to be the glory of the place. We sat nearly an hour in the sunshine on that fancy-iron seat and he looked away at the triumph of the weeds and in a soft voice as though talking to himself he told me about the fires in the German cities, night after night the terrible revenging fires, the firestorms in Hamburg and Dresden, the Russians advancing through the rubble of Berlin, and his chums night after night burned to death in their planes, going down in flames into flames, the smell of it, the sight and the din of it, the no-end of thinking about it, on and on, night after night, with time off now and then to be thinking about it and preparing yourself for the next time. And then quite suddenly he stopped and patted my arm and said, Trust our Glad to find a place like this and thank you kindly for bringing me to see it with my own eyes. And now we'll go home, he said, to Mother who has been waiting. And tomorrow we'll take her out for Sunday dinner in Heaton Park. Not too much damage there, so I believe. I met a lad on the train, barely twenty, I'd say, he'd been with 106 Squadron over the Normandy landings, a Jewish lad, a socialist, from Langley Road, he knew the Flight Engineer in that Lancaster that crashed into the Irwell by Regatta Street, not far from Reading Street, this time last year. He had seen bad things but I felt like an old man in his company, so determined was he to be cheerful. Now we get the country we deserve, he said, one fit to live in, one we'll be proud of, now. And he told me that as a child he'd gone most Sundays to Heaton Park and loved the place and as a young man, an airman, had always asked in his letters home was it spared or not and always went there when he got leave. And he assured me it's more or less business as usual in the old places now. So I thought after our Sunday roast we'd take Mother out on the lake, and row around for an hour. I think she will look quite the lady in her widow's weeds.

Then all the strength went out of her. Time you were gone, she said. Get home safe. They'll be worrying. Give them my love. We'll do that walk together when I get this sorted. You can treat me to Sunday dinner and row me around on the lake.

9

She died of TB, he said. Funny thing, that. I asked our doctor. He thought she must have had it when she was young, perhaps very young, down by the river, I'd say, in the damp, and got over it but it lives on in the body and takes its chance again right at the end. Apparently there's quite a competition of the maladies at the very end. She told me more than once her father was chesty. But he died of two cancers and heart failure. His firstborn's meningitis may have been the tubercular kind but more likely it was the group B streptococcus, which passes from the mother to the baby in the womb or the birth canal, working quickly. Yes, streptococcus, he said, after its fashion, mechanically, desires to live and not just to live, but to thrive and triumph. Rapidly redoubling its forces, every half-hour or so becoming twice its number, it soon overwhelms the defences that can be mustered against it by the new-born human child who also, dimly, inchoately, wishes to live and has her mother and father on her side who wish it heart and soul and with all their might. She, their child, has a birth certificate on which is the name they chose for her and that the priest baptised her with and which very soon will be entered on her certificate of death. Humans can't do without particular names. Adam and Eve in the Paradise Garden gave names to all things animal, vegetable and mineral they could see and dream and even halfways grasp. Later the scientists gave names to organisms, particles, moons and stars they could see with microscopes or telescopes and even to some they could not see but knew or supposed were there. But streptococcus, though it lives and reproduces, is not a living creature as Gertrude Adelaide Constantine née Patterson and Winifred her daughter were. In fact, he said, I'm not sure I should refer to it as 'it'. The life of bacteria and bacilli is that of the colony and species and in their way, self-replicating, self-cloning, their population ever more vastly doubling, they kill our named and unique loved ones. Winifred, born in their first home, 13 Littleton Road, 25 October, was baptized at St George's, 5 November, and died at home on the 8th. It's about a mile from home to that church. Was she already ailing and they wanted her made a Christian before she died? Or did the bacteria kill her in three days and nights after the ceremony at the font? No one knows now, no one can find out. And what is such suffering like in a human being so young, so small? Is it even imaginable? We can imagine distress in the womb, and the memory, or you might say the trauma, of the expulsion into separate life is a recurrent nightmare many have and never grow out of. And the symptoms of neonatal meningitis – the bulging of the fontanelle, the pin-prick rash, the blotches, bruising, cold hands and feet, fast breathing, strange grunting noises – these are, so to speak, the utterance of it. But the bewilderment within, he said, the barely dawning consciousness all at a loss as to what is happening, I doubt if there are words ordered in sentences for that. A healthy baby at two weeks knows pleasure from pain, knows want from relief, and even with eyes that can barely focus she knows and homes onto her mother's nearing face. She is beginning to make things fit. But born in the sickness, the bacteria at once overrunning the housing of her brain, how should she form the haziest least notion of what is afflicting her? I remember the right hand of our baby son reaching in curiosity for the left, as for a separate thing, a separate life. It was a lovely puzzlement to watch, nothing anxious in it, the right hand curious about the left and feeling for it and grasping it as a friend. He was beginning to comprehend the frontiers of himself, figuring out how what was him existed in the midst of what was not him. But surely in her, so small, so ill, the beginnings of such a distinction must have been annulled. All was inside; the eye, the brain, gave her no view onto anything distinct from her; and thoughts-becoming-language, thoughts becoming *thoughts-about*, this nascent faculty was stopped. Scarcely born, scarcely delivered out of the oneness inside her mother, she passes swiftly into a state which is, by us, unimaginable. And what appals me now, he said, is the thought that in that state, unspeakably, unimaginably alone, she was beyond consoling. The suffering in the parents is an easier thing to grasp but it sometimes seems to me, considering them and what would happen to a second daughter ten years later, that they themselves were not consolable by one another.

That day, he said – I had come on the train, and on the 373 bus from the station and walked from the nearest stop – when I arrived there was an ambulance outside her little house and they were just loading her in. She was joking with the medics, Be careful, I'm worth my weight in gold. She looked so small. We can hardly lift you, Mrs Gregory, they answered back. More than one a day like you we'd need a fortnight off. And seeing me hurrying up, and, when I leaned down to kiss her, seeing what it did to me to see her being carried away like that, she grasped my sleeve and smiled and said, Pity you've come all this way for nothing, I'd got everything ready, it's all on the trolley, ask Mrs Roberts to parcel some up for you, for the way back. And don't look so worried, she said, I'll get this fixed and we'll carry on where we left off.

I can't stop thinking about that dumb woman with a pass, he said. Gladys said she wasn't surprised she haunted me. For me she's *the* woman or *that* woman but in the book she's 'a dumb Woman with a Pass' to whom Constable Thomas Tennant paid sixpence on 17 January 1809. No name, but alone and unable to speak, she must have been very distinctive. The pass doesn't say from where and to where she was walking, but it certainly wasn't from nowhere to nowhere. On that road I could list the named places she must have passed through going west to east or east to west. In that book those without names far outnumber the named. On its pages a dumb woman is in the company of a sailor, a soldier, a vagabond, a woman with five children, a poor man, a woman in distress. The unspoken premise in all my chats with Gladys, he said, was always that every single human life is inexhaustibly, unfathomably, rich. The lives of the one hundred and forty-eight named inmates of Tadcaster Union on the night of 3-4 April 1881 in their connections, in their particulars, before and after the hour of their being counted for a census, are a galaxy in motion through an expanding universe. I doubt if the dumb woman could read or write very much. But I feel sure that for her survival she listened and watched very attentively. And who knows what her unuttered thinking, feeling, dreaming, remembering amounted to? No one. But for however long she lived those energies were working in her. To be honest, he said, I don't think Gladys specially valued the things I dug up on the internet and nor, listening to her, did I. I felt sometimes that typing in, say, 'workhouse' and getting 'about' 4,820,000 results in 0.61 seconds, was at best like poking a stick into an anthill. In some moods, I must admit, I felt it to be more like the heave and hyperactivity of decomposition than the makings of knowledge. I can say 'a dumb woman' and I can begin to imagine her, the singularity, holy individuality, of her, infinitely rich, though she came to me speechless and nameless with an indefinite article, she was herself a plural, inventive, endlessly surprising, pitiable, admirable, lovable abundant human life. The abundance of the bacteria that killed my grandmother's first child, their pullulant self-cloning, is quite another matter.

In her late eighties, Glad took our daughter shopping for knickers in Marks & Spencer's. Having tea with us afterwards in the Midland Hotel she opened the bags and in raucous delight held up their purchases for us (and everyone else) to admire. We sat in the car in the concrete multi-storey carpark with a view over Piccadilly Gardens and the people there among the flowers and fountains in the sun. Good as the Hippodrome, she said. Best seats in the house. Nearly ninety-one, he said, when I was round there once and we'd been talking about her Saturday nights on the Monkey Run, while I was siding the tea-things away, she looked at herself in the mirror and wondered did she need a bigger bra. 'Funny how they grow again,' she said. In hospital, dying, less than a year later, she murmured she was weary, weary. But sat up and listened and told me another story. I'll remember her in her talk, so alive, girlish and droll, conjuring up the dead with all their joys and griefs. She had the word that lives and gives life. 'Our Glad,' my father called her, his big sister. She was glad in the sense of cheerful and delighted, and in the old sense too, the sense the dictionary calls obsolete: bright, shining, beautiful, which is a sense that was living on, only dormant, among the common modern usages, only waiting for a life to call it up and embody it again: the bright shining of life through her mask of wrinkles, the fun, the joy and the courage of it.

Come on in, our Glad, he said. Start talking.

The Rivers of the
Unspoilt World

1

ANOTHER MIDSUMMER. HE WOKE in its small centre of
darkness, his face wet with tears. He lay very still, frightened
but attending. High in the town a public clock struck the
quarter but only faintly, as though considerately, and of what
hour he did not know or care. He felt his state to be unusual.
Most often if he woke in the night, and in summer always, he
could not lie there, his nervousness would not let him, he
must rise and pull a jacket over his nightshirt and leave his
room and go down the spiral stairs and begin pacing to and
fro in the garden by the river. There, disturbing no one,
permitted, he walked himself into a bearable state and some
nights could climb the stairs again and resume his sleep. But
this midsummer waking was different. After only a little
while expecting a worsening, the worst, he felt easier around
the heart. He closed his eyes, crossed his arms on his chest,
and waited. Quite soon he heard her voice. It – she – was
speaking a poem he knew every line of but never allowed
himself to utter even in silence, in his head, to himself. She
was saying:

Severed and at a distance now and in
  The past if I were able still to show you
    Something good and you with a sorrow
      Equalling mine should you still know my face

Then say how might she expect to find you now,
  Your friend: in the gardens where we met again
    After the terror and the dark or
      Here by the rivers of the unspoilt world?

Strange the feel of tears when you are lying as still as an effigy. The welling up, the flowing over, their wetting your cheeks, all gently. Lying still, face upwards, you seem a part of the earth and your weeping one of her infinite springs. What moved him especially on this occasion was a belief that she was not reciting something she had learned by heart. She was speaking in her own voice. And although he could hear the count and measure and pace of every syllable line by line, and knew the going over, the minute pause, the turning back below to begin the movement towards the next such ending and over-toppling, and though he heard two stanzas and felt as a small heart-shock the leap of faith through the gap between, the trapeze-girl letting go, flying through the air and reaching for a hold again, though he heard and knew and commended and rejoiced in all of that, the upwelling of his tears had another cause. He heard, more persuasively than ever in his life before, poetry being spoken as the first and native tongue of humankind. The lines with their strict count were spoken as natural. This is the tongue and tone of original speech, he thought, uncorrupted, it wells up out of her, it is her mother tongue, I hear it and I understand it.

Then came a shift, a disembodiment, that in the course of his madness he had experienced several times. It had interested his doctors at the start and encouraged them to try their science on him; but to himself, though always a shock, it was welcome. Eyes closed, lying still, he saw himself sitting at ease with her on a couch, his right arm, her left, resting along the back of it, in a sunlit room. She paused in her speaking the verses and looked at him, smiling. He smiled too. I wrote that, he said. She was wearing the light blue dress he had seen her in last and a necklace of small precious stones of a darker blue, his gift, which she only wore when she was alone with him and certain that nobody would intrude. She smiled again, and said, Well, in a way you did. And holding his gaze in hers, with not the least adoption of another voice, she continued the poem:

> I will say this: there was some good in your eyes
>   When in the distances you looked about you
>   Cheerfully for once who were a man
>   Always closed in his looks and with a dark
>
> Aspect. The hours flowed away. How quiet
>   I was at heart thinking of the truth which is
>   How separate I would have been, but
>   Yes I was yours then and I told you so
>
> Without a doubt and now you will bring and write
>   All the familiar things back into mind
>   With letters and it happens to me
>   The same and I will say all of the past.

Lying still and attending closely to this scene that was proceeding in a time and a place of its own, in wondering agreement he heard himself say, In a way I wrote those lines? Yes, she said, You heard me saying them and you wrote them down. Say what comes next, my love. I want to hear my voice as it sounds in yours. She took his hand.

So the poem continued between them, as dialogue

coming to them impromptu for their situation, in their time
and place. He said:

> Was it spring or summer? The nightingale's
>   Sweet singing lived with the other birds that were
>   Not far away among the bushes
>   And trees were surrounding us with their scents.

He paused. She continued:

> On clear pathways, walking among low shrubs
>   On sand, we thought more beautiful than anywhere
>   And more delightful the hyacinths
>   The tulips, violets and carnations.

> Ivy on the walls, and a lovely green
>   Darkness under the high walks. In the mornings
>   And the evenings we were there and
>   Talked, and looked at one another, smiling.

> In my arms the boy revived who had been still
>   Deserted then and came out of the fields
>   And showed me them, with sadness, but the
>   Names of those rare places he never lost

Without a pause he continued:

> And everything beautiful that flowers there
>   On blessed seaboards in the homeland that I
>   Love equally, or hidden away
>   And only to be seen from high above

And she, watching his lips, saw when to resume:

And where the sea itself can be looked upon
  But nobody will. Let be. And think of her
    Who has some happiness still because
      Once we were standing in the light of days

Beginning with loving declarations or
  Our taking hands, to hold us. Such pity now.
    That was our beautiful daytime but
      Sorrowful twilight followed after it.

That's as far as we got, she said. It just breaks off. I couldn't
think what else to say. – I couldn't think what else to write,
he answered. It's not finished. It just breaks off. Quite a few of
them were like that, as I remember. I couldn't bring myself to
go on. There's one at the very beginning when I had to break
off for the joy of it. This, she said, oh this:

Come and look at the happiness: trees in the cooling
                            breezes
    Are tossing their branches
Like dancers' hair and with sunshine and rain the sky
    Is playing on the earth
As though joy had hands and were raising a music...

That one? – Yes that one. I couldn't finish it. I heard a bit more
but I didn't want to finish it. I left the line of it hanging in the
air. But mostly when I didn't finish them it was because of the
sorrow, I knew I wouldn't be able to bear the sorrow. I learned
that very early on. The better I say it, the less I can bear it. Yes,
she said

Your beloved face has gone beyond my sight,
  The music of your life is dying away
    Beyond my hearing...

That one, for example? Yes, he answered her, that one. And several more.

In the silence then he heard her piano and his flute accompanying it. Hark at that, he said. We did that. It was ours. It can't be erased. They listened. Tell me, he said, you're the only one I can ask, you're the only one who'll give me a straight answer: Are you mad and I'm dead or is it the other way round? It's the other way round, my love, she answered. — I feared so. I'd very much prefer it was the *other* way round. — In truth I can't be quite certain, she said. In truth, my dearest, it doesn't greatly matter. Mine and thine, we never could tell them apart, nor ever wanted to. Last week, he said, this year or last or ten or fifteen years ago, they are much the same, I was mortally restless, the nights were getting shorter, there was nowhere near enough darkness, I couldn't sleep, I was mortally troubled, I went down in my nightshirt into the garden and walked to and fro, to and fro. And by the means of that walking I suddenly saw what would give me peace of mind. So clearly I saw it, as clear as the daystar on the pale green sky. So simple a thing, requiring only faith and a good pair of legs. Obvious really. Journeys end in lovers meeting, do they not? If they are lucky, they do, she answered, letting go his hand. If the lovers are lucky and the people they meet along the way are kind and if the roads conspire in their favour and if each has a good angel who will not tolerate the cruel injustice of their being kept apart. Given all those things, then, yes, my love, journeys do surely end in lovers meeting. He felt cold, he became aware that his hands, which had been resting open and quietly on his breast, now were clenched. Her presence was fainter, in a failing voice he said, I assumed all those conditions. I had assurances from the angel that the time was propitious, the soldiers had gone home, the constellations were just as they should be for such an enterprise, the nights were very short, the days either side of them were very long. – Yes, she said. In the lengthening days, in the shortening nights, I sickened. The shortest was my last. The next day never ended. – And I was walking towards you out of France in the heat of midsummer, I was making my way towards you as fast as any man could on foot, sleeping very little, walking long hours under the sun as fast as I could but not fast enough, for when I got there you had already left. – Yes, I knew you were coming. It was the last harboured secret in my married life. He is coming, he will bid me farewell. It was the last disappointment in the lifetime of our passion. But tell me your new plan, my darling. Last week's idea. Tell me. He knew it was no good. She was fading. The dress, the secret necklace, the couch she sat at ease on facing him and having a conversation, they were all giving up their existence and going back where he had conjured them from, the empty nowhere. Still, clenching his fists and shutting his eyes so tight they hurt, he continued, but as though by rote, with a version of a true story he had once placed great hope in. At cockcrow, he said, an unreasonable hour, I admit, I knocked at the bedroom door of my kind keeper's daughter. She appeared quite without trepidation on her threshold in a white gown. What is it now, sir? she said. Holy Maiden, I answered, I have seen in a vision that I must set off at once for Frankfurt, the Navel of the Earth, the City of Dreadful Night, and rescue Madame Gontard, my Diotima, from the jaws of death. I shall follow my river Neckar to its confluence with the Rhine and on to her river, the Main. She is expecting me, I cannot disappoint her. Please at once prepare me a breakfast and some provisions for the journey. I must leave before the cocks cease their summoning and the ordinary day begins. If I leave now I will be just in time, she will not have left, the harm that can never be undone will not have happened and we shall be as we belong to be, she and I, man and wife, living quietly, hurting nobody. Go back to sleep, sir, said Miss Lotte. I went dejectedly away, he said, and slept like a man under nine folds of lead and when I awoke the day was ordinary and when I asked for my boots to begin the long walk to your summer residence they would not give them to me, for my own good, they said, for the peace of their own consciences, how should they bear it if I died by the road or in one or other of the sacred rivers? You were entrusted to us, they said. We love you. So here I still am and there you still are and I begin to feel we shall never be reunited.

Then the panic seized hold of him. The blood in him seemed to be withdrawing from his body's frontiers, where he touched on the outside world, and hastening to a hole where his heart had been, all the mainstreams, all the tributaries, of his blood, reneged on their life-purpose, and rushed instead into the abyss at the centre of his being where his heart had lived. By force of very terror, he wrested himself from his underworld of trance and dreams, sat up, and barefoot and clad only in his nightshirt hurried down the spiral staircase and out into the garden there to begin the only therapy that helped, under the apple trees, among roses, night-scented stocks and clumps of lavender pacing rapidly to and fro, to and fro. After some time, exhausted, he sat down and leaned his back against the low wall outside which the Neckar was running fast. His sweat went cold under his nightshirt. He heard another quarter strike. The sky was lightening. Came the crowing of a cock, and soon the first solo voices, the makings of a chorus, the heedless, pitiless annunciation of further life, the din and beauty of it. He stood up, leaned a while for strength on the river wall, and it was then, as he turned towards the tower, the stairs, his bed, the hope of sleep, that he heard her voice in the unspoilt tone of truth saying again

    … and now you will bring and write
All the familiar things back into mind
  With letters and it happens to me
    The same and I will say all of the past.

2

I have met a poet, a real one, the wreck of one. I was staring
into the river, thinking it might after all be pleasanter to be
a cadaver in those waters than a student of theology in the
prison house, when I felt behind me – shiver down my spine
– the smiling of a saviour angel, I turned and saw her, no girl
more beautiful have I ever seen nor ever will, she stood in
the tower doorway, on the step, at her back I saw the staircase
into the upper room, and she smiled and said, Come in, if
you like. I suppose you wish to meet our gentleman lodger.
So an angel in the form of his keeper's lovely daughter,
knowing my heart's requirement, smiles and beckons me in.
Henceforth I have a calling. I will know him and love him
and the rest can go to hell. Hush, hush, write quietly and
exactly how it was.

    She stood aside, her arm outstretched, I climbed the spiral
staircase to a landing and there, at his open door, he stood. Go
in, she said, and left us. Quite a tall man, broad-shouldered,
stooping slightly. He wore a loose smock, and trousers belted
below the waist. His hands were in his pockets. As I
approached, he bowed, and I saw the balding crown of his
head. I begged pardon for intruding upon him. Continually
bowing he backed into the room, all the while addressing me
as Your Majesty, Your Grace, Your Royal Highness, and
speaking fast in a mix of tongues. I took his retreating and his
extravagant courtesy to mean I should follow him in. When

he halted, I did. The room is an amphitheatre, in it a bed, a chair, a small table, a piano, a dresser on which are a few books and a very well made model of a Greek temple. The walls and ceiling of his room are whitewashed, he has a view through the window across the river to the orchards and vineyards and behind them the level hills. In the window stands a lectern. Nothing came to me to say. I stared through tears. He bowed again and again, almost to the floor, freed his right hand and with it made strange rolling gestures of extreme deference. His nails are long. May I come again, sir? I asked. Ah, Your Holiness, he replied, forgive me, that is a question I cannot, I may not, answer. Then the rapid babble of tongues. He has an old man's mouth, his cheeks are cleft with sorrow, his frame is at times suddenly jolted as though lightning passed through it. His eyes cower deep in their sockets, they look out fearfully. Then I saw them find the girl, who had entered without a sound behind me, and at once they were reassured. They lit up with thanks. In that illumination, his face and his whole person were beautiful. I took my leave. In truth, I fled. Come again, sir, she said. I think he will grow to trust you.

★

Sleeping and waking I dream of him. In company I am absent, my absconded spirit is with him, night and day that absent self has haunted the precinct – the temenos – in which the poet has his lodgings. V. suspects I have fallen in love with somebody else and perhaps I have. This morning I uncovered his *Hyperion*, first edition, among piles of mouldering theology on a market stall by the church. Ah, said the dealer, You have found that. To be honest, I didn't know it was there. He took the book from me, examined it. The two volumes bound together, he said, 1797, 1799, a bit damp, a bit foxed and dog-eared, but nevertheless… Priceless really. Then he forgot me and read in it a little. Old man in a tasselled cap and a kaftan, one lens of his spectacles cracked. I thought, He will ask more than I can afford and I will borrow and pay it. But he handed me my find, saying, Yours, young man. In the insurrection of 1770, the year of the author's birth, the Greeks failed shamefully. Now they are becoming a free people. I felt I had arrived where I needed to be, among signs and wonders. I mumbled my thanks. He smiled, saying, I like the look of you. Ask, and it shall be given you; seek, and ye shall find; knock, and it shall be opened unto you. So encouraged, I hurried by alleyways and steps to the lower town and soon stood again at the low wall, looking over it into the river, which is high after some unseasonable heavy rain. I looked until I felt the presence of the same young woman, his divine gatekeeper, at my back. I feigned surprise, embarrassment. She smiled, seeing through me. You wish to know my name, sir. My name is Lotte. And you wish to visit our gentleman again. Gracefully she indicated that I was free to do so.

Climbing the winding staircase I felt greater trepidation than I had the first time. I felt that the shock of him would again be hard to bear. But also, in the intervening days and nights, in dreams and visions, I had learned that only through him, the mad poet, could my life find its proper course. Simple as that: I would be given or refused what my life could not do without. His hearing is morbidly acute. He had heard my footsteps and stood as before outside his room on the narrow landing – I can't say to welcome me, rather to assess the nature of the intrusion and the degree of agitation it would cause him. My deference almost equalled his. We were two creatures of the same species acting a fearful courtesy. I felt terror, but in it also a desperate pity for him in his trouble. I did my utmost to display myself as entirely harmless. But he backed away, one hand in his trouser pocket and with the other making rolling gestures of obsequious greeting and abasement, all the while mumbling, Your Grace, Your Imperial Majesty, Your Reverence, how kind, how very kind… So he withdraws. Is his self a citadel? I think not. At best the ruin of one and haunted. I held up my hands, as if to show him that I carried no weapon, and saw in my right what I had forgotten I held, the bookseller's gift, the poet's *Hyperion*. That was my *entrée*! I opened the volume at random, turned somewhat aside from its author, and read a few lines aloud.

> Oh look! Diotima suddenly called out to me.
> I looked, and gladly should have died there and then at the colossal sight.
> Like a shipwreck beyond all measuring when the hurricanes have fallen silent and the mariners have fled and the corpse of the smashed fleet lies unrecognizable on the sandbank, so Athens lay before us and the orphaned columns stood like the bare trunks of a wood that in the evening was leafy and green and in the night went up in flames.
> This teaches us to be silent about our own fate, said Diotima, whether it be good or ill.

The effect was miraculously beautiful. At the first words he fell silent, halted his retreat, stood upright, extended towards me his upturned hands (dirty as an urchin's, with long yellowing nails) as though he were offering me a blessing, and listened, how he listened! And when I had done and as I closed the book and looked him full in the face for his response, he said quietly, I had the honour of knowing the man who wrote that. Indeed, when he died he bequeathed me his own copy. See, there it is, on my little table always open. Never a day, never a night, goes by without my reading aloud from it. His face was entirely trusting and serene. I closed my copy, smiled and bowed, and said it was indeed a book of books.

There was stillness in his amphitheatre room. Through the open window came a blackbird's song and the soft steady rushing of the swollen river. His manner let me believe we might have some conversation. Your model of a Greek temple, I said, such a lovely thing, I have been wondering how you came by it. Ah, Serenissimo, he replied, I cannot, I may not, tell you. I tried to show him with a smile and by pressing his *Hyperion* against my heart, that he had already given me far more than I deserved. For a long minute he appraised me. Then he said, That temple, young man, sprang fully formed from the head of Pallas Athene. She appeared to me in a dream, wearing it like a crown, and said, The wars are over, you have defeated the wicked Emperor and his slaves. Return to the ruins now and rebuild the polis more beautifully than ever. Build my house after this image on the high hill in my city. And the goddess inclined herself towards me and when I awoke the Parthenon stood on my heart and my hands were clasping it.

Suddenly his face was stricken with anxiety. He said, clearly enough, But I must not, I cannot, speak of these matters to Your Eminence. Then his looks, his whole bearing, were bereft of all grace. His speech became a rapid muttering in several languages – I picked up scraps of French and German, Latin, Italian and Greek, as recognizable ingredients in a broth of nonsense. And yet not nonsense: there was a tone – panic – and even a purpose – to negate, to undo, to deny, as it seemed, the interval of grace and courtesy which had so touched me. I've never felt such pity for a fellow human being. Some devil of dread was forcing him to disown himself, all his best self. Or perhaps – I have thought of little else since I left his tower – some angel is warning him against divulging the secrets of his soul, and punishes him, for his own good, if he does. I have been told that in the clinic when he raved they fastened him in a straitjacket. Dr Authenrieth, they say, fits a mask of his own invention over the faces of patients who babble in any language he finds offensive. Perhaps this poet has been taught to fear utterance.

I found Miss Lotte in the garden. She had been picking cherries. When she saw my trouble she proffered the heaped basket. Oh the black red of those ear-rings of fruit! You mustn't mind him, sir, she said. It comes on him, he can't help it, he means no ill. In fact, she went on, I happen to know that he has taken a liking to you, so don't think of not visiting again. This heartened me. I stood by the wall with her, flicking cherry-stones into the river. I asked him about the temple, I said. And I told her his story of its arrival in a dream. Father will be amused by that, she said. Our gentleman often stands in his workshop watching him work. He stands there with his hands in his pockets, leaning forward, watching. Well one morning I was there as well, I had brought Father his forenoon bite to eat and stood till he paused from planing and could take it from me. And then our gentleman said to him, I'd be obliged if you would make me a temple, sir. A model of the Parthenon on the Acropolis of Athens. Father put down his plane and answered quite brusquely, I've a living to earn. I don't live in philosophical idleness the way you do. Our gentleman's face became very sad at my father's unkind words. All the strength seemed to go out of him. He bowed his head and he muttered, Forgive me, sir. I'm a poor devil, I am quite useless. And he shuffled away. Father was at once very sorry. I wronged him, child, he said. And he shook his head as though he didn't understand himself. I gave him his forenoon and kissed him and went out. Two weeks later, first day of spring as it happened, when I took him his snack he carried on working and nodded back over his shoulder, saying, Put it on that bench, my dear child, and give our poet what you see there, will you, please? So I put the platter down and took up the temple and went and placed it secretly on our gentleman's dresser while he was out at the far end of the garden pulling up tufts of grass as he does when it's bad for him in his spirits. Later when I went in for his bit of washing he was sitting on the bed with the Parthenon in his lap. That was her story. One man deploys his gift to comfort another.

3

That night, very tired, very agitated, fearful, he went to bed around 9 as usual. You close your eyes, your pale-red lids are too thin a protection against Apollo who mercilessly far longer, far more sharply, than is bearable illuminates the ruins of your life. Sunlit failure, absence, loss. That night, knowing full well it was hopeless, knowing *that he should not* (it is not in his gift), he tried to disembody himself and be with her and continue their conversation in some private place indoors or in the garden scented with blue hyacinths and echoing with the singing of birds. He said aloud but softly some lines he had written more than twenty years ago as magic against the facts, to force them to be kinder. There were times when the spell had worked, for a while at least, and had encouraged hope in him and in her. So he spoke the words again now, against the daylight and his terrible unease and her being far away, unreachably far away, against their severance:

> But we contented together like loving swans who are
> > Quiet on the lake or ride rocked on its waves and gaze
> Down at the mirrored silvery clouds in the water, the
> > > > blue of the
> Highest and purest sky flowing under them passing
> So on the earth we went our ways and even when
> > > > > Boreas,
> > The enemy of lovers, the maker of mourning,
> > > > threatened

Stripping the branches of leaves and hurling the rain
down the wind
We were quiet, we smiled, feeling a god of our own in
Our conversation, our unison souls, and each with the
other
Wholly at peace, like children, joyously alone.

He waited. And the unease seemed to rejoice, it ran all over him and all through him, it was in his hair and under his night shirt, it entered his body's bloodways large and small, rioted in every cubicle of his brain. Bacilli multiply like that, doubling and doubling till body and soul are one seething dis-ease.

Oh, it was all familiar! He had his routine. Dog-tired and all the workers of agitation wide-awake, he left his sweated bed for the piano, sat there and felt over the keys in which *in potentia* (so he still believed) lay harmonies. He rasped his long nails on their surfaces. Then, bending close, very gently, felt with his fingertips for order, process, connections, the amounting note by note and chord by chord into something able to combat the mere noise of his affliction, in part trying to recollect what was there, in part trying to bring into being what under his hands never had been there before. But feeling that the agitation around his heart would not be bearable much longer, he knew his too urgent seeking a remedy in the keys would itself ensure he failed. He could only make what amounted to a jeering, a diabolical laughter. He had not ears to hear nor hands to shape the harmonies that would help. Doubtless they existed, but remotely, among the spheres, inaudible to the damned. He pulled on his smock and his slouch hat and went down into the orchard and sat leaning against the river wall.

In these bad passages, day after day, night after night, it worked in him *mechanically*. Master of the ancient forms, maker of new, how he derided verse that was mere mechanics!

And lived now at the mercy of, merely hosting, the mechanical processes of torment. So he sat on the earth as a hot day passed very slowly into a warm night and to the left and the right of him his hands plucked at grass, tore out tufts of it and in the one movement tossed them aside. Returned for more. And so on. And in his head all the while the vile caricature of a conversation went to and fro, to and fro, a left-hand voice and a right-hand, arguing, but not better against worse, life against death, such a dispute would have been almost tolerable, even had the ill side always triumphed, still there would have been a contest, there would have been a bid, even if defeated, for the good in him. No, in him there was only the imbecile quarrel of negatives, of petty but life-murdering harms. He might turn his head this way and that, and his own mouth did perforce utter the ills, and his ears, as they had to, listened, but really it was all one, back and forth, back and forth, a cruel mêlée which he could only put a stop to by a violent out-shouting, a greater force of gobbledegook in four or five languages, or with the magic imprecation or command, Pallaksch! Pallacksch! Pallacksch! That shut it up, for an interval, and he leaned back exhausted, hearkening to the river hurrying steadily away.

A respite. After some minutes, hearing only the waters, he began wearily to hope that the shouting match of equal horrors was over for the night. The Neckar, strengthened by the downpours and rushing to unite with the Rhein, gave him some quiet in which, distantly aware of nightingales, he slept. And that sleep gave him access to the sustenance of dreams. He was admitted into the zone he and she had often spoken of, the place apart, the sanctuary, the island, the walled garden, the locus of their being allowed to meet and take hands and resume their conversation. His gift of beneficent dreaming did sometimes get the better of the mechanics of harm. They were dreams he could believe because he knew their origins in life

127

he and she had lived. That faith, won and lost and won again, equipped him to defy their enemies and denounce them as liars, as merely social liars. He and she had seen the truth, had stood together in the daylight of it, one dead now, the other mad, it made no difference to the fact of truth.

He heard her merriment. Too often mortally serious, she could, when let, tease and fool and laugh like a child. Then he opened his looks, the dark aspect she chided him for passed like a cloud before the wind when it clears a meadow and gives the wild flowers back their colours. She came to him now slumbering in the orchard, under the cherry trees, dreaming, and the river hastening by. My love, she said, I had a scandalous dream, so beautiful, telling the truth of it. We were in the big reception room, the grandest room, where you suffered so much, and it was full of guests and the necessary servants, and the noise was, as always, unbearable, the din of humans shouting into one another's painted faces, infernal, and through it, very faintly and all in bits came the music of a string quartet and I saw you from as far away as it is possible to be in that place, across a great gulf observing me, the wife, the mother, the hostess. You stood with a glass in your hand. I never saw a man more ill at ease. You seemed to me close to being annihilated by the simple fact of being there and knowing that our love was not allowed. Thus far, my dearest, my dream was usual and implacable. But then! Under the chandeliers, in the unsteady brilliance of scores of mirrored candles, amidst the roaring, grimacing and gesticulating, my clothes fell away from me, I stood there without shame, and seeing me in this revelation you became naked too, across the room through the lies, the bartering, the venom and stupidity we looked on one another as humans did before God envied them. I showed the marks of my four children on my body and you, my love, seeing me in my brave candour, you blazed with love, you were seraphic and indecorous. The crowd parted as though we were holy or leprous and we took hands, and through the French windows, that suddenly blew wide open, we exited and were as gleeful as the resurrected in Hesperia.

Dreaming, he smiled. She stepped closer, took his hands, leaned down to kiss him, her eyes closed – and her face seemed cast in alabaster, struck in sorrow, a mask, the death-mask of a woman who, dying, had grieved till the last moment of consciousness over all the life she had lost and been denied. Her breath on his dreaming face touched him like ice. Then she stepped back and was her living self again, but solemn. Write to me, she said. You promised you would write. I was not allowed to bring your letters with me. Write them again, say them again. Write new ones. Say one now, or at least a bit of one, from back then or one from where we are now. He said, 'Do you remember our untroubled hours when we ourselves were all the company we had? Happiness triumphant! Both so free and proud and awake and flowering in heart and soul and in our eyes and in our looks, and both in a heavenly peace with one another. I sensed it at the time and said it: you might wander the world and scarcely find the like of that again. And day by day I feel it with ever greater seriousness.'

Falling silent, he wondered at his writing and at her in the necessary deceit and secrecy receiving and reading it. He felt them, the two of them, true lovers, lifted into the figurative, emblem for all time, across the frontiers of lands and centuries, in many different mother tongues, and he felt it to be a cold zone and of no consolation. She was watching him closely. How often he had come out of a trance or absence or deep depression of the spirits and found her watching. Was that back then or now? she asked. Both, he answered. As you know, where we meet now and converse, it is timeless. And under his breath he added, And cold, it is very cold. My love, she said, reading his lips, reading his continuing thoughts, there is no consolation. I desire no more than you do – which is to say, not at all – to be lifted into the firmament as yet another constellation of thwarted love. You said – or did I? – We were right to weep as we have done all these years that we shall not have the happiness we can give one another. But it cries to heaven that we must think that we two shall perhaps perish with our best energies for want of one another. As I said – or was it you? – we cannot live on doing without and there is no virtue in trying. If they must remember us, especially other lovers, if they should hear of us in times to come, let them not grant themselves the solace of supposing there was virtue, glory, triumph in being put asunder and disallowed, let them not suppose an afterlife in thin air far above the lovely earth is any compensation. Loving as we did, we should have died breathless, mouth on mouth, and been discovered so, a scandal, naked, incontrovertible, beyond all excuses and hypocrisies. Loving as we did, we should have cast it in their faces, to stomach as best they could. But we were defeated, it was loss and a waste of life and that is that.

He woke sobbing. His face was wet with tears. The river ran fast with only a man-made wall between it and him. He plucked and plucked at the dewy grass. Yes, there were nightingales, yes there were scents. Earth is a sweet place, life here is a wonder and very sweet. What good is there in absence? None. None at all. I sometimes think, he said, that I went mad of my own volition to get to a place in which not being with you would be bearable. I must have been mad already if indeed I ever did have such an intention. We are famous. People climb my spiral staircase and ask after you. What was she like, your Diotima? Ah, your Diotima… And I read you aloud, mostly to fools and the morbidly curious, now and then to young men in love who remind me of me. So you haunt us. I bring you continually to life. My visitors attend a seance. The better I say it, the less I can bear it. – I'd rather be mad than dead, she answered. I'm glad you're alive, mad or not. Where would I be without you? Nowhere, my love, nowhere, my dearest, nowhere.

4

He writes on any paper he can get hold of. I have a sheaf of his newer compositions: odes in correct alcaics or regular quatrains of rhyming trochaics or iambics, the words fit the decided form but the sense is obscure. That is, the words themselves are entirely intelligible, but in that order and arrangement they are puzzling. The connections, the fittings, the transitions, are strange. Perhaps it is a new language that we shall have to learn? A new tone or logic or vision. Certainly a new tone of *voice*. A sort of innocence, but *after* the Fall. A man left wondering, at a loss, innocent only in the sense that he cannot now make sense. And another thing: the better I know him the more I suspect him of *feigning*. That's not quite the right word either. But in his own self-defence, so as not to disintegrate totally, I think he may be, to some degree, *playing* the fool, for spectators who think they know what madness is, and his acting contents them, they don't ask for more. His grotesque courtesies are a particular instance of the strategy. Apotropaic, placatory. The nicest strangers quicken some primeval dread in him. Perhaps he sees in them a power of harming they do not know they have? So it may be that in his 'innocent' poems they see something childish or childlike, reversion to simplicities, and that quality touches them and leaves them free to pity or condescend to him. But, if I am right, there is terrible sadness and dread behind the veil. I have longer poems of his too, in Pindar's style, harder still to grasp. They treat of Greece, of Oedipus, of transgression and of the merciless punishment visited on a man by a god.

*

I must write it. I shall put all else aside and write myself the *vita* of a poet who saw too much, desired too much and came into such happiness the gods were jealous and cast him back down into ruin. I shall write of his fall, his suffering and his continued revolt under cover of madness. Miss Lotte tells me he likes me, calls me 'that young gentleman'. I love and revere him. I say (to myself) he and I are kin.

*

He has visitors, especially in summer. Miss Lotte does her best to protect him, but they pull rank or wave what they say are letters of introduction. And sometimes he is to be seen on the landing, as it were on a high proscenium, waiting, absurdly beckoning them in. Other days, it is true, he lies on his bed curled like a babe in the womb and covering his ears with his dirty hands. Then nothing on earth will induce him to be civil. But even that rebuff does not disappoint a certain sort of visitor. On the contrary, they are thrilled, they feel they have seen the real thing.

Those admitted like to question him about his past, especially his Diotima. I have it on good authority that one lady, making such an enquiry, got this answer: Ah, Madame, my Diotima, thirteen children she bore me... And he began to count them on his fingers: the first became Pope, the second Sultan, the third Emperor of Russia... And do you know what became of her? She went mad, that's what. She went mad, mad, mad, mad, mad. Most, before they leave, if the grotesquenesses, the shouting, the deafening tunes on the piano, the monologues of a soul in torment have not sufficiently disgusted or saddened them, ask will he be so kind as to write them a poem? He almost always obliges, that being, I guess, the surest way of terminating the visit.

At their worst, his visitors conduct themselves as if at a freak-show. The ladies relish the gruesome indecency of it. But among the bourgeois and aristocratic rabble, there are a few, I gladly concede, who have read him, know something of the stations of his passion, and come to bear witness. I can't say – I have never entered when others were already present or stayed when they made their entrance – but I imagine that whoever comes in humility to witness the truth will be shaken to the heart by it, as I am whenever I see him again.

A freak on show is one image. Another, yet more distressing, is that of a caged animal still mindful of its former beauty, power and freedom. He will pace to and fro, to and fro, in his room or in the garden, for hours at a time, many hours, pacing fast in the confined space he is allowed, again and again arriving at the limit and there turning and returning. And all the while muttering or shouting to himself, ceaselessly pacing, in ceaseless colloquy with the tormenters in his head. Peace comes to him at last in the person of Miss Lotte, the good angel, telling him it is time to eat or time to try and sleep. Her alone will he allow to wash his hands and trim his nails. No wonder he addresses her as Holy Maiden.

*

Today, as I was leaving him, he took off his hat, bowed very low, and said, Excellency, I beg you, allow me to write you some lines of verse before we part. I stood in confusion, I blushed like a girl. Your Grace permits? And he turned, strode to the lectern, put his hat back on, took up his quill, and gazing out of the window became at once abstracted. If I close my eyes now I see him as a living presence as though I slept and dreamed. He raises his left hand, I see the long nail of his index finger pointing. It, like all of him, is watching, listening, attending. His lips move, the words are arriving sotto voce, his finger counts them in, they come in their metre, he nods his head as the first line ends. He closes his eyes, I see him saying it. I am closer than it is polite to be. I am drawn like a beast into the listening circle of Orpheus. I wish I had a beloved woman, a companion of my body and soul, to tell her what I have witnessed. I saw the moving lips, I heard the whispering, the breathing of words from the very mouth of Orpheus. I watched his hand write the satisfactory line across the foolscap sheet. And this too: I saw that his eyes, too often lustreless or scared, now with a look of grateful entitlement, of purpose, of belonging, searched beyond the river, through the trees, to the distant high levels of the hills, for the words, for their rhythm, for their couples of rhyme. I saw it! I watched!

Then he was done. There on the page, the poem, a quatrain, with much empty whiteness around it. He bowed, the floppy rim of his slouch hat obscured his face, Honour me by accepting this, Your Highness, he said.

*

Bastille Day went uncelebrated here. I did a pen and ink portrait of myself, head and shoulders. Now (same pen) I will describe that person: A mop of curls, black eyebrows, thin moustache. He wears a loose shirt, open and tied very carelessly at the neck. His look is inward, unsmiling. As I write, he is half-averted from me. He looks like somebody who doesn't at all mind posing and to be honest I have my doubts about him.

*

When I called on the poet this morning he was standing at the lectern with his back to the window and reading aloud from *Hyperion* to an empty room. He wore one of his several rather grubby nightcaps, the red one. Seeing me, he broke off his reading and began his ritual of bowing and scraping. I put my hands together and entreated him to resume the performance I had interrupted. As Your Majesty wishes, he said. It was a passage I had read aloud to myself many times and knew by heart:

> There was a time when I was happy, Bellarmin. Am I not still? And would I not be even if that blessed moment when I saw her for the first time had been the last?
>
> Once I saw it, the only thing my soul was seeking, and the perfection we remove to somewhere above and beyond the stars, that we postpone till the end of time, I have felt it present. It was here, the highest, in this circle of things and human lives it was here!
>
> I no longer ask where it is. It was in the world, it can be in the world again, it is only more hidden now. I no longer ask what it is, I have seen it, I have learned to know it.

Here now, the town's clocks having just struck midnight, I consider the slightness of myself and my generation. Born when *he* was, nineteen when the Revolution began in France, himself by then, like me, signed up to that grave-digger, that walking corpse, Theology, heading towards the priesthood and a suitable marriage in some Swabian dead-end, how he – with Schelling, with Hegel – rejoiced at the news of a livelier life being seized hold of and lifted up for all to see in Paris. The Chancellor of this Seminary then (and now, no doubt) was of the opinion (I quote) that 'It is good and salutary for one whose future occupation will be the care of souls that his will should be broken while he is young.' But I know – from Uhland and others – that the seminarists' watchword back then was 'Heaven now', here on earth, of our own making, in liberty, equality and fraternity. They swore their allegiance 'By the dead at Marathon'. I know – with horror or longing old men remember it – this place was a forcing house of Kantian ethics and Jacobin politics. It was reported to the Duke that here 'the anarchy in France' and 'the murder of the King' were being quite openly defended. Believe it if you can in the charnel house we inhabit today! They were in at a beginning which the ending, though vile, will never annul. Something was born then which will live for ever as a witnessed possibility of justice. But I was born in the dead time, amidst Metternich's spies and censors, and will die having seen no better. *He* was disappointed – beyond saying, even by him, the grief of that! But he had seen on this very earth and in the flesh and blood of the woman he loved the possibility of a life more fit for human beings at their best. They were in revolt, he and his comrades, women and men, and although they were defeated they point the way, they reach out their hands to me, saying 'Come, friend, into the open!' Only last week I wrote that he was flung down from a heaven of his own achievement by a jealous god. I correct that now and say that the heaven he meant to occupy was happiness here on earth for all humankind, beginning in his own country, he wished its citizens (not subjects!) to be glad and proud of their homeland and he was cast out and confined where he is now by kings and princes, bishops and priests and the vast armies of the deluded they had at their command. He and his comrades revolted in a cause worth fighting and dying for. Myself, born into the age of established disappointment, the restoration of tyrants, liars, spies, turncoats and servility, and nothing good stirring in the land or ever likely to – my revolt is all personal, all adolescent, entirely without any larger point or purpose. They will let me run my harmless course of offending the Respectability by my appearance and behaviour and when they wish they will haul me in and bow my neck into slavery. And whether I live that life or end it by the razor, the rope or the river matters not a fart.

*

Remarkable how much easier in the spirit he becomes out of doors. Even the view through the window into open country works quieteningly on him. More than once in his amphitheatre room when neither of us could bear his agitation any longer I have opened the window and turned him to look out. And into both of us, standing closely side by side, after only a minute or so, peace came, into body and soul. His muttering slowed and was quieter, he stood quite still, even the twitching in his left cheek, which I have always feared as the portent of some terrible crisis, even those helpless spasms ceased and he was still. We stood in silence, and although I could not become unaware of him, he could and did forget my presence, and I was thankful for that and in my heart I rejoiced.

Even better – the best in our acquaintanceship so far – today with his landlord's encouragement I walked out of the town with him to the summer house I have rented on the Österberg. It is at no great distance but being there shifts one's perspective. The town does not sprawl, you are soon out of it and life is other. It is *the country*. On the vineyard terraces, in orchards, allotments and flower gardens, people are quietly busy. The singing of birds is louder than their work or their conversation. No sooner *outside*, I felt him to be not just quietening but also attending. He looked this way and that, and his muttering, whose tone, if not the words, I am by now able to interpret, became almost peaceful. With only a little licence I might call it the bubbling of a stream, the soughing of a breath of air through leaves or a soft musical accompaniment. We walked among beeches, walnuts and sweet chestnuts and birdsong was everywhere.

The summer house itself is a small and ruinous property for which I pay very little and which gives me immeasurable delight. It is a tower (of sorts) and you ascend to its only usable room via an uncertain stairway. The 'garden' is a scrap of land in front of that. Arriving there, he halted and stared at me as though I were indeed one of the eminences he sees or pretends to see in all who approach him. I motioned him to enter in at the broken gate that cannot be closed. He backed away, took off his hat, bowed very low and began the tiresome rigmarole of, Your Grace, I cannot, I beseech you, Your Majesty, I may not... Taking a risk then, I imitated and outdid him in grotesque politenesses, bowing lower, cap in hand, sweeping it through the never mown grass. Serenissimo, I snivelled, Your Holiness, I implore you... Oh do me the honour, Your Imperial Majesty! And now let this be recorded as gospel truth: for a moment he was at a loss, for a moment I cursed myself as a clumsy fool. Then his eyes, cowering back suspiciously in their sockets, saw the truth and he smiled. That was a moment! Never have I felt better about myself than when the man I love and revere more than any man else on earth studied my antics till he trusted me and smiled.

I went ahead, pausing at the stairway to indicate the places of particular dilapidation. The rail is trustworthy, I said. Seize hold of it, and watch where you put your feet. I climbed slowly, he kept close on my heels. I heard his breathing – regular, easy, he is sound in the wind – and the uninterrupted muttering, his secret glossolalia, the tone of it now enjoyment. I halted only for a moment on the landing, wishing to see his uplifted face: I saw something scurrilous in it, he looked like a boy being very willingly led astray, going out of bounds.

Then we were in – in my lair, my eyrie, my rented tower of vision. Against his visit I had moved my table and chair away from the half-circle of window and pushed both casements, one of them wanting a new pane, wide open. See, friend, I said, and like a man with untold riches at his disposal I extended my open hand towards the view. He saw from on high the Neckar serpenting in from Rottenburg out of the haze of the distant uplands, passing below his own lodgings and then, to his left, heading away north-east among the places of his childhood. I saw him entranced, his lips were moving but the *sound* of his thoughts had sunk to the softest whisper. Stay, sir, I said. Stay looking. I will come and fetch you in a few minutes. His nod of agreement was, like the faint susurration of his thinking and feeling, barely perceptible. I left him and in the garden completed my preparations for our entertainment. When I came to fetch him, he was still at his post, looking, in a quietness I had never known him achieve or be given before.

I had dragged the heavy garden table to where the foliage opens and the hill slopes quite steeply away. Two lichened chairs in place; wine in a shapely, ancient, chipped, blue and grey jug and beakers to match; my handsome dark-red *Hyperion*. I served him and we drank. 'Blessed land!' I said. 'No hill of yours wants for vines…' And see there, along the Neckar's far bank, the lines of poplars. Might they not be cypresses, might we not be in Italy, even in Greece? I opened the volume and read

> O you groves of Angele, where the olive and the
> cypress, whispering around one another, cool
> themselves in friendly shade, where the golden fruit
> of the lemon trees peeps out from among dark leaves,
> where the swelling grapes climb as they please over
> the fences, and ripe oranges, like smiling foundlings,

lie there on your path, o you secret scented ways, you peaceful resting places, where sprays of myrtle smile up from the mirroring spring, never will I forget you!

Diotima and I walked for a while among the glorious trees till a spacious and gladdening place opened before us.

Here we sat down. There was a lovely quiet between us.

In the past, he said after a silence, in which night of which century I don't rightly know, but it was summer, that much is certain, I sleep very little in the nights around the solstice, and it was to me unsleeping that an angel came saying I must at once set off down the river you see there to a meeting with the Rhine and onward, as fast as I could, to a meeting with the Main, and there turn aside and find a certain grand house and a particular room in that house and in the room a woman was dying and only I could save her because only in me was there a love for her stronger than death, but I must leave at once, before daylight, and walk non-stop. Alas, my boots were in the custody of my keepers and for reasons well-meant (that I might die on the way, which would grieve them, for example) but not convincing (in a sense I was dead already), they would not give them up and urged me to go back to bed and I did so, for a week or more, in which time the beloved woman died. That said – muttered, whispered, requiring me to bend very close – he drank off his wine and lifted the beaker towards me, to be replenished.

*

This evening, already quite late, saying that after all one heard too much of Hyperion and not enough of Diotima, he took a sheaf of Madame Gontard's letters out of the drawer in his desk and read from them for the best part of an hour, allowing me to ask questions and giving me answers as veiled as the letters themselves were naked. Thereupon I told him that nobody would think of confiscating *my* boots and I would journey to Frankfurt in his stead. I wished him good night. But rather than make my way at once back to the summer house I went as far as the bridge and leaned over the central arch and watched the dark water. There was no light showing in the Zimmers' house, but in H.'s tower, in the window, there was. I felt a great love for him and also a gratitude that he was in their safekeeping. I saw the window pushed open and the dark shape of him leaning out. I could see that he was wearing his white night cap and again I felt: all's well. But then, chilling my blood, came this, a great cry, one word, one name, launched out of the body and soul of him, out over the hurrying waters into nothing, the sky, the cold company of the stars, the universe: Diotima! After it, silence but for the river. He closed the window, extinguished the light, and I sought my way back home.

*

There was a note on my table in the bay window, from C. Where are you? I thought we had an arrangement. I waited two hours and now I'm going home in the dark. – I forget people, she isn't the first.

5

Dearest, I woke in the certain feeling that my heart was a living creature incarcerated in my chest, shut in there by some casual tyrant and forgotten and what woke me was its despair, its flinging itself to and fro in the rib-cage, screaming and

141

pleading and knowing there is no hope. Forgive me my nightmares, dearest love, I wish you an innocent sleep. I went down into the orchard and was soon quieter. The river is not so hurrying as it was, there has fallen no more such violent rain, and I have resumed my night-time ritual of casting flowers on the waters. Some nights, some bad days, my terrors come together in an old suspicion I was perhaps born with and could never quite be rid of even in fair circumstances and when I had good health: that I am a person who must continually struggle to be alive or whether anybody notices it or not he will be dead, still walking around, still talking, but in all that matters dead. I remember seeing this as a fact and telling it to the young man in the mirror before I came into your house and you quickened me. I was twenty-five, the skies were leaden and I told him in the mirror, Friend, you and I are dead. And I saw him again, that myself, once I was evicted from your house and our future, solitary exile, had become clear to both of us. He looked at me and said, Alas, we have fallen back and are more dead than alive and I'm afraid this time it will be worse because we have lived for a while in the fullness of life and will never till the end of our days be able to forget what that was like. By 'flowers on the waters' I mean of course bread and by bread I mean the word, the words, that they should be carried by the rivers, the Neckar, the Rhine, the Acheron, and find you out. The dead are patient, I hear you say, they will wait for ever, if they must. But I have not yet told you of the young man who has taken to visiting me and reads from our *Hyperion*, asks after you, my dearest, asks after Diotima, and reads aloud the letters our fictional characters wrote to one another. On a sudden impulse, wishing that he should know her more closely, and seeing in him a chance, a willing helper, forgive me, love, I read to him some pages of your letters to me and there and then he offered to be our go-between, I will set off tomorrow, he said, rest easy, you and your Diotima, I will be back with findings and belongings of you both. He reminds me of me which is why I thought it right that I should let him learn, through your letters and my commentary, how in a blessed time we lived together under one roof and could meet and converse and read and go into the garden together, to the heart's content. And how often we discussed the likely fate of our invented lovers in the isles of Greece at a time of insurrection and disappointment. Till in the end, having bound ourselves body and soul to one another, become one flesh, we were dissevered and driven into subterfuge and arrangements that fretted the life in us to death for a glimpse now and then, a touching with the fingertips, of what in truth we could not do without, having so grown into happiness we thought it ours by right, inalienable. Such things I read aloud to him in your voice, saying that, loving as we do, it is not bearable to be sundered, forgive me, I thought him our last hope. Close to the wall, pacing the riverside garden to the limit, turning, pacing back and again reaching the limit, I thought (and it made me smile) that totted up these pacings through the hours and days and months and years would have got me to Frankfurt and back a thousand times. My visitors often congratulate me on my rude good health. Deranged you may be, sir, but incontrovertibly you have first-rate legs. With legs like yours a man might circumambulate the globe. Energy, Your Imperial Majesty, I whisper, I have the energy of love and longing, desire and disappointment, of a loss that cries to heaven for its making good, my feet and knees and thighs and heart and lungs are excellent, not a man among you could stay the course with me in my pacings to and fro under the sun, under the crescent, full and waning moon, not one of you, I have the energy of elegy that rises again out of its trough of sorrow, rises to a crest of joy again and pleads to bide there but must topple over, down, down, so on and on, that ceaseless onward drive of wave on wave having behind it the fetch of the whole Atlantic. And then another thing, reading your letters to me to my youthful alter ego, I came upon this that blinded me with tears: 'My thoughts which are often with you or rather are always in some connection with you often I write you entire letters but then there's such a mêlée in my head nobody would be able to follow it on paper…' In tears, I saw the infinite utterance of our love. The letters you wrote and got to me by secret couriers or thrust with your own pale hand through the hedge to exchange with mine, our hands ungloved and feeling in desperation for the letter and the flesh, touching, desperate to be held for ever and letting go, my letter in your hand, yours in mine, your rapid writing, as impatient of punctuation as lovers in a hurry are of buttons, laces, buckles, clasps and bows, those letters, how many words in all, so many, beyond counting, and beyond them, as you say, the endless letters you were breeding in your head while the children ran amok around you while you quietly sewed. I think of them, the letters never written down, those never having a life blood on white paper in black ink, those jettisons, that milt, that spawn, your letters to me, the written, the unwritten… And mine to you – is it true as some say that the guardians burned them or true as others say that they were allowed among your few belongings in the tomb but Charon, when you came to the river, would not let you carry them across? Since then in thousands of miles of pacing and no end of time I've done as you did in your small lot of years when all your hours were not your own, I've written at speed in the invisible ink of thought and cast them out like clouds of pollen in May, hoping that at least one word of my many millions would find you out and lodge in you and seed.

6

Half an hour north-east of Stuttgart, just beyond a wood of beech, oak and ash, sitting in a mown field with my back against a haycock, my notebook on my knees, writing. When I left J. the town clocks were striking 5, she was asleep. Yesterday, before going to fetch her, I made a fire in the garden of my summer house and fed *Phaethon* several pages at a time into the flames. I've rarely felt so sure of any act as I was – and am – of that. I feel it has halted me on a wrong way. I don't deny or regret the way I was on, it wasn't time wasted but it had to stop. Now I have stopped it and by walking I will try to find the new way. What was wrong is clear to me, but what would be right isn't – yet. Knowing what isn't right is a good start, I should say.

Phaethon is a novel by an author who took one look at his subject and saw and wrote not it but his *idea* of it. I'm ashamed that even after getting to know the man himself somewhat, even becoming to some degree his friend, I still continued for a while in my nonsense. I can learn from that. I had the person, the real thing, the life, before me, I loved him, he trusted me, and still I proceeded with a phantom, a mere idea. I was missing the experience for my idea, adolescent, fervid, vapid, all froth and phoney pathos, piss and wind. Yesterday after I had conducted him home and when I reminded him that I would set off for Frankfurt next morning and be away for some time, he nodded and smiled what I have taken to calling his *complicit* smile. And making a V of the first two fingers of his left hand he touched the tips of them like a divining rod against the shut lids of his eyes and said, But so simple are the images, so very holy, that truly one is often fearful of describing them. Leaving this morning, I thought I knew what he meant. Look, keep looking, let the particulars, the holy particulars, in through your eyes into the mind and very heart of you. See into the terrible beauty of things. Look, keep looking, for the words for it.

The Neckar is pleasant. For him, as for me, it has been a thread of life. Lauffen, Nürtingen – and Tübingen where, descending from the Seminary to the clinic and from the clinic to the tower he is as close to the waters as you can get. At the same time he loves where those waters start – close to the Danube – and more still, since his Frankfurt years, where they lead to: the Rhine and so to the Main and the Gontards' two big houses. But also, because of her, the Athenian woman, Diotima, his home river with its vineyards and its poplars that remind him of cypresses, takes him in the freedom of imagining to Italy and so, like the Danube (Black Forest to Black Sea) to Ancient Greece.

Easy walking, downstream, now the water is back to normal. Pleasant. Swabia is pleasant, hardworking, parochial, philistine and self-righteous. Its sons get out if they can. Its daughters never can, they bide at home waiting to be married. I will get out. Next summer I will cross the watershed, the Danube, the lake and mountains, into Italy. That will further improve my eyesight, further help my eyes and my soul and my circulating blood to take in the particulars, the images.

Strolling downstream today I noted what I will call signs – that is, things in themselves sufficient unto themselves whilst also being the indicators of (to?) something else. For example, the willows along the bank indicate how high the river *was* a month ago. Their branches are festooned with dead grass and weed. Bottles, boots, planks from a smashed boat, hay stooks, a dog, a bloated cow lodge in them. The willows capture and hold up to view such signs. Also, along the bank itself, especially where it bends, a varying tidemark shows the furthest the river overflowed. You see entire uprooted trees lying in it, prone and stranded. Just now, eyes down doing a slow search along the selvage here, I glimpsed a blue glass bead, then another, I kneeled and teased a girl's necklace out into the sunlight. It had ridden the flood in a tangle of leafing twigs. I pocketed it. Finders keepers, mine to pass on to whomsoever I choose.

I was in Nürtingen by mid-morning. He lived his boyhood there. The river brought him his first poems. Father and stepfather died in his infancy. His mother, after those two marriages, was very well off. I sat on the bridge surveying the Schweizerhof. That was the family home and she stayed on in it with the two sons and the daughter. She was anxious, the elder boy especially, the poet, worried her, he wandered abroad. She stinted him. In fact, Schwab says, ask anyone, in her disappointment and anxiety she sat tight on his inheritance. Still does. She moved in with her daughter's family by the church and the market about the same time as he moved from Frankfurt to Homburg, funnily enough. I strolled across and took a look at that dwelling too. I had half a mind to call and say I brought greetings from her son, which would have been a lie. Then I asked directions and on my way out assessed the paddocks, orchards, large kitchen garden, that were hers with the Schweizerhof. They're on the left bank, a little way downstream. I took a good long look. People noticed me. I was passing through, if word got back to her it will not signify. I am a collector of the circumstances past and present of my beloved poet. He writes to his mother when Miss Lotte tells him he must. Once he wrote a letter in his best copperplate while I watched and with a 'Be so very kind, Your Excellency,' handed it to me for my perusal. I never read a letter like it, and Miss Lotte tells me they are all the same. In a bizarrely convoluted language of filial dutifulness they are as cold as death or Mephistopheles at his most sardonic.

The river winding away north-east, I went due north over the hill, a very beautiful straight track across open fields under

skylarks, I chanted hymns of my own pagan making, so happy.
Down into Denkendorf. She signed him into bondage, he did
the first two years of it cloistered there. Free as a bird (for
now), I rejoined Mother Neckar at Esslingen and was in
Stuttgart by early evening.

My father moved us to Stuttgart when I was two. I don't
like the place. My mother's father was Vicar in Birkach, and
she took me out there sometimes, not far, and I did like that.
Grandmother told me stories. But Grandfather died when I
was six and the stories stopped.

On this walk I am orientating myself.

Four or five years ago my father moved again, to
Reutlingen. Last week I took a walk there, via the Galgenberg.
I was walking off the drink of the night before and, finding
myself on the way to Reutlingen, may have had some notion
of rapprochement in my poorly head. But when I got to the
family home I changed my mind. I stood on the street full in
the sun and imagined walking in and climbing the stairs and
knocking on the door of the room he calls his study. It would
have been an experience I could have written up in advance.
It is possible that he loves me but it is certain that he doesn't
like me. In fact most hours of most days he can't stand me.
And I doubt if he ever dreams of me lovingly. So that
afternoon he would not have been pleased to see me. He
would have wanted to know why I was not where I was
supposed to be, in Tübingen learning my Hebrew. And what
did I think I was doing instead of that? I should have told him
I had a hangover and had decided to walk to Italy to clear my
head and had called on him to ask for a small contribution to
my likely expenses. He has no sense of humour, my father, and
very soon it would have been a shouting match, me against
him, the tantrums, father and disappointing son in their usual
mortal combat but worse than ever because of my wish lately
to be more truthful. I didn't need to enter his house to know

how it would be. I opted instead for the unhinged slant on things. The son standing visibly on the public street in front of the father's respectable house, hands in his pockets, his slouch hat brazenly pushed back, looking. If he didn't see me himself (from behind a twitching curtain) some servant or nosey neighbour will have and reported. I think I can safely say he knew. The insolent eldest son, the – figurative – parricide, was there on a summer afternoon, looking without pity at the family home.

Here. Now. Twilight, bats, the last swallows and swifts, very faintly a town clock, the river birds noisily quietening down to roost. Bread, cheese, a handful of stolen cherries, my ration of wine. I trust it won't rain but if it does the wind is westerly and in the lee of my stooks I'll take no harm.

*

Early evening, just beyond Heilbronn. Easy walking, fine weather, right bank as far as Hochberg, track then due north over the rise (vast flocks of lapwing) to Marbach, from there track west to Pleidelsheim, across the river to Ingersheim, north-west to Besigheim, after that I stayed close to the Neckar to his birthplace.

I was happy all day. I woke to the noises of aquatic creatures waking. The river itself seemed to be waking. A fawn close up stood regarding me. I've never looked a fawn in the eyes before. I made no movement, only looked. She entranced me. Her look was cautious, appraising. Perhaps in a long overdue reversal of scripture she was thinking of a name for me. In her own good time, she lifted her head and loped away. I never saw such grace. I was damp and cold with dew but I relished the sensation. I saw that the sun would be a while getting over the eastern arc of hills. I ate the last of the cherries, swallowed a mouthful of wine, and set off, fast. I walked an hour, and in Mühlhausen then, in the square, warm sun and warm bread were mine together.

I saw a fair few people on my way, saluted them cordially and was answered cordially. I think I did not look *suspect*. Several times I halted and asked the name of a hill or a rich man's property and always learned more than the name. People seemed glad to impart what they knew. I felt I was a likeable phenomenon. I say that *impersonally*. I've found it to be the case when walking long distances that if you divulge a little, they nod, smile, are interested, are helpful. You like one another. Mostly I'd say they like the idea of the wanderer at liberty to pass through their domain and admiring it. Granted, I was well-spoken, not selling, begging, likely to thieve. I was just bohemian enough. (But only two days out. How will they view me when I stink and itch?) I told them I was making for Heilbronn, my place of birth. Two or three were curiously touched by that. I saw they thought it a pious purpose in a young man. Walking on, I retained in the mind's eye for quite some distance an old woman's very blue eyes and a shock of her white hair under her black shawl; an old man standing up from ridding his ploughshare of an entanglement of bindweed and brambles and suddenly clutching at a pain in his back. I must train myself to see better, retain more, and more exactly. I came into Ingersheim at noon. Swifts were screaming round the church spire that shone bronze against a sky of the purest blue. I sat by the fountain eating black bread and very peppery radishes. A man led a mare across the flagstones to drink. He led her with his left hand. When he was close by me and we had exchanged a 'good day', I saw that for a right arm he had only a stump. He saw that I saw. While she drank at the trough he told me he had been in the wars and suffered that damage. He was fearful of coming home, he said, to show himself so impaired. He feared he would lose the girl he was betrothed to before he went away. But no, they married as soon as they could and have two children. How old are you? he asked. If you don't mind me asking. Eighteen, I answered. He looked me up and down. I'm thirty come Michaelmas, he said. He saw that I had thought him very much older. I'm content where I am nowadays, he said. I wish you well. And he extended his left hand. Awkwardly I took it in my right. I saw he was used to that.

People tell you things when you are passing through and they know you will never pass their way again.

The Klosterhof is a little way out of Lauffen, on the Zaber, just before it joins the Neckar. In an angle between two waters. Nothing much is left of the ancient nunnery. They pulled it down. An antiquarian might identify its stones in recent wealthy houses in the neighbourhood. Where it stood, on the living tumulus, there's a joyous welter of grasses, flowers, bushes and sizeable trees. Such colour, scent, leafing, blossoming, fruiting! And the sweet birds sing. Creamy elder, beloved of bees, is doing especially well. Only last week Schwab showed me a drawing he has made of the Hölderlin family's coat of arms. It plays on their name: Hölderlin/*Holder*, and bears two sprigs of elder in flower, one embraced on a shield, the other sprouting, as though in further birth, from a crown supported by that shield. And he showed me also an early poem – it will be in the volume they are preparing – in which the hedge of wild elder around this birthplace is celebrated. Tree of good luck and bad luck, of virgins and witches, perfumed and rank. I have a sudden memory of my Birkach grandfather forcing out the pith from a tube of it, for a Pan-pipe. And another: of my fingers, face and best shirt stained with the berries' black gore. The Klosterhof and its land and outhouses are still walled around. So, in H.'s day, it would have been an enclosure within an enclosure. Sacred precinct of childhood within the precinct of the brides of Christ. He mentions an ancient elm at the gate through the elder hedge into his inner world. Surely a child would have felt benignly encircled there. And it was a busy working zone. Much is still present: an orchard, a kitchen garden, an acre of vineyard, stalls for cows and horses, a sty, a dairy.

I was at the gate, looking, when the woman of the house came out and invited me through. I took off my hat, I wished I might have been her returning son. But I said I was a friend of an old man who had lived the first four years of his life here. When I said his name it meant nothing to her. But I saw that she liked the idea of my journey on foot for the sake of him. When I praised the flowering elder, Wait, she said. And came out two minutes later with a cold beaker of its wine.

I wonder has my poor garden house ever touched him be it ever so faintly with a memory of his place of birth? And in the interludes when the fits leave him does he feel *any* of a child's contentment in his amphitheatre room or in the orchard by the river that connects him still to the small tributary stream and the house within two enclosures in that angle of two waters where he lived long enough for memorable things to lodge and last? And a loving surrogate family whose Miss Lotte, Holy Maiden, particularly cares for him – do these match at all with back then? And the rhyming poems he will write for keepsakes and sign with strange names and date in times long before and long after his own, in those poems, in their holy images, behind which I have felt a sort of horror of the void, is there not also perhaps a breath of the innocence, joy and safety that were surely there at the beginning in the Klosterhof behind its hedge of wild elder?

I had nothing to look for in Heilbronn. Now by our river writing these notes, I feel an onset of the sadness I fear one day will extinguish the life in me.

That year in the season of short nights and lingering twilight he had hours without raving or convulsive picking and fidgeting. With sympathetic interlocutors then he was at ease and, though he still spoke in the language of otherwhere, in their different ways they understood him. Indeed, his talk continued in their hearing afterwards, when they were no longer in his company, phrases and his tone of voice and certain characteristic looks and gestures lingered in the air around them and they attended. In some what he had said remained for the rest of their lives, still working and differently. Others remembered his face when he sat in silence. Desolating, said one. In a level sadness he seemed to be contemplating a landscape all of failure, loss and wreckage.

Also that year in that season, as another effect of his brief remission, the gift of disembodiment came back to him and for a series of nights he slept at once and entered the space that is both boundless and magically encircled, the locus of conversation with the dead beloved. It might be a summer house in the park in Westphalia when for whole afternoons they were quite unsupervised, or even a room in one or other of the Frankfurt houses when there was no likelihood of any intrusion. But they were safest, left most to themselves, in places that had no name and were of their own poetic making. My friendly sanctuary, he called his verse. My asylum. And there they were at home, they had a house they owned and could dwell in as they pleased and pass from room to room. They could say what they liked for as long as they liked.

Their conversation in these sanctuaries was of such candour, their understanding so complete, at times it felt like triumph. This was our allowance in circumstances forced upon us, and see what we made of it! Is it not fit to be looked at by the angels? To which the answer was another question:

whose angels, yours or ours?

That summer in the short nights he was able to meet her in the walled garden whose whereabouts were known only to them. They made no arrangements, each desired it and so it came about. They met in daylight, and walked or sat in the sun or the shade, just as they pleased. The flowers, trees, bushes and paths of the place were on every occasion familiar but never the same. Once, for example, as though to illustrate some previous dream or conversation, a bed of periwinkle appeared. They spoke of the past, remembering good and bad, and of a future too in which they would be free to do as they wished and would cross mountains, follow south-flowing rivers, come to ancient shores, embark for the islands, and always when they spoke of such a past or a future it was there alive in them present. So it was in their speech and listening as it is in the lines and stanzas of poems, always present, here and now, sorrow and happiness, present. Only on parting, when they had kissed and stood for a moment in silence, did they see in one another's faces the resumption of ordinary time. It was so, we were so, we did and said those things. It was then, it was back then. And we have no future. And she vanished, leaving him.

Some nights, in his sleeping and dreaming, they were together not in the elsewhere garden but in his bed. Knowing that he suffered, she came and slipped in beside him in the tower above the river. The nights are short, she said. I can stay till cockcrow. Tell me how it is. Believe me, love, where I am, the air (call it that) is full of the murmuring of the living who can't get through their days, cannot face the nights, without telling their beloved dead how they have been managing without them. The whispering of the living in all the tongues of the sunlit earth, that is the white noise of where I am now. My thoughts are merciless without you, love, he answered. I have the devil in me telling me I didn't fight, I wasn't bold enough, I was compliant. We should have claimed our own and faced the world for it. – Have you forgotten? she said. I told you to leave. Over a stupid altercation with my husband, your employer, I begged you finish with him there and then, and leave his house. Obeying me, after that it was all broken into bits, into fearful little scraps of being together, never a hope of fashioning our own salvation. You left to protect me, you feared I'd be disgraced. The fault was mine, I should have been cleverer, I should have lied, lied more and better, to buy us time and when we knew our way I should have told him to his face I had seen the light and the light was at last a life I could call my own. Instead, only furtiveness and endless devious scheming and arrangements. – You told me he was surprised to learn I had left. And that was because it never crossed his mind that treating me like a lackey day after day in the end would drive me, even me, to revolt. They say time heals even the worst of wounds but we are different, love, I think you and I will never again be whole till we're in one place. When you were dying I was going mad and my alienation has been thorough ever since. Not in your state nor in mine can we be mended. I should have done what love demanded and hauled you out of his moneyed residence. – And the children? – They were his property. At once he forbade your son, my pupil, who loved me and whom I loved, who had written me a letter, I have it still by heart, I can't bear it that you've gone. Dear Holder, come back soon, how shall we learn without you? Here is some more tobacco for you. The father forbade him all further dealings with me, the father claimed him, aged eleven, out of the woman's care into his, as a future asset in the banking business. And the girls I am sure he made good matches of.– Hush, my love, hush. I can hear the river and the nightingales. Remember that summer, that first summer, over the hills and far away in Westphalia, lying awake with the windows open and moonlight coming in and the singing of the nightingales, I lived six years after that, day by day, week by week, month by month, the good of it, the happiness, being added to. Few women are given so long so passionately in love. And though year by year it got more difficult and anxious, it did so only because the love itself was greater and wanted more. Had we wearied of one another, would that not have been worse, oh so much worse? Had one of us loved not more and more but less and less, would that not have been terrible beyond all saying? Remember they married me to him at seventeen, I had four children, I adorned his home, he was glad of me, ours was a house the business men liked to come to. You forget, perhaps you still don't know, how many women slumber in that fashion till they die. But you came into my world as the living proof of an elsewhere I had heard of in music and poetry, and I awoke. Don't let the devil ever lead you into regret. For so much love we had an equal suffering, so it was, so it had to be, your poems, that swing continually from presence to sundering and absence, say the truth of it.

He called her Diotima after the woman of Mantinea from whom Socrates got the understanding of Eros which, in Plato's *Symposium*, he passes on to the other men there present. Again and again in his poems she is his teacher. Casimir Boehlendorff, who became destitute and mad and killed himself, said with peculiar certainty, She taught him what love is. Sometimes he called her 'the Athenian woman', because she would have been at home in the city of Pericles, Aspasia and Phidias. Introducing her to Neuffer, who toed the line and became a vicar and a complacent know-all, he whispered, Is she not a Grecian? (A bust of her done by a contemporary sculptor shows her as exactly that.) He called Frankfurt 'the navel of the earth' which was Pindar's name for Delphi, the holiest of places, sacred to Apollo, site of countless shrines and temples raised up on a terrace above the sea in a natural amphitheatre, eagles forever slowly circling above it and back-dropped by cliffs and slopes that rise to the twin peaks of Parnassus, the one sacred to Apollo, the other to Dionysus. Up there is the source of Castalia whose waters give the frisson of deep cold that is the mark of the hitting home of a line of true poetry. Yes, he lent Frankfurt, the banking city, the name the ancient poet gave to Delphi, and did so because Frau Susette Gontard, née Borkenstein (also a banking family), mother of four and one year older than her lover, lived there with her second-cousin husband, Jakob Friedrich Gontard whose personal motto was 'Les affaires avant tout'. And she did not become less Diotima when she wrote to him soon after his sudden ceasing to be one of Gontard's employees, 'I have already noticed that I am being treated with great courtesy, every day new gifts, treats and excursions, but accepting the smallest favour from him who had no mercy on the heart of my heart would be like taking poison so long as this heart still feels, for who after the fall of her friend could enjoy the good life (as they call it) and still uphold any sense of herself and her finest feelings?' On the contrary, he answered, the better I understood that between our selves and theirs, between their good life and ours, no negotiation would be possible, ever more clearly I saw you as an exile from the ancient land where you belonged. I felt found out by you to be your friend and ally in the Age of Lead and that you were given to me as lover and comrade in the struggle without mercy for the life that was rightly ours. – The struggle demeaned me, my sweet friend, what it cost me in lies and subterfuge, evasion and endless scheming to be with you for an hour, for ten minutes, for the touch of your hand, for a glimpse from my window of your appearance, as arranged, and your passing and going out of sight, as you promised you would, it left me shaking like a woman fevered, and furious at the insult done to my soul by the effort of trying to have even an interlude of life worthy the name. So full my head and heart were with your absence I saw you *when you were not there*, and nothing was in that vision for my comfort, only more fear as though you'd got the arrangement wrong or could not help yourself but came where and when you shouldn't have and let me see you and all I felt was dread. Say it again, he said, my love, say that letter again, I did not read your letters, I *heard* them off the page, their haste, their urgency, I saw your face, I heard your writing on your lips, no correspondence was ever closer than ours, the hurrying whispered exact voice of feeling, say it again… My love, she said, what I wrote and what you hear is this: 'I thought that before my eyes I could see your shape in the allée. Was it you really? I wasn't on my own, the visitors were with me. It struck me like a bolt of lightning I went warm, and cold, and soon the others noticed that I wanted to be alone, and left, It seemed to me then that it was really you and some anxiety was driving you to me, you had to come to me, I went to the window and stood there, my eyes fixed on the place, and again the illusion came upon me, I saw your face through the bushes, then you were leaning against a tree and spying out and sorrow seized my heart with a cold hand and threatened to squeeze the life out of it, my thoughts were freezing cold, it was as if I had gone to embrace you and you had become a shadow and this beloved shadow would still have been able to comfort me and when my senses asked for this it too vanished from me and a nothingness, if that is conceivable, remained. Out of this dumb sorrow I had to tear myself and then from the depths of me came a groaning a whimpering a torrent of tears which for a long time were so violent I could not halt them and since then I have felt such a heavy sadness, and as though in your heart you have something against me, and I can think of nothing else, Oh God! never appear to me again like that! Oh never doubt my love! - - - - It is you I love, you alone, and will in all eternity. - - - -'

Long before cockcrow you have left me, love. It is because I quicken your visiting ghost with the sorrow of being alive. We shall have no rest till we are both together in one place. You wrote, 'I feel very keenly that without you my life is wilting and slowly dying.' All the while knowing for certain, you continued, that any step you might take to see me in a secret and anxious fashion would eat at your health and peace of mind every bit as much. And so it was and is. I shall perhaps have to believe in miracles, you said, because I can't see how else we shall be together. And wish it passionately, but to be together without fear, careless as in the beginning of our love. Lovers have better things to talk about than how they might contrive to be together without fear. I suppose it was then, witnessing our erosion, that we began to think of parting *by our own decision*, severance we could call our own. In poems we tried it out, I wrote at *our* dictation. We thought we knew ourselves and soon learned that we didn't. Each throttling the other's soul, that's what it felt like. I saw blank incomprehension in your eyes and you in mine. Though we knew that love is frightening to the loveless, that lovers are as welcome as insurgents in the body politic, we never courted martyrdom. And offering ourselves, you to me, me to you, the Lethe drink was no more a free act than Socrates smiling at his judges and quaffing the hemlock. Then, bled-white and wandering the earth apart and meeting again as strangers and in some park or garden walking a while and speaking of this and that, we come unawares to the very place of parting and the heart leaps to life and flings the blood through the veins, the astonishment, the inrush of present life, all that would have been in equal measure true and unbearable. So we settled for the lily, white, very beautiful, strangely fragrant, lifting towards us over one or other of the streams of death.

8

I should be north of Mosbach by now, in a hayfield. Instead, I'm in Mannheim in a common lodging-house. I got turned back at the border, the guard – a drunk enjoying himself – said he didn't like the look of me and when I showed him my passport he said it might serve for an arse-wipe and when I showed him Professor Conz's letter of introduction to the Esteemed Director of the Court Library in Bad Homburg he said that might too but for nothing else was either any good and I could fuck off back to wherever I had crawled from. So I crossed over to the other bank of the river, whence I had come, and thought to walk it and then the Rhine and the Main to Frankfurt but the skipper of the *Florian*, a timber boat, who had watched my going and coming, said, What's your trouble, Sonny Jim? and when I told him he said, Shysters, they are over there, all of them without exception, and that particular swine is the worst of the lot, if you looked like a smuggler or a bit more respectable, he'd have said, Welcome, my friend, bribe me. Anyhow, not to worry, you can sail with me to Mannheim and I've a pal there who will convey you in style to Mainz. So I helped him load up and once we were on the move I swabbed the deck and scrubbed and brushed and polished. He told me tales all the while but what with his accent and me never still and him sitting cosy at the tiller I didn't take in very much, it seemed to be mostly about the fortunes you could make smuggling salt out of Wimpfen, he had a few sacks stowed below, nothing to speak of. In Mannheim, nearly dark, I helped him unload and there, lo and behold! was his best mate, skipper of the *Liberty*, and he's sailing first thing tomorrow with iron ore and assorted contraband and me. So now for a short night I'm in with the low-life smoking my pipe, drinking a beer, eating some sort of meat and feeling quite pleased with myself.

*

My skipper down the Rhein is a man called Emil, taciturn himself but wanting me to sit by him in the stern and talk. Without saying the name, I told him I was on a sort of pilgrimage to a couple of places very important in the life of a dear friend three times my age who is not allowed to travel any more. For some time he made no reply which oddly enough did not make me feel in the least uncomfortable. I sat watching the traffic on the river. I thought, I've lived in places on the Neckar but when I got to know H. I felt I knew nothing much about even that river. And now this: the widening, the multitudinous life. And I was not ashamed of my ignorance, rather I rejoiced in it. This is the beginning and the opening, I said to myself, I shall learn, every hour, waking and dreaming, I shall be open and will learn. Then Emil said, When I was about your age I killed a man old enough to be my father. It was at Valmy. I didn't want to kill him or anybody else for that matter but if I hadn't he would certainly have killed me. From the start I had wished to be fighting on the other side. Instead, I fought for the kings and princes and their priests and lackeys. – I said nothing and he paid close attention to avoiding the mudbanks between two long low islands. A good while later – we had just passed by Worms – he said, à propos of nothing I had been talking about, Our men were very much bigger than theirs. This was obvious when they were lying all together dead. The Prussians especially looked monstrous. The French were fighting *for* something, we were just fighting against it, and only the Prussians with any conviction. Nobody liked the Prussians except the Prussians. Seeing how big they were dead really turned my stomach. And yet most of them were only peasant boys. – He had big hands which you might expect would be clumsy. But

161

managing the sails and the tiller and keeping his eye on the traffic, he fitted new hooks to a line and I marvelled at the finesse and rapid dexterity of his fingers. He had a bite pretty quickly and hauling the line in and seeing the catch to be two good-sized trout, he said, They will do us nicely, and snapped their necks with quick mercy. We moored for the night at Gernsheim. He cooked the fish, saying very little, filling my glass. Don't mind me, he said, my humour is melancholic. I took up this trade soon after I got out of the army. I wanted to be on my own. What will *you* do with yourself? I told him I was signed up to be a vicar but had not the least intention of ever becoming one. I told him I wanted to learn and what my teachers taught me I would use the way I liked. He nodded. I saw that he was steeped in his solitude but wasn't misanthropic. He listened, wanted to know. Much to my surprise – I've never used the term before – I told him I wanted to be *a man of letters*. Good, he said. You might be able to show people that things don't have to be the way they are. He gave me a blanket and I slept on deck. All through my sleep I heard the river continuing without us. Waking for a while, I saw the giant Orion stepping through the heavens. Emil said we'll be in Mainz tomorrow late afternoon.

*

I left Emil and the *Liberty* in Mainz. He was waiting for his cargo of grain to take back to Mannheim. He said to look out for him, ask after him, if I come back by the rivers. Though walking might be quicker, he added. And don't worry about the frontiers. Just don't try and cross where you're supposed to. Ask the locals, they'll put you right, there's always someone will row you over for the price of a drink or two. – Parting, he embraced me. I'm an hour along the Main now, weather uncertain, but there's a barn in the corner of this field. Oh these rivers! Neckar, Rhein, Main, and the ghost of him on all three, ghost of a man not dead but acquainted with Charon, crossing the Acheron when he pleases, crossing back again and talking to me. Emil behind me, H. closer and closer ahead of me, H. in his passion, H. on the frontier of madness. I am rather full of other people's lives at present. But that is good. *Promeneur solitaire*, people talk to me, day after day the meetings and farewells, and during the miles alone they continue in me, I turn their confidences this way and that, try not to grasp, try not to conclude too soon, but listen, listen again, try to learn. I have to assimilate other lives and shape myself against them. It will be what H. calls 'a loving quarrel'. Tomorrow, uninvited visitor, snooper around the boundaries and under the windows of the Gontards' winter and summer residences, I shall need charm, cunning, and, to get to the quick of the matter, the cap of invisibility.

★

I'm in the Weidenhof, a lot pricier than my doss in Mannheim, but Schwab told me it's where H. put up when he came in for the meetings or glimpses of one another. It's about half-way between the Gontards' town house, Der Weisse Hirsch, and the place in the country, Der Adlerflychtsche Hof, they moved to for the summer. I'm surprised how close the two are. In town they were next to the Grosser Hirschgraben and in the country just beyond the Eschenheimer Gate, barely a mile apart. Hardly worth the upheaval, you might think. From the country Gontard came into town for the working week, to see to the one thing that mattered, his bank, leaving wife, children, house tutor, governess, servants, visitors, hangers-on to amuse themselves. In a couple of passages H. read aloud or dictated to me, Diotima – I've noticed he always calls her that and with a sort of scurrilous delight when she is most struggling for a life of her own against the forces that were denying it her – Diotima tells him how they might manage at least to exchange letters after the move into the country in early May. According to Schwab, the arrangements must have been known, in broad outline at least, to people in Homburg. Hard to see, Schwab said to me, how he would have kept secret his early settings off from Homburg to Frankfurt, summer and winter, often (though she begged him not to) in foul weather. His close friends there, Muhrbeck, Boehlendorff, Sinclair, for example, knew of his love and saw close up what the thwarting of it was doing to his spirits. And among those who love and revere him now (the few, the growing number), his passion and hers seems a great good, a thing to be glad and proud of, fit to be shown as proof of what humans are capable of, its course and tragic outcome, the horror and the waste, are known but not much spoken of, out of tact, respect, a sort of *pudeur*.

*

In the family church, not listening to the sermon, Frau Gontard, conjured up the image of her lover and told him how they might manage their summer assignations. So you come, she said in the hurried undertone of love, on the first Thursday of the month if the weather is fine and if you can't then on the next or the next but only ever a Thursday so that we won't be confused by the weather, so then you can leave Homburg in the morning and when it is striking 10 o'clock in the town you appear at the low hedge by the poplars and at that time I'll be upstairs at my window and we can see one another, for a sign rest your stick on your shoulder, I'll hold a white cloth and if then after a few minutes I close the window that's a sign that I'm coming down but if I don't, I can't risk it, if I come you walk to the end of the drive not far from the little arbour because behind the garden we can't reach one another because of the ditch and we're more likely to be seen but the arbour will hide me and you will be able to see in both directions that nobody is coming and that we'll get enough time to exchange our letters through the hedge. Next day when you are going back you can risk it again at the same time if it hasn't worked the first or if there are things in the letters we have to answer.

*

I shall be his witness. Feels like years ago that I left my *Phaethon* as a pile of ash in the garden of my summer house. Since then, on this pilgrimage and enquiry, I have learned more of the truth, or have come more into the heart of the truth, by being *in the places of it*. I am not a chronicler but a feeling witness, going back certain years before I was born, in search of surviving evidences of what I feel to be the truth of his life. I have some of his poems. I know people who knew him around the turn of the century and know him now, as I do (but not so closely as I do). Close up I have seen the myth. I have talked for hours with the man whom Apollo struck, who saw too much, who converses still with the woman of Athens. But I must learn more of the holy particulars of their myth, the grit and dirt of it, the plans and subterfuges, the deceits and lies, the anxiety, the fret, the abrasion, the killing disappointments. Love starved, love going without, day by day less bearable. All their efforts to get at least the living word across the frontier, from hand to hand. Once or twice they employ a friendly go-between. Or he sends by some normal courier a parcel of books for the attention of Frau Gontard: letters are hidden in the secret heart of them. And very near the end, facing the nothing, she wonders – he read me this in the tones and with a look of loving and desperate disbelief –

might a mutual friend, Landauer say, be willing to *mention his name* in her company! Just that, the beloved name, a mention in company, a contraband gift, a crumb to live on. And this – with his permission – no, encouragement, almost insistence, as though in a lucid space in his remoteness, he wanted it known and said, he wanted recognition of this waste of life, a memorial, a sort of justice – this I wrote down at his dictation in my notebook: When you think of me in the future always picture me in some occupation that I enjoy. And I shall think of you that you are doing something that rewards your kind heart, and so we shall think of one another with cheerfulness. And bravely, with the rapid passage of time, hasten towards reunion, whenever that might be. – So in the teeth of the facts, in despite of them, she begged that they would think of one another happy, as they moved out of even the possibility of even the most fleeting, unsatisfying, distressing encounters, into the immovable fact of absence and towards her death and his madness. How should he now, mad, conjure up and be content with images of her contented?

*

A small public road runs outside and along the hedge of their summer residence. I strolled there like any other stranger with time on his hands. The house stands back, its upstairs-windows showing between six Italian poplars. To and fro I strolled, glancing up now and then as though for her signal, not knowing which of the windows was ever hers. Unknown, never likely to return, I felt myself noted and appraised by local people passing and pausing, and even that very little made me uneasy. I, having nothing to lose, felt *perilously* visible. From there I walked to the town house, stood first on the corner where he could be seen by her in her room watching out for his appearance. Boldly then I strode into the large courtyard, ambled there as though I had a visitor's right to. Her room was on the first floor, very likely at the far end, quiet, with a private way down into the garden. But in another wing of the vast house, on the opposite side of the courtyard, other rooms were occupied, facing and looking across at hers. I glanced up there, saw myself watched in my to-ing and fro-ing by an old man wearing a night-cap and a dressing gown, I supposed him to be sick and spending all his daylight hours at that window, watching. In the winter, after her signal, H. stood in the dark below her window. Will she throw her letter down to him or will she have been prevented? He will reply overnight if she does; if she doesn't, he will expand his letter to her which he has with him, show himself on the corner at 10 the following morning, and at 11 they will cross on the street, holding letters to swap.

*

Homburg. I took my time getting here. Stopped often, looked back over the city. From either Gontard house, the place of his retreat was visible high on the hillside, the Feldberg rising massively behind it. I wanted a sense of each looking to where the other now in separation dwelled. It is a clear relationship. I climbed here through vineyards, hayfields, woodland and birdsong in evening sunlight. In the past few weeks I have grown close enough to the two of them to recognize this as what it must have been for them: a simplified landscape of feeling. I wanted to sleep among trees just below the town but thought better of it and am well – that is, rather expensively – accommodated at the *Golden Pony*. I can't present myself at the Court Library tomorrow with twigs, or worse, in my hair.

*

East of Darmstadt. I never went to the Library. From the *Pony* (on their impressive notepaper) I had written for an appointment with the Librarian at midday and before then went to locate the three addresses H. lived at. He had got to know Homburg during the first weeks and months in Gontard's employment. His radical-republican friend Sinclair was there in the service of the Landgraf of Hesse-Homburg, a deeply pious man, and H., in an increasing happiness, often climbed to see him. After the separation from Susette, Sinclair found him a room in the Haingasse, number 36. That house, owned by a glazier, is derelict now and likely to be pulled down soon. He was there for the two years of his correspondence and assignations with her. He looked out on gardens, a hill with oak trees, meadows, open fields and the descent to Frankfurt. The other two were his dwelling places when Sinclair urged him to come back to Homburg to be among friends after her death and the onset of his madness. The first was in the very respectable Neugasse, at the lower end, number 133, and again he had a view south to the towers of her city. His landlord, a French clockmaker, after less than a year couldn't stand his piano-playing and he was taken in by a saddler, back in the Haingasse, number 38, a room upstairs looking down through its one window into the yard, till 11 September 1806, on which day his life as a free citizen ceased. So far the bare facts, as I knew them before I visited their locations. But I met a living witness, a woman in her early twenties, wife of a silver-smith, she stood in the open doorway of no. 38 with a baby on her hip, watching me, expecting me to address her, so I did. And after hearing what she had to tell I felt quite incapable of presenting myself at the Library with my letter of introduction from Professor Conz. Really, I fled. What I learned there in the Haingasse has brought me as close into his life as I can bear. I fear seeing him again. I fear he will know what I have learned and will give me that look of his which says, Well now, my young friend, what do you make of that?

*

Camped here by a small river, nameless to me, that comes down from the Ödenwald, only now have I begun to breathe easily again. I fear Professor Conz will cast me out of his heart. *Tant pis.* I've had a long day's walking, at top speed, down the path into Frankfurt Hölderlin walked so often and I shan't walk again, past the two Gontard houses (I have seen enough, I have by heart the topography and logistics of torment). Had a drink or two in the Weidenhof, called for a sheet of their excellent notepaper and wrote grovellingly to the Court Librarian, apologizing. Crossed the Main without trouble. Perhaps they just wanted rid of me. My arse-wipe of a passport has served me thus far homewards well. Tomorrow at dawn I shall climb this river and up there will sense my way over the watershed south, south, down to our river Neckar. Starlings, thousands of single birds in an undulating, clenching, expanding, soaring and swooping vast black cloud, are readying themselves to settle for the night in a pale bed of reeds on the far bank. They will fall like the blanket of the dark, with much noise, and quieten little by little as I lie down and mull things over under countless stars.

*

It occurs to me that I still know very little about his 'other' life in Homburg, the work he was doing there, his efforts to become an independent man of letters, the revolutionary friends he consorted with. Instead, I have followed what seemed to me (and still does seem to me) the imperative issued by the confiscation of his boots. He felt commanded to follow the rivers and be reunited with Diotima in Frankfurt. With his blessing, I went in his stead. I am answerable to him.

169

But there are things I learned about him that are not sayable to him. But I fear he will know what I know as soon as he looks me in the eyes.

★

The woman standing with her baby in the open doorway of Haingasse 8 was watching me. Her expression had become serious, almost fearful. Are you looking for where the poet lived? she asked. I took off my hat and answered her with a like seriousness. Yes, madam, I am. She nodded backwards. Here, she said. Up the stairs. His room was rather dark, it had only one small window and no view, only of the yard. I was playing with my little sister just about where you are standing now. I was seven, she was five. Nobody had told us to keep off the street that afternoon. Perhaps nobody knew. We were playing, a few of the neighbours were out, it was a sunny autumn day. Then a coach came into the street and halted here, at our house. Two men in black got down and knocked at our door. My father opened and without a word let them in. I don't think he noticed me and my sister. He looked very serious. Soon the two men came out carrying the poet's trunk between them, lifted it onto the back of the coach and strapped it tight. Then came my father, leading the poet gently by the arm. I remember how silent the street had become. My father looked so unhappy. When the poet saw the coach and the two men standing either side of the open door he turned his face towards my father for an explanation, and began to shake. I've never seen more fear in any person's face. My father motioned him towards the coach. Then the scene began that nobody who witnessed it has ever forgotten. The poet tried to run away, the men in black seized hold of him, he struggled, and shouted again and again, They've come for me! They've come for me! The two men couldn't hold him and my father wouldn't help. The coachman got down and together the three overwhelmed him. He had the looks of an angel and he fought like the devil. His nails had grown very long, he would only let my mother cut them and not often, and he scratched at the faces of the men who were holding him, one of them you could hardly see his face at all for blood. But they bundled him inside, the two big men got in, with him in the middle. I saw their fists and I heard his screams. The coachman slammed the doors, climbed up, took the reins. And still you could see the poet fighting with all his strength to get out. Then it was over, they drove him away. My father came across to us and took us indoors. He said not a word, nor did any of the neighbours speak. I've never forgotten that silence.

I said nothing either. Only looked at her and her child. If I'd met one of the women years after the Crucifixion and heard from her what it was like, I think I'd have felt much the same.

I was making to leave when the woman said, There's another thing, sir, if you have a minute. Yes, I answered. Do, please, say it. Two or three years later, she said, my sister and I were playing in the attic. We had a sort of house of our own up there at the gable end, just a space in all the jumble really. Nobody minded if we rummaged around for more things to play house with and that day we found a nice leather case, soft leather, with a coat of arms on it, and when we opened it there inside was the poet's flute. Neither of us could play it, of course, but I put it sideways to my mouth and blew and moved my fingers up and down the way I'd seen him do. My mother had told us he could play very well before his illness got so bad. He had been a very good pianist too, and when he was living at the clockmaker's house, the Princess gave him a piano, thinking it might heal him. But he smashed it in one of his fits. My mother and father were busy outside somewhere but Grandfather was home with us and when he heard me with the flute, pretending I could play it, he came to the bottom of the ladder and shouted up, What's that you've got? Bring it down here. So I did as I was told, came down the steps and gave it to him. You don't play with that, he said. It's been in the madman's mouth. You'll catch what he had. They'll come and take you away. And he laid the flute across the edge of the hearth to the floor and stamped on it and broke it in half. Then he trod the two halves under his boots for good measure. Our mother and father were very angry and sad when they found out and for a long time there were bad feelings in our house. Why are you so interested, sir? If you don't mind me asking. I know the poet, I said. He is my friend.

9

This afternoon I walked with him some distance into the woods, along the hill, west, towards the chapel. I had my first feeling of the nearing of autumn. He said not a word but walked at my side and did seem to be attending closely as I spoke of my time in Frankfurt and Homburg and my route there and back. I was anxious and spoke quickly, and if withholding things is untruthful then I was untruthful. I said I had visited all three of his lodgings in Homburg but withheld what the young woman in the Haingasse had told me. Mostly I spoke about the two big Gontard houses and said – without alluding to the letters he had read aloud to me or given me to read – that I had a much closer sense now of how much the arrangements he and Diotima were forced to make had harmed them in their love. Being there made all the difference, I said. At that, and at one or two other points in my *récit*, he nodded. But said not a word. I didn't mind. I should not have liked it had he questioned me too closely. And perhaps my boatman on the Rhine had helped me trust the listener. As we walked back towards the town, I spoke quietly and with no uneasiness about Lauffen, his birthplace, the benign enclosure, the elder tree at the gate, the courteous woman who brought me a beaker of elderflower wine. 'Holder', I said. It brought it home to me. Coming into the garden of my summer house, we paused at the gap in the trees that allows the view up the valley. I told him about the rivers, the boatmen, the bringing in and giving out of the goods people need. Still he kept his silence. And I had the strange but kindly feeling that talking to a beloved shade might be like this. Since getting to know him I have taken more notice of the bereaved, especially the poor, in one or other of the town's graveyards who sit telling their dead about their day. And none among the other visitors thinks it foolish. Climbing together into my living room and setting the two chairs, the table, the two beakers, two wooden platters and the shapely jug in the bow window, I was thinking perhaps day and night wherever he is he is doing that. Perhaps – how should we know? – his unintelligible mutterings are such a conversation. Not his loud gabble and raging and muddle of tongues. But the *sotto voce* muttering, his eyes elsewhere, perhaps that is nearly always his telling her and her listening intently.

At the table in the window – it was early evening by now – I should have been content to sit in silence with him, breaking bread with him, drinking the wine, and having whatever feelings we liked about the river coming peacefully towards us and passing below. And so I was shocked when, wiping his mouth on the back of his hand, he looked me full in the face – and we were sitting close – and said, He only had one eye, you know. Oedipus had two and put them both out with his mother-wife's golden ornamental needles, but my Diotima's keeper, my master, he still had one and spied around with it, the other he poked out with a pair of scissors when

he was a child, by accident, they say, but in a fit of rage. You
didn't meet him? He is alive and well, I believe. He married
again, and then again, so I hear. Will you be a house-tutor, my
young friend? In my day it was the usual course if being a
curator of souls did not appeal. His gaze close to is sardonic
and frightened in equal measure. But it is an occupation full
of peril, he went on. You are assigned to the world of the
woman of the house, you are paid to help with the things that
are her concern, the education of the children, the music, the
charming recitals, all the ornaments, extras, amenities the man
is quite glad to come home to late in the evening or at the
weekend, from the vaults of his bank. And the most dangerous
of all the ingredients in this bouquet of flowers, this pot-
pourri, these domestic adornments, is poesy. Playing the flute
to Madame's piano is risky, writing poems is suicide. Tell me,
young man, does anybody still read Lenz? I thought not. He
went mad. He should be compulsory for everyone your age
thinking of going into private education. *The House-Tutor* is
the play, its hero, Läuffer, by no means a poet, falls in love with
the daughter of the mother of the house. In my case it was the
mother herself. And he cuts his balls off. At least I never did
that. Why did he? I asked. So it wouldn't happen again –
falling in love with his pupil – to fit him for future
employment, he could list among his qualifications that he
was a eunuch. I was compliant – Our Lady of Cythera forgive
me – I let the Cyclops-banker treat me like a lackey, but I
didn't do what Läuffer did. He drank off his wine, I poured
him more, he got up and paced around the room, alarming
me. I went to him and led him gently back to the table in the
window. See the river, I said. I know her better now because
of you. He was quiet then, abstracted, not exactly peaceful but
I could see the lovely curve of the Neckar under the
woodlands, and on the far bank, on those slopes, the orchards
and the vineyards, all of that and more being taken in through

the eyes at least steadied him. Tell me, he said, does anybody still read Heinse? He's dead too, died a year to the day after my Diotima, he showed us the statues in Cassel, he accompanied us into Westphalia, he appreciated her, he said she had a complexion like that of Titian's women, and her dear young friend Marie, her confidante, the French governess, she was also with us in Westphalia, so beautiful too, he would gaze at them both, in gratitude, or stood between them beaming like a pasha. For as the French revolutionary armies advanced on Frankfurt, the Cyclops sent us away – could he not see, did he not care? – while he stayed behind to look after what mattered. The roads were crowded with refugees, poor people with their babies and belongings, we had trouble getting through, they were desperate, the rich shoved them aside, we saw carts upturned in the ditches. At that time I was still telling my mother not to worry, pray for the French, I said, they are fighting for the rights of humanity, but ourselves all we wanted was to be somewhere quiet, and Heinse was with us, as companion and accomplice. Heinse, philhellene, you know, author of *Ardinghello and the Isles of the Blessed*, man and woman created he them, naked, dancing the Crane Dance, labyrinthine, ecstatic, under the sun, under the vast white moon, the salt-swell phosphorescent, they sang and danced the dance of the resurrected flesh. He made a book of this and sent it forth, it was his bread upon the waters, food and message, we fed on it, Father Heinse, we called him, and he viewed us benignly like children who are drawing nearer and nearer to what they know they should not do and know they will, as soon as they are let. And so it came about and he smiled on us next morning and went his ways, leaving us in possession, in the living gift of it, never to be taken from us, it was inalienably ours, we made it mouth on mouth, we blew the holy spirit of it deep into one another's heart and lungs and soul through all the ways of the blood, she is dead, I am

175

mad, but it lives and when she comes to me in these short summer nights, slips in beside me as she did that first night over there in Westphalia, I tell her again, heart's love, it was so and is so, ungainsayable, and will be till I join you on the far side of Acheron and we are together and are both beyond harming any more.

Communicating this and much else to me, suddenly fatigue came over him, a hopelessness, and he halted and became very anxious and asked where am I and how will I get back into the care of the Holy Maiden Lotte, having no living daughter of my own? It was twilight, the swallows roosting, the swifts still circling very high, the first bats, their velocity and last-split-second evasions. I told him not to worry, we'll go now, we'll take a lamp. Slowly we made our way, so lovely the dusk, star after star, singly and in shapes, becoming visible. The path was clear but I felt his anxiety. Now and then he clutched at my arm, which he has never done before. Ah, your Reverence, he said, I burden you and all my friends and relations with my past. When I halted to light the lamp he looked at me in wonder. You do not fear what you might attract? he asked. Only moths came. It's true their compulsion was distressing. We continued on our way and he resumed his mutterings, too low and fast for me to catch the usual meanings of the words but, as often before, I felt that I understood the tones of voice and subsong of his deeply foreign language and that he knew I did and was glad of that and expected it of me. We were soon home. Lotte was there on the landing of his spiral staircase, which was lit. He doffed his disreputable hat to her. I never saw love and reverence so simply and wholly expressed. I waved to her, she answered. So I set off for my tower, hastening, carrying in my head the undercurrent and burden of his hurried account. I knew that he wished to have me as rememberer, as witness, as imaginer to the very limits of my poor ability. Speaking, he held me to my commission by his lips and his eyes. All this I have written down, fast as I could, I took dictation from his muttering lips or eavesdropped when he sank into soliloquy, I ingested it, I was scribe and feeling re-incarnation, theirs, the thing of their doing, fit to be set as a constellation in the winter sky, for lovers and all believers in love despite and still to get their bearings by and pledge themselves again. I got it down on paper before first light, fast as I could, in fear that the voices, his and mine, would be overwhelmed by birdsong and that his speech, my script, would sparkle only very briefly and fade away then under the sun like the morning dew.

10

As I left him today he gave me this manuscript and made a motion with his right hand that I took to mean I was at liberty to copy it. Back here in my garden house by lamplight and the moths knocking gently at the window, I will. His script, so flowing and beautiful, mine a poor fist. No matter. I think that here and now my life is more fortunate than it has ever been or will be again.

Bordeaux, 8 May 1802.
After we parted – two years ago today – I was on my own and I knew at once that is how it would be for the rest of my time this side of Charon's river. I had friends still and I can honestly say I loved them and they showed me with many acts of kindness that they loved me. But I was on my own. To make what is called a living I did the only thing I knew how which was to educate other people's children. I always got on well with children. The only child I had of my own died of smallpox aged one year, nine weeks and six days, and I never saw her anyway. I arrived in Frankfurt trailing not clouds of glory but that scandal. She was called Louise Agnese. I have

worked out since that when she died I was in Cassel again
with Susette on our way back to Frankfurt after Westphalia.
Stäudlin drowned himself in the Rhein around that time too.
It was weeks before I learned of either death. When we got
back to Frankfurt, Gontard was away in Nuremberg, so we
were allowed a while longer to live in something like joyous
freedom. Heinse visited, smiled on us. Then for a further year
and a half we continued under the same roof. Lovers know
what they want but, instead of it, we were often obliged to
stand at opposite sides of a room with a multitude of loveless
people shouting into one another's unlovely faces between us.
I remember the noise – and also the mirrors, the infinite
reproduction of what you could scarcely bear one glance of.
After that period of what we would look back on as the gods'
indulgence – we had hours of every day together – there
came the last act, the end-game, during which I had to walk
three hours for the possibility of a glimpse of her and the
touch of her fingertips. We lived in plans, arrangements,
disappointments, breathlessness. We learned that the state of
constant anxious longing is at length not bearable. We never
loved less, still don't, but she said, and I saw it, that it was
killing her. And we agreed that I had to make a living. And
like none other, she believed there was a poetry in me, in the
pen in my hand, like none other. My belief was that, as in the
making of a longed-for child, it would come, if at all, of us
both. When I smuggled the second volume of *Hyperion* into
her possession – she saw me passing below her window as
arranged and saw also that I was holding a book and guessed
what that book might be – I reminded her that she was
comrade and co-worker in it, and asked her to forgive me that
on a point of not-quite agreement I had in the end taken my
way against hers and made Diotima die. Then the distances
got greater – Stuttgart, Nürtingen, Hauptwyl, and now here
– further and further apart and no letters. Every so often we

heard of one another. In Stuttgart, living with the Landauers, teaching their children, I saw what a family might be like. Also, with Christian I could talk about her. In the midst of those good and loving people I was on my own. Since the day I quitted my employment with the banker I have been walking further and further, deeper and deeper, into being on my own. In January last year I set off to teach the two adolescent daughters of another business man under the Alps. That winter, for all the kindness of my friends, I had been mortally agitated and several times, even in the midst of laughter and easy conversation, icy cold around the heart. I remember the look Christian gave me when I told him I felt a great need of peace and quiet. He might have been hurt that his loving hospitality had not helped. But his look was of sorrow and pity. You are thirty years old, it said. Too young to be wanting peace and quiet. Forgive me, I said. That winter I often asked forgiveness of people I loved. But from Stuttgart Christian and another three of them walked with me in the brief wintry light as far as Tübingen. And there too I met friends who showed me – with joy for me – a favourable review of that second volume of *Hyperion*. Now writing of this, the amity, the encouragement, I shake my head over the young man who could not be helped. Climbing next day alone into the defencelessness of the high Alb, seeing few travellers and those of the kind who look fated to walk exposed under the empty heavens for ever, greeting them as my similars and passing on, I felt glad of my good boots and the strength of my legs. The soul in me might flutter timorously and peer out through my eye-holes at what she would have to contend with next, but the frame she housed in was by now lean and fit and inured to cold and striding. On that high road, crossing another watershed, I felt my calling, it and I were closing the gap between us. At Sigmaringen I took the coach, dozed and wondered for twelve hours, made no conversation, and reaching Überlingen looked across the water to the mountains, the day's last sun just leaving them for another night under the implacably freezing brilliant constellations. So be it, I said: the cold, my loneliness, my being shown without mercy what I have to do in the time allowed. That crossing of the water into the mountains seemed to me conclusive. I did the rest of the way, with one night in Konstanz, on foot easily and in a steadiness of the spirit. It was a hospitable house I arrived at and I liked my new employer and my pupils. Dog-tired, I lay awake for a while listening to waters hurrying below my window. Next morning at first light I looked down into the garden and saw the stream and the poplars and willows through which it flowed. I dressed and let myself out and climbed a small hill that is behind the house and saw the summits and the rosy fingers of dawn herself playing over them and those vast mountains were stepping down out of the very heavens, out of the blue, down and down, nearer and nearer, to the threshold of my life. No sooner arrived, I was granted proximity. I thought now, for a while at least, I will see things close up, there will be little clothing between us, it will be shocking as ice, and the flames of sunrise and sunset upon these phenomena will themselves be as cold as the never unfreezing snow. And I turned and lifted up my eyes to those close remote mountains on the day, 23 February, my employer came to me in the garden and told me that peace had been agreed in Lunéville. I was like a child, bashful in my joy, I showed the tears of it only to the white summits. Their descent that morning felt like the coming of a demand upon me, a commission. Who else, if not you? So with very great difficulty over the following weeks I discovered the poem that was in me to be written about the peace. Pretty soon then my employer informed me with, I think, sincere regret that due to circumstances beyond his control he had no further need of my services but he would be more than happy to write me a reference for whichever house-tutorship I moved to next, and this he duly did and a good one it was. I was three months under the Alps. In the boat to Lindau I looked back continually at the flames of daybreak over the high snow-lands and then, turning my face to my own country and beginning the walk from Lindau along roads whose accompanying trees, the cherry, the plum, the pear, the apple, were snowy with blossom, I measured the long lines of elegy, their coursing onwards, their toppling over, their lovely sinuous flow, their varying pace and pitch and tone, in through the soles of my boots to the making heart and soul and brain and lips of me, I walked the many couplets into being, yard by yard. I with no home to go to, no hearth, no wife and child, no abiding stay, I who in the coming winter, to get a living, once more would be driven abroad, wrote 'Homecoming', and was glad of it. In much the same way, the morning I learned of Lunéville I saw peace stepping down out of the mountains into the space vacated by revolution and war and desiring a new community there of free and equal citizens and I did as I was required to do and fashioned a house and home for it, line by line and with much labour and was glad. Did I simply disregard the fact that Bonaparte was dictator in France by then and everyone knew that his and all the other nations would use the peace to make their citizens ready to resume the war? As though I put my head in my hands and close my eyes and wish and believe that if I wish hard enough it will be there, a better humanity, and I will be at home in it, in a country I need not be ashamed of, when I uncover my face and look around me. I was home all summer, unhappy, wrote to Schiller and other influential persons asking might they enable me into a job lecturing on Greek literature in Jena, but they did not answer. Instead came an offer of another house-tutorship, in Bordeaux this time, my employer would be Consul Meyer, from Hamburg. Yesterday, after he had told me that very

regrettably he would have no further need of my services but
would, of course and with pleasure, write me a reference (and
it would be a good one) for my next appointment as house-
tutor wherever that might be, I walked out to the Bec
d'Ambès where the Garonne and the Dordogne come
together and, wide as a sea, set towards the ocean. That
promontory is the farthest she and I have ever been apart and
tomorrow I will present myself at the bureau of the
Commissariat-Géneral de Police de Bordeaux for a pass to
make my way back to Strasbourg. But for all the nearer I will
get to her on foot in that direction I might just as well – and
the fancy is quite attractive – go as flotsam on the married
rivers into the Atlantic. As last year ended the thought of going
abroad again became unendurable. I wanted a homeland, to
have a living and be useful in, and I saw that my countrymen
had no use for me. I felt my loneliness become a state of exile.
I wrote to Casimir – my dangerous kindred spirit – that I was
full of farewell. I wrote to Karl that it would be better for me
to be outside. If now I were in Homburg and woke with the
singing birds and left the day's first footprints across the
meadow's lustrous dew and greeted the earliest workers in the
fields and vineyards and stood before the line of poplars till
her window opened, still I'd be outside, still I'd be in exile, still
I'd be full of farewell. I had the colloquy the mad have in their
heads. I spoke my watchword – 'Whatever happens, make it a
blessing!' I answered, This is no life, I answered, This is your
only life, I answered, 'Whatever happens, make it a blessing,
turn it to joy!' And I wept, oh how I wept! Then footslogged
off upstream against my river that December had overburdened
with cadavers and deracinated lovely trees. Deep snow after
Freudenstadt, deeper crossing the Kniebis Pass, now and then
the snow-capped tops of shrines to Christopher or the Virgin
who might save and of crosses raised to travellers whom they
didn't. I was sole on that high road, I had wrapped my face

and left my eyes the necessary slit. Then on the west slopes some warmth stole back into me and wrapped me in her arms. Here in the Consul's warm spring garden, saying to my soul, Have courage, I review small broken passages of journeys, I see myself but cannot quite place myself, I seem to be looking down on me from a height and am a creature making all the speed it can, infinitely slowly through interminable forests that do not cover the bare-rock frozen-snow mountains even to the waist and the road unrolls before me and disappears behind me. Where I crossed the big lake last year in spring I saw the Rhine in it, of it, and moving fast as an identity through it. There is something in that mix and self, that insistence on individual purpose, calling, shape that I have sought to understand and hold on to and must, in the coming days on the roads again, for there's a whispering in me, like a beginning of waters underground, that says let go, dissolve, tiny struggling self, let go. I stood on the bridge at Kehl for a while and bowed my head over the tawny river. I suppose there must have been other humans there, crossing, halting, musing, but I see only the one, he is face down over a breadth and depth and hurry that clarifies him into what he is: a speck, alive. So I crossed into France, where Bonaparte was busy making himself Consul for life. But the border police addressed me as Citoyen and when they asked me my profession I replied *Homme de lettres.*

11

This morning I went to see Prof. Conz, to apologize for my flight from Homburg. I was anxious, he was genial. My dear boy… He had already heard from his friend and colleague, the Director of the Court Library, who appreciated my 'gracious note of apology', he said. In a rush then, having told nobody before, I related my encounter with the young woman in the Haingasse. When it was finished he said nothing, only looked at me and I at him. There was a sudden chill in the cosy room. The French would say, 'Un ange passe'. But it felt more like a shade from Hades flitting by. (NB: I have not made enough of this: H. lives and breathes and has his being a stone's throw away from Prof. Conz's rooms. Beyond this town people who have read or heard of him do quite often suppose that he is long since dead. But I visit him, walk and converse with him, know him to be intensely alive. Still I have often felt him to be one whom Charon ferries to and fro, never even asking to see his passport.) Then the Professor heaved a great sigh through his bulk and said, My young friend, you did well. In the Library with my courteous colleague you would have learned a few things no doubt, but remotely. He took up his post some years after our poet's removal, never knew him, only knew *of* him. Through that young mother in the Haingasse, through her *récit*, you touched the life, which in that particular scene is quite unbearable. Again he fell silent, became absent, I imagined he might be back in 1790 and his Euripides classes, and H. among his pupils and the most agreeable to contemplate. With a deep shudder then he resumed his place in present time face to face with me. I hear you went forth like a journeyman, he said. To learn. I should have enjoyed your boats, but I was never much of a footslogger. Don't imagine there was ever a lean young man in me. We were always, give or take a few stone, more or less as you see us now. Sir, there's another thing I suddenly want to tell you, I said. Well...? he said, apprehensive (I thought) for both of us. Before I left, I said, I burned my *Phaethon*. I immolated it in the garden of my summer house. Having got to know him better, himself, I was writhing in shame at *the use* I had made of him. So I left my error or sin as a pile of ash and walked to come nearer into the truth of him. He looked at me with a sort of friendly pity, wonderingly. My dear boy, he said, I congratulate you. Few of your age correct themselves so soon. Many never. This emboldened me. Sir, I said, you would do me a great kindness by seizing all the copies you come across and using them in the winter months to feed your stove. I have learned how cold *he* was in winter in Homburg, he could not afford to heat his room. So please burn me a *Phaethon* whenever you can, it will be honourable to end in flames and giving warmth. Then I reached for my hat and got to my feet and thanked him from my heart and bowed. He heaved himself out of his capacious throne and opened his arms for me to be embraced. Dear boy, he said. You will never be a fat and easy man. Still there are things to be said in favour of not dying young.

★

Telling Prof. Conz about *Phaethon*, then spending an hour with H. in the Zimmers' garden (he was very agitated, talked incessantly aside in an undertone with his devils, bowed and scraped towards me and lifted up his face as though asking could I or any other living fellow-human give him peace?) and coming back here to my summer house, I felt not any regret, the thing deserved extinction in the fire, but a sort of grief at failure, the commission not carried out, and that I am being asked to try again. I *know* quite a lot. I have friendly dealings with half a dozen men who knew him before she died and he went mad and know him still but rather as though he were death-in-life, severed, ghostly, unspeakable. But I, born into the gap between her death and his committal to the clinic and the tower, am I not called upon peculiarly to do him justice? And have I not, perhaps unknowingly, begun to put a life of him together – yes, by talking to the surviving comrades of his youth, but also, and more, by going over the ground itself, by journeying to where he was a child and where he was a lover? I am already thinking I might give up my 'studies'. I had already decided next year to walk via Hauptwyl through the holy places of the Swiss insurrection and the making of their democracy and over the Gotthard into Italy. Well, perhaps I shall. But perhaps my first duty would be to cross the Kniebis Pass and the valley of the Rhine to Strasbourg and Bordeaux, and from Bordeaux back again to the holy places of his homecoming? Journeymen – some walk seven years, so I have heard. For every serious calling there is so much to learn. Meanwhile...

*

I was interrupted by a messenger from Prof. Conz, with a package, the gift of a book. It is a copy of H.'s *Tragedies of Sophocles*, published by Wilmans in Frankfurt in the year I was born. And a note with it: My dear boy, I bought this for a friend. He died before I could give it to him. It has been on my shelves ever since but because it was for my friend I have never wanted to part with it, though of course I have a copy of my own. Now I should like you to have it. K. P. C.

*

I am a believer in signs. That market trader who gave me *Hyperion*. And this messenger coming to me from Professor Conz with the gift of *Oedipus* and *Antigone*. Encouragements. So... H. is not, never was, Phaethon, nor Icarus either for that matter. He did not steal the chariot of his father the Sun God nor did his father, Daedalus, make him a pair of wings. He did not fly too close to the sun, melt the wax of those wings and fall into the sea, nor did his father blast him out of the sky to save humanity from extinction in fire. He had two fathers, knew nothing of the first and very little of the second, if they affected his life then chiefly by their absence. He was not overweening nor a threat to his fellow-humans, nor is he either now. But the hero of his novel on which he laboured for years and could not finish till he fell in love with his own Diotima (the needed rush of reality) and can't leave go of even now (as the Greeks again fight for their freedom) but often reads aloud from, that hero is called Hyperion, a sun god, and in childhood his mentor, Adamas, took him to Delos and climbed the marble steps of Cynthus with him and seized his hand, lifted it to the sun and said, Be like him! And in half a dozen of his poems that I have read, the sun is the maker and giver of light and life. In the loveliest, Diotima becomes almost a sister of the sun – without him, without her, no life fit to be seen is possible. In the great crisis of that life, his homecoming out of France, some of the friends he so distressed arriving among them, supposed he had walked too long in too hot a sun and his mania was 'only' that: sunstroke. So in the imagery at the heart of it my *Phaethon* was not wholly false. Things I have learned since its publication have even lent it a tad more truth. But it was false and only fit for burning on account of its vapid *elevation*. The giant Antaeus drew his strength out of the earth and was invincible only so long as he kept contact with it. My *Phaethon* drifted up and away like a swelling hot-air balloon amid a rant of tinny trumpets. Contrary to what I said in Frankfurt, I *do* want to be a chronicler – to witness and to chronicle – but to write a *Vita*, to chronicle a life lived mythically, the hero conscious of living his own myth, in the here and now in all the din and fret and busyness, the life of a hero with laughable idiosyncrasies, a life in folly and error and making amends and small and grave failures, and faith and the loss of it, and hope and the loss of it, and love and hate, humility and vanity. H. is remembered in the Seminary as appearing in Hall with the grace and beauty of Apollo – also for tearing the cap from the head of a junior student who had not shown the proper respect and doffed it himself. The arrangements to commit adultery with the wife of a Frankfurt banker belong in this *Life*, in the living heart of it, the shame and rage and the day-by-day abrasion of love by thwarting, secrecy, fear. This man who stood his ground under God's lightnings was afraid of his own mother who sat on his inheritance like an anxious spider and stinted him. His letters to her from the tower are grisly masterpieces of a thorough alienation (he has read me one or two with *relish*). He is a great poet, like none other, among my country's very best, and poetry is won in struggle not just against the times and their mores and their politics but also against the self, the failure of the will, frivolity, dishonesty, fatigue, and (in his case desperately) against the more or less always constant threat or temptation of dissolution and disintegration. Schwab mentioned to me only the other week, almost in passing, as though it were very well known, that every day H. faced the fact of his immense *destructibility*. This master of ancient and complex forms knew how close he was to not being able to hold *himself* together. The poet struggles to make of the stuff of his life a *Vita*, a myth, a chronicle laced with the figurative, one that will hold together beyond his death and be a present help in the lives of others. The way to that success is certainly not through a sifting out from the lived life of all that is mundane, tasteless, distasteful, dirty, broken and petty. The Life I write cannot omit close study of how he made a living. The *conditions* of life are in large measure the stuff the poems are made of. They do not need to be the *subject* of the finished thing, nor even very visible in it. But poems arise in the lived life, and they draw their strength, their power to touch other people, by continuing in it, by being, so to speak, up to the knees or the neck in it. Poetry is not an act of catharsis of poet or reader or listener. It will not cleanse you of the muck of being human. It will show you living in self and time and mores and politics and not (never!) triumphant over them but surviving in them. That's the triumph: surviving long enough to have your say. I begin to believe I could write his life in accordance with that understanding of biography.

*

H.'s homecoming in the summer of 1802

(NB: this will want revising once I have gone over the ground on my own two feet.)

Schwab — already wondering about a brief biography to accompany or follow the publication of the poems — tells me that H. wrote to his mother from Lyons en route for Bordeaux; again as soon as he arrived; and a third and final time on Good Friday (16 April). In that last letter, Schwab says, there was nothing unduly alarming. He spoke of his need, after so many trials, to preserve and hold himself steady; but the family were used to that. The next sign of life was the delivery of his trunk to Nürtingen around the middle of June. It is twenty years ago and the hero of this story is still alive and in good physical health. But he will never be a source of trustworthy factual information about his homecoming from Bordeaux in the early summer of the year 1802. How strange that is. And soon after that arrival he crossed a frontier into a land and a dwelling place from where, however long he lives, he will never be able (or willing?) to give a plain account of his own life. And yet and still he has the power of speech in his native German and in French too and Italian, in Latin and in his beloved ancient Greek, and in a mix of all those and more. And courteously in the tower he will go to his lectern and in a clear and flowing hand write verses that scan and rhyme and have a haunting beauty.

And there Schwab is and here I am even before his death wanting to gather the materials of a Life, wanting to write it. And this will go on beyond his death and beyond the deaths of those living now who remember him as a child, a scholar, a writer, and see and love him still on this side of the caesura, the rift through his life, after which he remembered things as the shades in Hades do and spoke in tongues and was closed off and shut in and few could get close to him and then only in brief slants of light like sun through cloud or deep black forest and briefly understood and could answer in his tongue. The person who knew him best, of course, and conversed in that foreign tongue with him whenever they were alone, is the person who loved him best, and she is dead.

The trunk, dispatched from Bordeaux and entering Germany via Strasbourg and across the Rhine, arrived in Nürtingen before its owner did. The mother opened it. But the first anybody knew of its owner's whereabouts was his appearance among his friends in Stuttgart. I walked there last week and called on one of them, Matthisson. He said, Schwab's been already but I don't mind telling you as well. In truth, he looked very uneasy, not at all, despite his exquisite hands, nails and necktie, his usual suave self. I was sitting here, he said, behind this desk, as I am now, and the door opened, as it did a moment ago when you knocked and I called to you to come in, but he didn't knock, he came in unbidden and gave me no greeting, nor did I him, not knowing who he was, and he stood there for a while, he was pale as death, all skin and bone, with long hair and a beard, his eyes cavernous and wild, in the clothes of a beggar man, and he stood there and said nothing. I rose to my feet, in terror, and at that he strode from the door, leaned over the desk — I remember his hideous long fingernails — and close to my face in a tone that seemed risen out of an echoing sepulchre he said the one word: Hölderlin. And with that he vanished. I heard later that he had appeared similarly to another friend – Haug perhaps – and to him managed to convey that he had been attacked on the road and robbed. Matthisson fell silent and we looked at one another wonderingly. I found nothing to say. Soon I made to leave. He stood up, and shaking my hand and opening the door for me and as I thanked him with all my heart for his account, he said, Something else occurs to me, from further back, from a happier time, end of June 1793. I was on my way home to Switzerland and, with Neuffer and Stäudlin, spent an afternoon with H. in the Seminary. He was becoming known, had begun *Hyperion*, Stäudlin was publishing him in his *Musenalmanach*. France was Jacobin by then and the mood among the seminarists was revolutionary. H. read us his hymn 'To the Spirit of Boldness'. I, nine years his senior and already the agreeable travelling-companion of Princess Luise of Anhalt-Dessau, was moved to tears by it, by him, so youthful, so beautiful to see, and there in high-flown verse praising and summoning up boldness to be the comrade of all who wanted the end of venal power and instead of it for all the earth's people the right to life, liberty and the pursuit of happiness. Two years previously he had done the pilgrimage to the sites of Swiss independence and democracy. He seemed to me that summer afternoon, declaiming his poem, to be the risen hope of our generation against all the centuries of stupidity and wrong. I crossed the room, embraced him, pressed him against my heart. – There on his threshold at the open door, I liked this man who could reach back nearly thirty years into a self still recognizable as his own. Yes, I said, a fortnight later he was with Hegel and Schelling and scores of other young men and women in a field just across the river, in full view of the Elders and Authorities, celebrating Bastille Day with the setting up of a liberty tree and the singing of the Marseillaise in a translation said to be by Schelling. We grew up into disappointment, said Matthisson. Yes, I answered. And *we* were born into it.

From Stuttgart H. walked to Nürtingen, home. Lately, dwelling so much on his homecoming from Bordeaux, I've scarcely been able to imagine him *walking*. I see him hastening, actually running. Even now in the Zimmers' orchard and garden, continually coming to the limit and turning back again, he never paces, he never strolls, it is always a hectic hurrying to and fro, to and fro, his only pauses being to tear out grass. Only with me on the way to the summer house and in the rough garden there, have I seen him – such gladness I had seeing this!– measure his steps with mine so that we walk for all the world like two people in conversation, attending, answering, even occasionally halting, to muse aloud. Several nights lately, on the borders of sleep, I have had a nightmare vision of him leaving the Consul's house *at a run*, in a mad haste to cross France and be nearer to Diotima. And so I think of him running from Matthisson's to Haug's and from there out of town, into the fields, towards home. I followed him, but slowly. The family's shock at his appearance very soon became terror when he discovered that his mother, opening his trunk, had not only taken out things needing washing or mending, as any mother might, but she had also rooted around in it and discovered what is always described as 'a secret container' and she opened that too and found in it Susette Gontard's letters to her son and read enough of them for the concealed truth to become clear. His rage was terrible and to escape it she, his widowed sister Heinrike and the servant girl ran out into the street. So the mother's grief and shame became public and if neighbours and strangers never quite knew what the matter was they saw in his behaviour not just that he was mad but also that she had done him some primitively cruel wrong. Taking my time, I arrived at that house in the market place. It was late afternoon, vespers, people were coming in from the fields, the orchards and the vineyards. Watching the door, I felt the scene of twenty years ago might play itself again, the son home from the far western coast, in rags and raving, cursing and threatening the shrunken mother, and a small crowd gathering, like a chorus in Sophocles, to take it all in, witness it, speak of it down the generations thereafter, the lost son, clutching a bundle to his heart, turning back into the fields at a run, and still having more and worse to learn.

Susette Gontard died on 22 June. She had been sick for ten days after nursing her four children safe through scarlet fever and catching it herself. But what killed her was most likely consumption, which she was liable to and had suffered from in the last winter. Sinclair, thinking H. still in Bordeaux, sent the news to him at Landauer's house in Stuttgart, to forward, but in flight from Nürtingen he was living there, his kind host handed him the letter. A few days later he fled again, from that hospitable house where his grief was understood, back home to the mother.

Uhland urges me to go and visit Ebel in Zürich. It was Ebel who arranged the job in Frankfurt. He was a friend of the family, of Susette at least. He decamped to Paris before H. got there because his translation of Sieyè's *Que'est-ce que le Tiers-État?* had just been published and he feared imprisonment if he stayed in Frankfurt. He had mixed feelings about the Revolution in its practice but stayed in Paris at the heart of it for five or six years. He was back in Frankfurt as Susette's doctor, at her bedside when she died. 'A good man, you'll like him, he'll tell you things.' Uhland, and he's not the only one, seems not to expect me to serve my time in the Seminary.

★

Some quotations from H.'s *Oedipus*

THE PRIEST.   Death
She spots in beakers of the fruitful earth,
In herds and flocks and in the unborn births
Of women, and fire from inside
The plague god brings and empties Cadmus' house
And Hell grows rich with sighs and howling.

★

TIRESIAS.   You, having seen, don't see what you are at
In evil, where you live, with what you house.
Do you know where you are from? You are in secret
Detestable to your own kind below
The earth and here above...

★

OEDIPUS. It must not be that I, on signs like these,
Should not uncover what blood I am of.

JOCASTA. By gods, do not. If you're chary of life
Then do not search. I have sickened enough.

★

MESSENGER.   Thereupon the sight was terrible.
The golden needles ornamenting her
He tore them from her dress and opened them
And stabbed into the bright of his eyes and said
This thereabouts: it was to not see her,
And not what he was suffering and what bad he had
                                        done

So that in darkness in the future that would be
How he saw others whom he must not see
And those that he was known to, unbeknownst.
And so in glee he stabbed, often, not one time,
Holding the lids up, and the bloody apples
Of the eyes dyed him his beard and not in drops
As though spilled from a murder ran but blackly
Spilled the blood was, pelted down.
It issued from a couple, not a sole evil,
An evil got together by man and wife.

First: the language is very removed from the usual. It is uniquely his and I am in a better position than most to understand it and love it because I have spent many hours with him and listened very closely to his speech.

Second: Reading his notes on *Oedipus the King*, which are opaque to me in many places, I did grasp this, again perhaps because I have spent so much time with him, he seems to trust me and I have attended as closely as I can: that in H.'s reading of the play Oedipus' sin consists less in murdering his father and marrying his mother than in helplessly, compulsively, manically rooting out and bringing into the light and uttering things too frightful to be seen or said. The knowing herdsman warns him off, 'Unlucky man, why, what do you want to know?', as does his wife-mother Jocasta (who also by then knows). But he is compelled to continue, into that which is unspeakable. The Messenger, recounting the catastrophe, still cannot utter the things welling forth from Oedipus himself: 'He speaks/Unholinesses I am not allowed to say.' In the end, blind Tiresias foresees all, and Oedipus sees too much. He goes 'blind from seeing'. The line I came across among the sheaves of poems H. let me look through (a line I lifted for my *Phaethon*), 'King Oedipus has an eye too many perhaps', says just that. And the audience likewise see too much when the great doors are opened and he appears with his eyes put out. Then, as Creon says, he is not fit to be seen by the sun. The compulsion in H.'s own poetry is not to say things which are unholy but rather to say things so truthfully and beautifully that their holiness is revealed and it is not bearable. That degree of vision, of seeing, still shimmers, to most readers harmlessly, through the lattice of the rhyming quatrains he writes in his tower, to oblige or get rid of the sightseers.

★

Late afternoon today on impulse I called and seeing nobody climbed the spiral staircase as Miss Lotte has said I may. I paused on the landing, the door was open. They were sitting face to face across his table and turned their looks towards me when they heard my step. She was holding his left hand steady in hers over a white towel and with the clippers in her right cutting his fingernails. And so the scene paused and their faces were turned my way. His feet were bare, his trousers rolled up to the knees and there was a copper bowl of soapy water close by. She had been washing his feet and clipping his toenails. The two faces, so very different, both entirely untroubled by my appearance, if I close my eyes I see them still and pray I always shall. Such composure, goodwill, beauty, it would steady any witness all his life long.

★

Uhland tells me that Sinclair, having got H. the sinecure in the Landgraf's library, wrote half a dozen times to his mother to reassure her that he was well. In S.'s view – shared, he said, by several other men who encountered him in Homburg – H.'s 'madness' was no such thing but a way of expressing and conducting himself, which for very good reasons he had

adopted and sustained. So 'an antic disposition', like Hamlet's.
By 'for very good reasons' S. seems to have meant that H.
wished to conceal his 'real' life as an active revolutionary. This,
in Uhland's opinion, has more to do with S. and *his*
involvement in plotting an uprising in Württemberg, than
with H. who by then (August 1804) would have been quite
incapable of such adventures even had he still felt drawn to
them. Several people recall him at this time continually
shouting, 'You won't make me a Jacobin! Away with all the
Jacobins! Vive le roi!' A Württemberg court-enforcer and three
soldiers came to arrest Sinclair at 2 in the morning, 26
February the following year. When S. protested, they left; but
came back for him at 10 and a crowd of about 100 gathered
at his door to watch him being carried off.

★

Since Uhland told me that I've been thinking more about
incarceration. I remembered Schubart, whom H., just beginning
to write, venerated, and who, when they met in 1789, had done
ten years in the Aspberg for offending Duke Karl Eugen.
Schiller would have suffered the same (for *The Robbers*) had he
not fled the country. So H.'s unwillingness to be thought a
Jacobin in Homburg comes most likely from a dread that for
his politics the authorities would put him away. Sinclair's arrest
will have compounded that foreboding. And evicted for being
disruptive from the room in the Neugasse that had a view south
over Frankfurt, he was moved to the room in the Haingasse that
had no view at all. Followed the realized terror itself, his forcible
transportation to the clinic. The authorities excused him his
supposed politics on the grounds that he was mad. Then put
him away for being mad. And the tower after that? The
Zimmers are good people, not jailors, but it was a while before
he could believe in their goodness.

*

Today, Sunday, while faintly from the town to me here at my table in the garden the bells were ringing (I love them at a distance) – out of a deep thought of him I woke and saw him, really and very close, rounding the hill through the trees into the opening, led by Miss Lotte, holding tight to her right arm with his left hand. This locus already so often blessed will be in me now like an illumination in an ancient holy book. I want to live long, to harbour it in my innermost treasury, close my eyes and consult it whenever I am in need. There they stood, smiling at having surprised me. He looked older. I bade them be seated, I hurried to my tower room to fetch the beakers, the jug of cold elderflower, some cinnamon biscuits. When I returned they were sitting quietly side by side, the view of the Neckar before them. I served them, sat down facing them, could think of nothing adequate to say. Then Miss Lotte said, We came here once with Mother and Father, all of us, when I was very small. I think nobody lived here at that time, not even in summer. How strange to be here now. How lucky I am. – I'm going to Italy, I said. I shall defer the study of Theology for the afterlife. Till this very moment I didn't know for sure but now I do and you are the first to know. In fact I shan't tell anyone else. I will write you letters, if I may. Both nodded. Then H. said, This holy maid and I have a longer journey ahead of us. I dreamed it and told her of it as we walked to visit you. Blind Oedipus arrives there with his faithful daughter. A local man extols the beauties of the place when she asks where they have come. In our tongue this is how he would have said it. And H. began to speak, softly, in an undertone, so that Miss Lotte and I leaned close like children rapt and wanting to learn. He murmured:

Famous for horses, there is none
More beautiful on earth
Than this place you have come to, strangers
Bright Colonus where
The many nightingales sing loud and clear
Amid deep greenery and under the wine-dark
Berried ivy, down
The untrodden ways that no storms shake
Nor fierce sun burns
The god comes, Dionysus comes
For revelry
With the undying
The ever-fostering nymphs.

The Greek came back to me, my got-by-heart, that I took
from my teachers for I knew it would help, I heard it
shadowing my mother tongue and I rejoiced.

Here in the dew of heaven
Day upon day narcissi thrive
Whose clustering beauty
The goddesses have always worn for crowns
With the golden shining crocuses and never
Do the unsleeping streams
Of Cephissus dwindle but they roam
For pasture and every day
With undefiled waters
Over the swelling land
Give easy birth. The Muses
Love to dance here and the golden-
Reined Aphrodite rides...

And there he halted, weeping. Cephissus, he murmured, loveliest of the unspoilt streams. Help me there, Holy Maiden, and all will be well again. She looked at him with love and pity, patted his hand. Come, sir, she said. Father and Mother will be worried. We take a walk together, as a family, after our midday meal.

★

The blue necklace I found – that came out of the river – I will give it to Miss Lotte.

12

Yes, the dead walk who were withheld their due in life, they walk still hungering and thirsting, but those they loved and who loved them, the living left trying to live without them, they walk, they like the restless dead are restless and they walk. I leave the house and my bewildered mother and my widowed sister in it, I leave early and go into the fields, I walk and walk and have the makings of poems in my head that are not strong enough to help me in living with the fact that you are dead. Oh we lived without, we lived two years and many miles apart and utterly without, but this is lonelier still, this fact to consort with, that you are dead. Stay in earshot, love, walk the earth, come nearer, listen, answer, however soft your murmuring I will hear and understand. Come closer, my dearest, walk beside me, simulate the decorous strolls in parks and garden we were once permitted. Lovers dissevered by death have as much to tell one another as they ever did and if you are silent now, in the daylight, I will still believe that our silences are as eloquent as they always were. I walked to Schelling's, I didn't know I was going there or anywhere else for that matter, I crossed another field and there I was, miles from home, in Klein Murrhardt, at his window. A man seeing himself reflected in a window pane will often be greatly affeared. Often I have sat with just a candle for company and looked out through the window and seen myself looking in. I would not risk it now – sit there looking at myself– not now that I am on the edge of going *very* over, into somewhere I shan't be able to claw myself back from. But it was a sunny day and looking in I saw myself reflected in the face of the *Wunderkind* who everyone said would do well and he has not disappointed, he looked up from his writing and I saw my reflection in his face. I believe there are no mirrors in monasteries and nunneries. But if I keep my eyes down in a skulking or modest or terrified fashion in the outside world that is because all the humans I encounter lately have mirrors where you might expect faces. Some cats and dogs and horses have gone the same way. So in the face of my former friend who is doing well I see that I am as frightening as I am frightened. I ask: were you still alive in the usual understanding of the word would you be frightened of my face as everyone else is nowadays and not just my face but the face is where the self is most evident, I should say, in the eyes and the mouth especially, would you back away and only slowly recognize me and your terror turn to a sorrow beyond telling? I answer: I would not look like this if you still lived and moved between heaven and earth as other mortals do. You would quieten me, my lips and tongue would begin to form the language you and I spoke together even in hostile company. My former comrade Schelling did soon know me and though he couldn't keep his eyes off me, the whole forked creature that I am from head to toe, he was courteous, more than that, I felt he felt pity, which very nearly became too much for me, too touching, too much the truth. I would have liked to tell him of my journeys, the winter and the summer journeys, how cold I was at times in bed high in the snow, how hot at others on the long straight ways that had no trees and I having only my pilgrim's hat between my busy head and the sun. One day I met Apollo, he strode towards me down such a track, when he was close I stepped aside and doffed my hat, he halted a moment and regarded me, so close I saw only the light and no shape of him, the light went through my eyes like Jocasta's needles, then he turned away and sauntered on and that much I could see, the dimming shadow of him proceeding on its way. Fire and ice. Have I not always swung between them as between two equally harmful poles? I don't think the snows of the Auvergne or even meeting Apollo on a track through fields somewhere near Lyon made it all that much worse. Possibly I see even better since the icicles or the red-hot needles were pushed into my heart and brain. But, I grant you, it is the sort of seeing that will not help me in my everyday dealings with my fellow human beings. In fact such everyday dealings are over now and were, if I'm honest, not often very satisfactory. Was it only an interlude with you, a sort of intermission or reprieve the gods granted me on your account? My Diotima begged my Hyperion to be calmer for her sake. As well ask fire to cool your brow. She parched when he sought death instead of her. Was I never quiet? All the tranquillity we had I think of now as magically encircled, the lease we negotiated on it brief and the cost our ruin. And now the aftermath is not a compensation. When I tell you perhaps I see better now it is that the clothing, the veil, the mist between me and things-not-me some days for some hours seems to have been entirely removed. Then I see things in their simplicity, their holiness, and, trying to say them, I have to choose my words very carefully indeed, for any wrong word, any imprecision, any less than perfect articulation of such words-for-things in a line and in the joining of lines in verse is a fearful matter, one's best never being good enough, nowhere near. I sift my muddily remembered whereabouts and bright as electrum in the sand of Pactolus shines, for example, one tree, a miraculous slim nut-tree, overhanging a source of water, or the ocean itself lies across the whole span of my vision, level, deep and incandescent. They were brighter than that, of course, sharper, closer, they terrify me, these scraps, if I try too long to see and say them adequately, the life in them, their being, is so much surer of itself than mine now is. Our love was radiant, of course, but as a quiet fire that nourished and rejuvenated us and did not consume. When let, which was not often, we undressed, remember, and bathed in it, in the pool of it which lay at the heart of our enclosed garden, the trees stood back from it in a ring, like the trees and beasts and rocks who were drawn by the singing and playing of Orpheus and gathered around the space he made, their mixed kinds all together, of many different substances and ages around the pool as though our love and our bathing there were a music and they came to listen. Is that not so, my dearest? So it is not as though I have had failure, insult, fret and a troubled mind all my thirty-three years and nothing but. On the contrary. I'm a poet who has had no need to invent alternatives to tribulation. Here on this very earth I've seen – more than seen – I've kissed, embraced, lain with, talked and laughed and slept and woken with the liveliest life that the defeated and deluded think they must postpone until they ascend into the empty mansions of heaven. Desolation now, my love, and the unhinged and random hither and thither. Life at the mercy, life a prey to, at risk of, life without, life with a rift through it, life walking in circles in search of a place of solace. And all the while knowing, conceding, even almost accepting the ancient equation: for so much joy so much sorrow, for so much living in presence the like deal in absence. On the roads I met many who struck me at first as kith and kin. But when I looked closer, halted where they halted, and saw them note my foreignness and class and yet suppose me to be suffering as they were, exposed and one way or another burdened, so that they shared bread and wine with me and wished me luck, then I was ashamed and said to myself if I had my time again I would learn more about these soldiers, for example, told to go home, however far away home is from where they happen to be when peace broke out, go home, they were told, come back when we tell you to and off they went, a hundred, two hundred, three hundred miles, with their visible and invisible hurts, go back till we want you when the fighting starts again and see what life is left you in your natal place. And the women… Trailing the long roads from or back to where they once belonged, in groups for greater safety with babes and toddlers and bewildered older ones, sharing the provisions and the care and the anxious watchfulness. By these, and pedlars, poxed and scabby loners, haloed pilgrims, quacks and holy mendicants, brawlers, whores and upright journeymen and crazed musicians I was alerted to my failing. I never stood deep enough in the muck and desperate cheerfulness and endless accidents of life. But it is too late now and I'll do what I do best in the time allowed me which will not be long. I tire very quickly, I said to my kind host, Schelling, I walk for miles turning a dozen words this way and that and swapping them for others till exhaustion conquers me and I sleepwalk back to Mother. I began to tell him of the gypsy woman I encountered I don't know where, perhaps in Gascony, the road wherever it came from and was going to was dusty white, I remember, and the air was humming with heat, and I remember I had got further into the state of a somnambule wide awake and more sharply alert than he is in the ordinary daylight and at dusk Venus appeared on a sky of quivering green, I saw her pulsing, I saw the clasping and unclasping of her brightness, and very suddenly, I remember, I was dead beat and felt I might fall over and lie face upwards by the roadside and keep my eyes wide-open on her as long as possible and drift off into the sort of sleep in which all my saints and heroes, dwellers in Hades, jostle for my particular attention, the throng of mortals and immortals as I see them lately in constellations of my own devising. It was then that I noticed the wood and bethought myself and said, You'll do better in there, and struck off at a diagonal across a stubble field, I remember, and pretty soon I saw in the dark heart of that wood a fire and from that fire came singing in a woman's voice and I was sore afraid and entranced and I said to myself as I did often on that journey, So be it then. And as I went in, the crowns of the trees flung up their rooks in a detonation of cawing and I laughed to be so very noisy in my arrival. She sat, the songstress, at her campfire on a pile of sawn logs in a dress of red and gold and black and stitched with silver open from above the waist, her dark breasts showing large. She wore a headscarf strewn with silver stars in their constellations and sang in a tongue I supposed Egyptian, lifting up her sun-black face and showing teeth as stained with tobacco as my own but set also with gold and black here and there with gaps. I had begun this narration to my philosopher friend but guessed before long that I was speaking too fast or in the wrong order my sentences on a subject beyond his ken and to him only bizarre and of pathological interest so I desisted and took up my hat said in the voice of everyday courtesy I will be on my way and thank you for your kindness to a self afflicted. At which he sprang to his feet and begged to accompany me a mile or so, it was a fine evening and his head was tired. So off we set, much like, but for my unholy appearance, two ambulant scholars step by step getting a little closer to the truth. What tires my head, I confessed, is my compulsion to undo things, very finished things, I open them up again and the lines that were compact and fitted nicely tip out and sprawl all over the page like guts. He said that was a pity.

Crossing France, I said, Apollo very fierce, I entertained the idea there might be coolness in bolts of lightning. Did you indeed? he answered, and arriving at Sulzbach remembered he had letters to write. The sky was a mild pale green, Venus – I suppose as a courtesy to him – not too pulsating. I saw that he did not wish to embrace me and I did not blame him but gave him my hand, having wiped it first on my trousers, and he shook it warmly and looked me in the eyes and wished me luck, for which may Hermes, god of the roads, bless him. He did not ask me where I was going next, just as well, I had not thought that far ahead, very likely to my worried-sick mother. Soon as his back was turned I sat down on a stone pile and resumed my narrative, aloud but to nobody, of the swarthy gypsy woman who had by then ceased her singing and moved into speech in a tongue which I could in parts understand, it had something of Greek, Italian, French and Swabian in it, and I gathered that she, the Egyptian, had pains in her legs from too much travelling, she was the mother of thirteen children, she said, but they were scattered over several lands. Be seated, she said, so I moved a few logs to face her by the fire. She gave me wine, I gave her bread, she gave me figs, I gave her olives, grapes and a cut of sausage and becoming more accustomed to her tongue I essayed it myself and in a rush I told her I was heading home to the navel of the earth as fast as I could to rescue my beloved wife-to-be from servitude and insult. She nodded and with her right hand, sunburned and unclean, she made a sign of what I took to be blessing on the smoke-scented air and stuck a stub pipe into a gap in the gold of her teeth, tamped down the tobacco, lit it with a glowing twig and puffed in a deep contentment till I had said a poem and another poem and another concerning you, dear heart, sweet love, so you will be remembered by the gypsy woman and word of you will be borne from land to land. I rose, bade her good-night, she nodded, removed her pipe and grinned. I lay down on dead leaves in my cloak face up at a decent distance from her camp and she resumed her singing and I drifted into sleep still listening and there were waters in her song, streams and a river, the gifts of high snowy mountains to the sea not far away and over her and her singing and me and the dying fire all night there were owls and they were calling to and fro. Waking I heard the start of day in little trials and hesitations and a growing confidence as from this side and that a couple of notes of birdsong were caught up and answered and augmented, like spring to stream and stream to lake under a lightening sky and on the waking sleeper, me, through foliage, that risen music seemed a sweet downpour. The fire was dead, burned ends of sticks in a circle on the grey-white ash, and the Egyptian had gone her ways but her singing and her swarthy face and naked breasts, the constellations sewn in silver on her scarf, her pipe, the pains in her legs, her kindly listening and her blessing I had taken over into my sleep and made them mine, rob me of that, none can, Susette, my love, all of it I was hurrying to tell you, all and more, there was always so much more to tell, and I'm weary now, weary to death, and you are dead, the star I steered by has fallen from the sky, I run this way and that in futile little sallies without hope of comfort, since you are dead, Susette.

13

Late summer undoing into autumn, yellow spear-head leaves of willow on the Neckar which is fast and near to overflowing after a day and a night of torrential rain, he disembodied as easily as any lover divests to be naked with the beloved in her bed but found himself not there but walking in the garden with her, clothed and side by side, conversing quietly, and so long as there is this – this place, this possibility, this way of being together – he has promised her he will bide out his time in the quotidian world and keep her alive by thinking of her and speaking of her and reading aloud from the book in which, by the implacable truth of his fiction, she had to die but, that notwithstanding, he swears one work after another of his will bear her along through many lands and languages and down the rapids of the years and she will live as surely as if the gods themselves had set her as a new constellation visible to humans of both hemispheres in turn in the winter sky. Thank you kindly, she said. In my last winter it was bitter cold in Frankfurt, a fog came off the river and my old complaint revived. I hope the devotees you speak of won't locate me in the even colder heavens by my coughing. Are there no warmer places you might enshrine me in? You always did have a sense of humour, he replied. Well, more than I did. Hard to have less, she said. Perhaps men don't need to see the funny side. My young friend has gone to Rome, he said. On foot, of course. He says he wants to see the Alps stepping down into my former employer's back garden. After that he'll call on Ebel in Zürich. His good friend – I might almost say his patron – Professor Conz has provided him with a letter of introduction. I told him Ebel knows things I don't know and only you do and, of course, he can't ask you. I'd be no help anyway, she answered. I don't remember dying. Does anyone remember being born? Everything is shadowy apart from you – me and you – and we are very clear, which I suppose is on account of your having, if not much of a sense of humour, at least a very powerful imagination. In that poem I love and don't love, 'The Parting', when the lovers meet after a long separation and walk to and fro in the garden as shades, bloodless, and arrive suddenly at the place where they said goodbye and the blood comes back into both of them in a rush – that's how imagination works, with warm blood. And if *you* don't quite love it, he answered, what follows, I have grown to detest, the lily, the golden scent of the lily over the stream, as though anyone would be happy with that. In the garden by the river in the summer nights I run to and fro tearing up tufts of grass and cursing myself for not imagining us in flesh and blood walking out of that damned city and south by river and lake and mountain pass through the snow and ice and down into the sunny country. On the roads in France I saw couples who looked like us or like we would look if I'd had the courage of my imagination. – Again and again you wrong yourself, my dearest. I had four children, do you not remember? – I loved them and I was exiled from them. From all children. Sometimes I climb the steep alley by my tower and watch the children up there on the street. At first I would approach them and speak to them but they are terrified by my appearance and run away and at a safe distance chant spells against me till I go back down out of their sight. – But, she said, halting and turning to face him, You loved my children and they adored you. How happy that made me! – Some say you died of their scarlet fever. – I'm pretty sure I died of my old consumption. Or because I could not live without you. Causes of death: a trinity, three in one and one in three. I confessed to Ebel what I had told nobody but you: that without you my life was slowly withering and dying. I saw that though he did not say so he thought such a cause of death perfectly possible, at least as an ally of whatever else might come along. It is not fanciful nor was I just feeble. When I met you, I saw what my life needed if it were ever to become fit to be looked at. That wasn't a delusion it was the simple truth. With you my life flourished, without you day by day my life lost heart. I did try living without, living on lack, but it didn't work, just as you said it wouldn't. In a way that's all there is to it. I did my duty, at least to my children. One illness or another took advantage of my weakness and finished me off. And long before you died, he said, I was only just clinging on. I promised you – did you hear me promising? – that I wouldn't kill myself, and though by every rising of the river in torrential rain I was sorely tempted, here I am still, a walking bedlam, and all manner of poor lost souls with their wits astray are domiciled in me like bats. On the roads in France as I headed home to you, I saw tribes of women without their men, I observed them closely, how they looked after one another, schooling the children in the necessary courage. I saw a mother gather a dozen around her under a glorious murmuring linden at midday and sing them songs and tell them stories, saw their eyes, spellbound and concentrating, in the midst of such distress. She fed them the encouragement that couches in fables. I watched, I took it in. And now you pass it on, she said. I loved you at once for that. You see and tell so believingly I felt you at once to be a witness of the truth. You had been in my house an hour, in our first conversation already it was dawning on me that I did not have to continue to be the woman I had become. Hark at that bird! he said. Singing his heart out. And the waters, the springs, the streams, the rivers of the unspoilt world. Here in this garden they always sound so close. Even the sea, distant, distant, but not beyond hope. But only the other day I learned that in Frankfurt when you died they were blaming me for your death. I don't mean somebody took the trouble to inform me. They were contemplating me in my tower, and speaking of Diotima one of them leaned to the other and said, not even lowering his voice, as though I were too imbecile to understand, In Frankfurt when she died the family said, We know who to blame for this, do we not? Yes, she said. That would be Jakob's brother. And Jakob himself said it, You know who's to blame for this, don't you? Yes, I do, I answered, closing my eyes. They walked a while in silence, he in the appearance people were mostly used to in Tübingen but visitors found comical or distressing, she in the blue dress he liked and wearing the necklace of blue stones he had given her and with

210

the marks of the illness on her face and hands. They paused together, if a point were hard to express or understand, resumed their pacing of the paths together, hearing the blackbird and the thrush, quietly the waters and a murmuring now and then, a parley of soft voices, in the foliage of the larger trees. Truth is, she said, you *were* to blame, of course you were. But then so was he, only too stupid to see it. He made it clear from the start to me, the seventeen-year-old, that I was to bear his children and adorn his house. By 'adorn his house' he meant dress nicely, see there were flowers in vases, pictures on the walls, some music at weekends – and even some poetry, if I liked, why not? And, within reason, he would pay for it. I haven't forgotten the look on his face when I told him I loved you. Astonishment, far more than anger. And then a peculiar pity, as though I'd fallen sick of some incomprehensible female malady and he would have to be gentle with me or I might do something silly and become a burden and a disgrace. So he was to blame in his stupid ignorance of me, his wife, and what my love of music and poetry might lead me to ask of life one day. And my blame? her lover walking with her in that garden asked. – You were to blame for things I thanked you for with all my heart every day back then and here in the hereafter still. I knew of you before you entered his employment, don't forget. I had *read* you, as they say. So my soul was curious and alert when he told me you were coming to our house. And before that, don't forget, he left me alone during the week with my books of fiction and poetry and my piano. He is to blame for never once supposing any of that mattered even half as much as telling the cook how many would be dining on Saturday. Also I had Marie, at home, over there in Westphalia, and at home again. Do men like Jakob never think two women friends might speak to one another of the heart's affections and demands? French being one of my social accomplishments, with Marie I liberated myself into it, got better at it, in the gardens or in her room or mine fluently and exactly I told her the truth through the veil of foreignness. Unrest, he said. In the Seminary with Hegel and Schelling as comrades and news coming in from Paris with every post, I wrote hymns to the spirit of boldness, to friendship, beauty, freedom, all rhyming abstractions. And from the demolition of the Bastille to the September Massacres and the Terror, I kept faith. After Valmy I wished the unrest would spread into Germany and on through the whole wide world. Spoken or not, the preamble to all my poems was, We hold these truths to be self-evident... When I met you, the Athenian woman in the city of buying and selling, I felt not just confirmed in my vocation but also, if I would learn more, better able to carry it out. Meeting you allied me with real possibilities. There you were, living and breathing and walking this earth, this very earth. Not enough, never enough, did I mix with the blood and dirt. But what I did do, for all my weaknesses, was spread wherever I housed and wandered what I felt in myself: unrest. I furthered the cause of unrest. My verse, whatever the subject, whatever the form, in its rhythms, its onward drive, its reaching over the line-ending for more and more, in its rising and falling, presto, lento, ritardando, my verse embodies unrest. And I myself am the living image of it. You are quiet here, she said. Even speaking of it. Only here, he answered, in this strange otherwhere and in our otherwherish language, dearest, am I quiet. In the tower, for all the lovingkindness of my foster family, I exhibit the extremest form of my unrest. In France, seeing such movement of people on the roads, I remembered our making away into Westphalia, our slant intention among the desperate refugees, our desire to get through, get beyond, get out and away, and though for a while I continued wishing the armies of the Revolution victory, perhaps it was then, so in love with you, that I shifted my hope for myself and the peoples of the world into the answering of the demands of love. Perhaps it was just that you knew what you wanted more, she said, and what invasion and chaos were making possible for you, for me, for what I wanted most to come about? Yes, he said, and Heinse, libertine, advocate of jouissance, lover of Greece, Father Heinse, was our smiling Pandarus. Well, she said, guiding him left at the bed of periwinkle down the sand path she loved particularly, the path of the lavenders, cistus, thyme and rosemary, loud with bees, did you mind that? I didn't and don't. I caught the unrest from you at first sight. Livelier life you woke in me. I conceived in our first exchange of courtesies. Ah the quickening, the kick of life in the deep heart of me! Thinking about it in church sometimes, when the preacher man rose in the pulpit and began to sermonize, watching him, not listening, I said to myself he is trying to bend me into the paths of righteousness, he is trying to excite the fear of God in me, he wants me dissatisfied with the present state of my soul. He is doing his damnedest to kindle unrest in me. And I thought: my unrest is there already, love started it, the excitement in me is spoken for and long ago found its own direction and faces starvation now and runs to and fro in the heat of the day, thirsting, whimpering, desperate for water from my love's cupped hands. And I began my next letter to you in my head, giving you exact instructions for the diminished practice of our adultery, how to exchange our letters through the hedge and shock one another to the heart by the touching of our bare finger-tips. Remember, he said, her distress becoming very palpable to him,

On clear pathways, walking among low shrubs
  On sand, we thought more beautiful than anywhere
    And more delightful the hyacinths
      The tulips, violets and carnations.

Ivy on the walls, and a lovely green

Darkness under the high walks. In the mornings
  And the evenings we were there and
    Talked, and looked at one another, smiling.

I will, she said. And you, my dearest, remember this:

  In my arms the boy revived who had been still
    Deserted then and came out of the fields
      And showed me them, with sadness, but the
  Names of those rare places he never lost

  And everything beautiful that flowers there
    On blessed seaboards in the homeland that I
      Love equally, or hidden away
        And only to be seen from high above

  And where the sea itself can be looked upon
    But nobody will. Let be. And think of her
      Who has some happiness still because
        Once we were standing in the light of days

  Beginning with loving declarations or
    Our taking hands, to hold us…

Yes, she said, turning to him and seeing that already the space
between them had widened, Yes, I was yours then and I told
you so, without a doubt, and now you will bring and write all
the familiar things back into mind with letters. I will, he
answered, entering the shallows of sleep, hearing the cock
crow, I will say all of our past, I'll say it till it becomes one
more of the many tongues of the verdant earth that surface
into the light of the sun and stars and run for the love of it
and are persistent, crossing frontiers, wanting listeners.

Note

The chief characters in 'The Rivers of the Unspoilt World' are:

Susette Gontard (1769-1802), wife of the Frankfurt banker Jakob Gontard (1764-1843).

Friedrich Hölderlin (1770-1843), poet. He came into her household in January 1796 as house-tutor to the oldest of her four children, a boy of eight.

Wilhelm Waiblinger (1804-1830), writer. In 1822, as a student, he befriended Hölderlin who by then was living in a state of severe mental alienation with a carpenter's family in Tübingen. Hölderlin liked and trusted the young man, who later published a sensitive and intelligent account of their friendship. Waiblinger himself lived the brief life of a thorough Romantic. He died in Rome of a rapid tuberculosis and is buried in the Protestant Cemetery near Keats and Shelley.

This story is set (with some licence) in 1822 and moves between the three characters, one of them dead, largely in their voices but with some reinforcement now and then by an 'omniscient' narrator. In that year – as several visitors noticed – Hölderlin had intervals during which he was capable of, and, especially with Waiblinger, willing to engage in, lucid dialogue. The story takes advantage of this. Also in 1822 the

215

Greeks made good progress in their bid for independence from the Turks, and Hölderlin's publishers, with an eye to the market, brought out a second edition of his novel *Hyperion* which deals with the failure in 1770 of the Greeks' first try for freedom. Born in that year, as were Wordsworth and Beethoven, Hölderlin, like them, invested great hope in the French Revolution. Hope and disappointment is a chief theme of this fiction.

In the course of the story Waiblinger, increasingly viewing himself as Hölderlin's first biographer, talks to people who knew him as a student in Tübingen, as a young poet, and during his mental collapse. Among them are Ludwig Uhland and Gustav Schwab, already collecting the texts for a first edition of his poetry; Karl Philipp Conz who had taught him; and Friedrich Matthisson who had studied with him. The story lets Waiblinger get from them and others what he needs. In addition he learns the life by walking to places important in it. Following the Neckar, he entwines Hölderlin's life with his own.

In no very strict order, the fiction moves from Hölderlin's childhood to the state he is in when Waiblinger gets to know him. It shifts through many locations too. The letters Susette Gontard wrote to Hölderlin during their separation have, mostly, survived. He seems to have had them with him in his lodgings.

Citations

All the translations from German – Hölderlin's poems, his novel *Hyperion*, his letters to Susette Gontard and hers to him, and his own translations from Sophocles – are by the author. References are given below, to the page they appear on in this book, to the author's *Friedrich Hölderlin, Selected Poetry (SP)*, Bloodaxe Books 2018, and to volume and page in the *Große Stuttgarter Ausgabe (GStA)* of Hölderlin's works.

pp. 112-15, 'Severed and at a distance now …' *SP*, 212; *GStA*, 2, 262

p. 115, 'Come and look at the happiness …' *SP*, 22; *GStA*, 1, 210

p. 115, 'Your beloved face …', from 'Another day …', *SP*, 44; *GStA*, 1, 313

p. 122, ' Oh look! …', from *Hyperion, GStA*, 3, 85

p. 125, 'But we contented together …', from 'Menon's lament for Diotima', *SP*, 84; *GStA*, 2, 76

p. 135, 'There was a time …', from *Hyperion, GStA*, 3, 52

p. 139, 'Oh you groves of Angele …', from *Hyperion, GStA*, 3, 87

p. 144, 'My thoughts which are often with you …' *GStA*, 7 i, 74

p. 157, 'I have already noticed…' *GStA*, 7 i, 74, 60-1

p. 158, 'I thought that before my eyes…' *GStA*, 7 i, 82

p. 159, 'I feel very keenly…' *GStA*, 7 i, 90

p. 164, 'So you come…', *GStA*, 7 i, 77-8

p. 166, 'When you think of me…', *GStA*, 7 i, 103

pp. 194-5, 'Some quotations from H's *Oedipus*', *SP*, 259; 272; 295; 303

pp. 199, The author's own version of Hölderlin's translation of a chorus from Sophocles' *Oedipus at Colonus*.

Special Thanks

The author is grateful to the following people who helped him in the writing of these stories: Nicola and Matthew Constantine, for their discoveries in family history; Perrine Chambon, Helen Constantine, Phil Davis, Sasha Dugdale, Charlie Louth and Monika Szuba, for their close readings; and Ra Page, for his faith and encouragement over many years.